Secrets

Also by Frederick Ramsay
Artscape
Impulse

Secrets

Frederick Ramsay

Poisoned Pen Press

Copyright © 2005, 2006 by Frederick Ramsay

First Trade Paperback Edition 2006

10 9 8 7 6 5 4 3 2 1

Library of Congress Catalog Card Number: 2005903226

ISBN: 1-59058-286-1 Trade Paperback

Poisoned Pen Press
6962 E. First Ave., Ste. 103
Scottsdale, AZ 85251
www.poisonedpenpress.com
info@poisonedpenpress.com

To my father, A. Ogden Ramsay (1904-2000)

Known to generations of McDonogh School students as "Bugs,"
he remains, even now, an inspiration for many and a standard
against which I will always measure my life.

Acknowledgments

My thanks to the many readers and commentators who critiqued this story in its several incarnations—John Rundle, Bette Laswell, David Bishop, P. J. Colderon, Cindy Chow, Jean Jenkins, Nancy Clarke, my wife, Susan, and, of course, the folks at Poisoned Pen Press who have magically turned this sow's ear into a silk purse.

I would be remiss if I did not also mention the countless people who constituted the eight congregations I had the privilege of serving, at one time or another, in the Episcopal Diocese of Maryland and who taught me so much about people. I assure them that none of them ended up as a character in this book, although there were times when I had to fight very hard to resist the temptation to use one or two.

The same holds true for my clergy brothers and sisters. They may, however, see something of themselves in Blake Fisher, for when all is said and done, he represents both the best and the worst of us all.

Chapter One

The church huddled in a small grove of pine and oak set back from the road at the town's northern edge. Featured on postcards for decades, it was in great demand for weddings by Callend College women, area residents and, on occasion, visitors from as far away as Washington, DC. The previous vicar, in order to reduce the number of requests for those events from outsiders, imposed preconditions on its use. If you wished to be married in Stonewall Jackson Memorial Episcopal Church, you had to be a member in good standing for at least six months or you had to pay a user's fee of five thousand dollars. Every year, membership rose from January to June, then fell off precipitously.

Constructed entirely of local grey limestone, it contrasted sharply with the rest of Picketsville, whose architecture leaned toward antebellum. Nineteenth-century tastes dismissed limestone as ordinary and ill-suited for erecting a modern city. The only correct façade for a building, they believed, was brick. Some of the town's older buildings still displayed bullet holes chipped into salmon red bricks, acquired when the Union Armies began their descent down the Shenandoah Valley into the heart of Dixie.

At night, the church sank into the shadows cast by surrounding trees. On a moonless night like this one, it disappeared completely.

Waldo Templeton moved cautiously toward the church doors, jet black in the night's palette of grays. His shoes, dusty from the gravel path, grated against stone steps. He extended his right arm its full length and pushed gently on the right-hand door with his fingertips. Not locked. He frowned. Why not locked? It swung silently inward. He could smell oil recently applied to its ancient hinges. He paused. The church often went unlocked. So many people had keys; it probably didn't make any difference. He moved forward to a second set of doors, his hand caressing their smooth glass surface. He pushed through them as well.

Starlight outside, black as a raven's wing within, and only a flickering red candle suspended over the aumbry showing him which way to go. He fumbled to his right for the light switches. He hesitated and then withdrew his hand. If the doors weren't locked, better not turn on any lights. No one was supposed to be here at this hour anyway, and light attracted attention. He might have been followed. No, no lights. He hesitated and then started forward again, submerged in black velvet darkness. He crept up the center aisle, his arms outstretched like a blind man. He stubbed his toe on one pew, banged his knee against another. He sucked in his breath and waited. Nothing stirred. His eyes adjusted to the dark and he moved forward again, a bit more confidently. He recognized the looming bulk of the organ to his right and could just make out the communion railing in front of him. But before he could steady himself on it, he tripped. This time he cursed and dropped to his knees. He held his breath, marking time with the pounding of his heart. He stood slowly and swung his head around, eyes boring into the unyielding gloom, searching, listening for any sign of danger. He rubbed his shin and took three more steps. His hand touched the altar's cool marble and starched linen. Feeling his way along its smooth edge, he slipped behind it. He'd need the key.

The first bullet ripped through his shoulder, knocking his hand away from the altar and spinning him around. Before he could react, the second gave him a third eye and sent him reeling into the nineteenth-century bas relief carved reredos behind him. His slow descent to the red carpet left a matching smear on its white painted facing. The odor of cordite, like New Age frankincense, drifted upward to mingle with older high church incense ingrained in the ceiling's dark oak beams.

His killer flicked on a small Maglite and carefully retrieved two shell casings from the carpet, then knelt and rifled Waldo's pockets. The figure stood with a grunt and, flashlight upended on the altar, fumbled with a key ring, removed one, and pressed it into a wax container, first one side then the other. More key jingling and the ring and its keys were returned to Waldo's pocket. The wall clock by the open sacristy door read 11:03. Clad entirely in black, except for a splash of white at the throat, Waldo's executioner walked the length of the nave, slipped out the door, and pulled it to, making sure the lock snapped shut. The car sat parked out of sight on the church's auxiliary lot, well behind the building and nearby under a copse of oaks. The headlights wouldn't go on until the car bumped onto the main road.

In the Middle Ages anyone on the run, in fear for his life, or simply in danger—if he were able to reach a church and place his hand on its altar—would then fall under the protection of the Church and, presumably, God. He would be granted Sanctuary and made safe—safe in a consecrated place, on holy ground. Felons fleeing the King's men could gain a respite from their flight, perhaps just long enough to confess their sins, receive unction, and go to their maker shriven and clean. But for others, it bought time. Time for bribes to be paid, for innocence to be proven, or a covenant struck. Unfortunately, for Waldo Templeton, none of these possibilities materialized. He had managed to find Sanctuary of a sort, not the kind he sought, not one with permanence, and certainly not one that could save his life.

His problems began when Picketsville filled with news people, stringers, and hangers-on from around the country. All the major television networks had sent trucks and reporters to cover the robbery of five hundred million dollars in fine art from Callend College for Women the previous spring. It had made headlines on the national news. And then, with the establishment of an apparent link between the robbery and a terrorist cell, a second wave of media personnel washed in to become a beast in need of constant feeding. The sheriff's office and its laconic leader, Ike Schwartz, could not have kept it satisfied if they had tried. So they didn't. Reporters with network connections, local stations to supply and deadlines to meet, scoured the town looking for news—any news. In the feeding frenzy that followed, they overlooked very little.

Waldo should have known better. He should have holed up in his little town house and waited out the onslaught of media mania. Then, too, he had a run of bad luck. He went to the Crossroads Diner at ten o'clock for coffee as he always did and sat in his customary bench in a back booth. Buried in his paper, he failed to notice the commotion at the front of the diner. When a woman reporter with impossibly curly red hair arrived with her camera crew in tow to do a color piece on the locals, Waldo did not move. If only he had been sitting with his back to the door, or had not lowered his paper at that precise moment, or if he had just this once resisted the urge to add caffeine to his system, he might still be alive. But for reasons known only to him and now forever lost, he remained seated, smiling, and staring into the camera's red eye, his blurred image broadcast on television stations across the country.

It is one of life's great ironies that critical events hang on small decisions made on the spur of the moment, decisions for the most part irrational and impulsive. Red lights are ignored, cocktails are consumed, drugs are sampled, a phone is left ringing—and people die. Most of our lives are played out as a series of these small, singular determinations, made without thought to the consequences they carry. And one by one they pile up, each knocking into another, into those of others, like dominos, until their effect is enormous. Lives are ruined; vengeance is sought, wars begun, and all because someone chose to turn right instead of left, or, in Waldo's case, to remain seated and smiling. Small decisions—massive changes—the Butterfly Effect.

Chapter Two

Millicent Bass' sole source of income, aside from a modest sum she received from a trust fund, came from the meager salary she earned as a part-time secretary for Stonewall Jackson Memorial Episcopal Church. She believed she should be paid more. But, because she had access to all of the church's files, she knew the bottom line on the budget contained no money for a raise. Furthermore, the new vicar did not come cheap. And that rankled. He did not conform to her strict standards of what a clergyman ought to be. In fact, she counted the very fact he had taken the post in Picketsville as a mark against him.

Millie grew up in Alexandria, before outsiders moved into that historic town and turned it into just another chi-chi bedroom community inside the Washington Beltway. She had very decided and mostly negative views of those living in the Commonwealth west of the Blue Ridge Mountains. "If he were any good," she declaimed to her mah-jongg club, "he wouldn't be forced to take a job in a mission church in a backwater town like this one." The internal contradiction implicit of this analysis eluded her. It was just as well.

Millicent had been the church secretary for over two decades. "Vicars come and vicars go, but Millie," the saying went, "was forever." Her years of service, she believed, endowed her with certain privileges. She could be selectively rude to some parishioners, share gossip with others, and be outraged when one of those not in her select set dared to gossip without her knowledge or permission. She knew secrets.

Over the years the church had fallen into gentle decay and now existed as an insignificant parochial mission. Most of its parishioners, including Millicent, were content for it to stay that way. She felt certain this new man with his endless talk of evangelism and his plans for what he called "outreach" made her and everyone else very uncomfortable. Well, not everyone. Some of the new families, the ones with noisy children who disturbed the collective piety of Millie and her friends who were, after all, like Saint Peter, the rock on which the church had been built—those people thought outreach wonderful. Millicent pursed her lips. She and her friends agreed that those people really belonged farther up Main Street at Saint Mark's Lutheran. There, they were told, children ran wild up and down the aisles, people sang dreadful praise choruses, and the minister told jokes from the pulpit.

She hung up her coat and flicked on her computer. She would need to do the Sunday bulletin and print copies. She searched her desk for Waldo's hymn list. She needed it to fill in the blanks where the hymn numbers went. She searched in her in-box but could not find it. She tried calling Waldo at his office, discovered he had not yet arrived. Real Estate people, she thought, no better than gypsies, the way they kept hours; and the money they made selling other people's houses. Outrageous—no answer at his house either. She decided to wait an hour and call again. In the meantime she resumed her search for the old vicar's files.

No one knew that he'd kept notes and even tape recordings of his counseling sessions in a locked box. Well, no one except Millicent, who had a duplicate key, which she had made one afternoon when the vicar thought he had lost his. Millicent "found" it for him the next day. Those files contained some very juicy stuff. But ever since the old vicar died, she could not find them. At first, she thought his widow might have taken them with her when she came to clean out his office after his funeral. But Millicent called on one pretext or another and discovered they were not with her either. She wondered if the new vicar had them, then guessed he did not. She had scoured the office before he came, and removed anything she thought might be useful. Where could they have gotten to?

Aside from her main task of producing a readable bulletin for the upcoming Sunday service, she helped the Altar Guild set up every Friday. She enjoyed that part. The ladies joining her were old friends and it gave her a chance to gossip about everyone else in the congregation. Four members of that august body—pillars of the church—would arrive in a few minutes. She cleared her desk, checked her watch, and went into the vicar's office. He would not arrive until well after ten.

He claimed to be making pastoral calls but she held to the opinion that he slept in. She switched on the fluorescent lights and surveyed his office. As she passed by the door that led into the sacristy and then into the church, she thought she smelled something. Not a nice odor. It seemed stronger nearer the door. She opened it. Nothing in the sacristy. She passed through the small room with its cabinets holding silver and communion supplies and peered into the church. With only early morning light filtered by dark stained glass, she couldn't see very much. The main switches were at the far end of the nave next to the glass doors leading from the narthex. But the switches controlling the sanctuary lights lay at her fingertips.

She flicked all four and stepped around the corner to look. Something had happened during the night. The altar cloth, the Fair Linen, hung askew, one end in untidy folds on the floor. One large brass candlestick lay on its side, its candle crosswise on the altar. She thought at first the Brogan boys had broken in again. She would call their mother, but that would be a waste of time. Mrs. Brogan was notoriously blind to her boys' behavior. "Just boys being boys," she would say, never acknowledging that boys did not normally set fire to barns and that if they did, they went to jail.

She made an awkward genuflection at the communion rail and stepped up, thinking to restore the damage. A pair of shoes caught her eye first and then, stepping to her left, she saw the body. At first she thought Waldo was sleeping. It did not occur to her to question the likelihood he would be sleeping in the sanctuary at a quarter to ten in the morning. She tried to say his name. Croak. She tried again and managed a ragged whisper. When she saw the blood on the reredos and the bullet hole in his forehead, she screamed. When the first of four Altar Guild members joined her five minutes later, they found her collapsed on the floor, mouth open and moaning.

One had the presence of mind to call the sheriff's office.

Chapter Three

"Ike," Essie Falco yelled through the open door, "it's Billy's momma down at the Stonewall Jackson Church for you. She says it's urgent."

"Essie, we have a new office intercom, you know. You push that little button and speak in a normal voice—"

"I know, Ike, but I been yelling at you for more than three years and can't get used to all this modern stuff."

Ike Schwartz, Picketsville's sheriff for the last three and a half years, sighed and let his feet drop from the windowsill where he'd propped them only minutes before. He usually took his feet-up nap in the afternoon. But Thursday night had been a long one and he knew from experience Fridays could be difficult as well, so he decided to grab a quick doze between morning coffee break and lunch. He swiveled his chair around and gritted his teeth at the shriek it made in the circuit. He'd have to put some oil in there someday.

"Which line?" he yelled back. Two of the four green LEDs on his phone were lit.

"Line three."

He punched the third button. "Sheriff," he said and listened to an excited voice race through a litany about a Ms. Bass and a man, who seemed to be dead, named Waldo somebody. He waited for an opening.

"That you, Dorothy?" he asked, and wagged to Essie to pick up. She already had and was making notes.

"Dorothy Sutherlin here, Ike, yes sir, and you'd better get on out here *toot sweet.*"

"Did anybody call 9-1-1, Dorothy?" He knew the answer but figured he would ask anyway, you never knew. "No? Well, no need to now, we'll see to it and be right out." Small towns—the last to acquire technology, the last to use it when it finally arrived. In the past, Picketsville folks always called straight in to the sheriff's office when something happened, so why change now? Only newcomers, city people, and tourists called 9-1-1.

"Essie, get a hold of the County. It looks like we might have a homicide. Then call whoever's on and tell them to meet me at the Episcopal Church and, oh, get an ambulance down there, too, just in case."

Ike heaved himself out of his chair, patted his pockets for keys and wallet, considered whether he wanted to strap on his duty belt, decided against it and stepped into the main office, belt and gear in hand. Sam Ryder, his newest deputy, walked in as he closed his door. Sam—Samantha—Ryder had her own space in a renovated jail cell down the hall. They had never needed more than two holding cells anyway, and Sam needed space to set up her computers and their peripherals. The Picketsville sheriff's office had joined the information age. He had no idea what she had assembled in there. It seemed like every day another box, envelope, or package arrived and disappeared into the cell.

"How're we doing, Sam?" Ike didn't know if he'd understand the answer if she told him, but as her boss he thought he ought to be kept informed.

"Almost there." She picked up a thin package labeled *Software* and retreated to her *sanctum sanctorum.*

"Right, good," he said and left shaking his head.

◇◇◇

Ike noticed the New Jersey tags on the car as he pulled around it. Another out of state driver. The area had been attracting people from all over the country lately. The regulars at the

Crossroads Diner were full of it, some worried, most simply annoyed. Chester Starks muttered darkly about "foreigners." In another age he might have said "Yankees," but Californians and Arizonans didn't fit.

Flora Blevins, who had run the diner since the Carter Administration, said she'd told Marvin down at the print shop to run her up two different menus—one for townsfolk and one for newcomers and outsiders. The difference between the two would be found in the prices, not the cuisine. She said she'd been fixing to do it ever since the diner became the "in" place for the girls from Callend College to bring their dates. That started last spring, just before the big robbery. The regulars said they felt like they were in a zoo when those bright young people in their fancy clothes descended on their sanctuary, like they came to study the animals. They reckoned the double menu idea a fair tradeoff for their discomfort.

Ike had a notion what sudden interest Picketsville held for the neo-carpetbaggers filling the motels and renting houses up and down the highway, but he also knew he couldn't do anything to stop it. If what he supposed turned out to be true, historic old Picketsville would soon become the Freeport, Maine, of the Shenandoah Valley, and probably end his tenure as sheriff.

The thought gave him pause. He'd run for sheriff because he needed something to do in the time of his life he referred to as his Job Years—years he'd spent, like the biblical sufferer, sitting on a metaphorical dung heap wondering why God hated him so much. He had gotten past that, but now he wondered why he stayed on. He didn't need the money and he certainly didn't need the aggravation. Yet something held him in place and, several times a week, he wrestled with it. He tried to remember who wrestled with God. Not Job— he just sat and waited. Isaac? Ike's full name was Isaac. Isaac didn't wrestle, did he? Jacob. Jacob wrestled with God, threw his hip out or something—too many years had passed since he'd been to *shul* and no way to make it up now. Biblical metaphors weren't going to get him his answer. Not today, anyway.

He pulled onto the gravel parking lot in front of Stonewall Jackson Memorial Church. Only in this part of the country could a house of God be named after a Confederate general. Billy Sutherlin and Charley Picket were waiting for him in the parking lot.

There were at least four police cars in the parking lot when Blake Fisher, the Reverend Randolph Blake Fisher, Jr., Vicar of Stonewall Jackson Memorial Episcopal Church, drove up. His father, Randolph Blake Fisher, Sr., owned a seat on the New York Stock exchange, a seat he'd inherited from his father who, in turn, got it from his. A big man in many ways, Randolph Senior so completely occupied the name Randolph that Blake had had to settle for using his middle name. He noted with some annoyance that someone had parked in his reserved space. As he climbed out of his beat-up sports car, Dan Quarles rushed across the parking lot.

"Father Fisher," he yelled, "where have you been?"

Dan sounded accusatory, as if he'd been personally inconvenienced.

"Someone steal the safe again?" Blake asked, ignoring Dan's disapproving stare.

"Waldo," Dan sputtered.

"Waldo stole the safe?"

"Waldo's dead. Shot twice."

"Shot? You're kidding."

"Not a kidding matter, Vicar, very serious. And Millie Bass is hysterical. She found the, ah, you know, the body."

Blake walked quickly to the back stairs and climbed them to the offices. He crossed through Millie's, his own, and on into the sanctuary. A bored-looking young man in a light blue jumpsuit with *RCPD* stenciled on the back waited for a signal to wrestle Waldo Templeton, or what remained of him, into a body bag. Millicent Bass sat hunched up and tiny in a front pew, attended to by several ladies from the Altar Guild whose names, except for Dorothy Sutherlin, Blake could not remember. He had not been vicar very long, so this memory lapse could be excused, but the real reason he could not remember their names had nothing to do with his tenure. They all seemed to behave like they were doing him a favor, that they, not he, were the ones to decide how and when various things got done, not an attitude unique to this particular church. He found it so off-putting he kept his distance, and thus their names had not made it into his memory bank.

"You the Reverend here?" This, from a tall, lean man in a rumpled uniform—hard face, soft eyes. Southern cop, Blake thought. Great, just what I need, Buford T. Justice parking his size twelves in my church.

"I'm the Vicar, yes," Blake said.

The man studied Blake for a moment and led him to the pair of front doors. He held out his hand, inviting Blake to step outside.

"No sense burdening the ladies," he said. "What can you tell me about Waldo Templeton?"

The two men walked slowly away from the door toward a stand of pines. "Not much, nothing, really. I've been here less than three months. My predecessor hired him. He is, excuse me, he *was* a very private person. I saw him only in his capacity as our organist and intended to replace him."

"Why?"

"He was a mediocre organist and a little creepy to boot."

"What do you mean by creepy?"

"It's hard to say, but he sort of drifted in and out, you know? One minute you thought you were alone, the next minute, there he was. I'd swear he walked through closed doors. He would just appear in the office. That kind of creepy."

"That's not normal for single men who play the organ in churches?"

"Excuse me?"

"Skip it. Just a thought. Oh, another thing, before I forget. Do you know anything about a church called Saint Katherine's?"

Blake stopped in mid stride. "Maybe. I used to be a part of the ministry team at Saint Katherine's in Philadelphia. Why do you ask?"

"He had a note in his pocket that said, 'Find out what the Vicar did at Saint Katherine's.' The Vicar, that's you, right?"

"Right." Blake felt his stomach turn over. Anger, misplaced perhaps, but very real, dislodged his usual easygoing nature. He resented this country cop even while he knew it had nothing to do with him, really. He turned and faced the church.

"Well, Reverend, you be sure to stick around, will you?"

"Reverend is an adjective, Sheriff, not a noun," he said.

The cop spun on his heel and raised his eyebrows. "Say again?"

"The correct form of address to a clergyman is Mister, or Doctor, or Bishop, etcetera. The use of Reverend as a title is incorrect. As I said, it is an adjective modifying Mister, Doctor, and so on. The Reverend Mister, or the Reverend Doctor—"

"Thanks for the English lesson. I think I knew that, though I haven't had much call to use it. The important thing here is, if you plan on preaching in this part of the world for any length of time, Son, you'd best get used to being called Reverend because, usage or not, that's what everyone is going to call you."

"So in this corner of the State of Virginia—"

"Commonwealth."

"What?"

"Usage. Virginia is a Commonwealth, not a State, as are Pennsylvania and Massachusetts. Down here, people are picky about what they're called. You can understand that, I assume, what with Reverend and all. Commonwealth—not State."

"Right."

Chapter Four

Ike suppressed a smile. It seemed the big city boy had issues about country cops. Nothing changed. He turned to admire the church's entrance and its solid double oak doors.

"Tell me something, Reverend, why do churches, especially older ones like this one, paint their doors red?"

"I'm not sure," Fisher said. "There is an old tradition that congregations paint their doors red when the mortgage is paid. I don't know what you do if you have to borrow money again, as this church has. I suppose we should get some paint remover."

"I don't think anyone will notice."

The benefit of the church's stone construction became immediately apparent when Ike stepped back in. Sixteen inches thick, the stone walls maintained the interior at a comfortable ten degrees below the outside ambient temperature in the summer and retained the heat in the cooler months. So far, the church's leadership had not felt the need to air-condition. Ike let his eyes adjust to the relative gloom and then moved toward the front of the church. Dorothy Sutherlin waved to him from the first row of pews. Dorothy had raised seven boys, one of whom, Billy, worked for Ike as a deputy.

"Well, thank goodness you got here, Ike," she said in a decidedly unchurch-like voice. Dorothy did not bellow, as some of her critics alleged, but over the years, as the result of raising seven boys, she had developed impressive volume. "It's all I can do to keep these ladies away from the...scene. I had to tell Mavis here not to touch anything after she started to put the Fair Linen back on the altar. The candlestick has been set to rights, too."

The woman Dorothy indicated as Mavis began to protest. Ike cut her short as kindly as he could.

"I'm sorry, ladies," he said while he stepped carefully around the altar to inspect the dead man. "You'll have to leave everything as it is until we are finished here. That may not be until early next week."

"We're supposed to have services here in two days. I'll need this area cleared and the altar set by then." Fisher looked worried.

"Not this Sunday, I'm afraid. I'll ask the FET, that's the Field Evidence Technicians, to work as fast as they can, but with the blood—" Ike stopped in mid sentence. He leaned forward and looked closely at the blood smear on the reredos.

"Who...? Which one of you left a fingerprint in the middle of this stain?" Ike felt his calm beginning to slip away. One of these four biddies had put her nose or, to be precise, her finger, in as well. He glared at the ladies. He realized there were five of them and he still needed to find out who they were and why they were in the church in the first place. "Well?"

The ladies hung their heads and then their eyes ping ponged back and forth at one another. Finally a woman he thought he remembered as Millicent Somebody raised her hand.

"I'm afraid I did, Sheriff. I didn't think. When I saw Waldo, I unconsciously touched the...blood. I guess I couldn't believe...."

The county FET team arrived in the middle of this exchange. Ike waved them into the area and asked their leader, Bart Franklin, to take the fingerprints of all five women. Franklin peered at Ike over the top of his glasses but nodded and gave the order to one of his men.

"You, too, Mr. Fisher," Ike said. "Anyone inside the crime scene—we will need your fingerprints and a sample of your DNA. He saw Franklin flinch. Ike figured once the word got out that there were consequences for tampering with a crime scene, however small, he would have fewer problems in the future.

"With all due respect, Sheriff," Blake said, "I don't think I'll go along with all this."

"I can make you," Ike said.

"Probably, but I believe you are over-reaching. We do not have to submit to DNA sampling without cause."

Ike studied the clergyman, trying to look behind his eyes. "Very well, Reverend," he said. Franklin looked relieved. Ike set his team in motion, interviewing the women, taping off the area, and searching the church and grounds.

"About the services Sunday," Dorothy Sutherlin said, "Billy here could string a piece of clothesline across the front of the sanctuary and put up some fabric. There's the little altar in the basement we could set up in front...." She paused and looked inquiringly at Blake.

"Yes, yes, that will have to do, Dorothy, thank you," he said.

◇◇◇

The police left after, what seemed to Blake, an interminable amount of time, but probably amounted no more than three hours. Millicent gave her statement. He sat in on that, as much to find out what had happened as to provide pastoral support for Millicent. The look she gave him indicated she did not wish his support and probably wished he were somewhere else. Dan Quarles told the police he'd answered a call from the church when Blake could not be located. This he said with a scowl and a sidelong look in Blake's direction. The ladies of the Altar Guild clucked a joint statement. They came to set the altar. They always did that on Friday, they declared, with the serious-ness only dedicated volunteers possess. They found Millicent in hysterics on the floor. They called the sheriff's office, then Blake—unsuccessfully—and finally, and successfully, Dan (bless him) Quarles. Blake had nothing to add. Schwartz asked to see the rest of the building.

Blake thought of the church as a large, empty, stone box. But what it lacked in spirituality it more than made up for in aesthetics. It boasted stained glass that might be Tiffany, some artwork he had not yet gotten around to checking, and a well-proportioned carved marble altar. The latter, now free standing but once positioned on the east wall against the reredos, stood in an apse created by the sacristy on the left and an enclosed stairway on the right, clearly marked with a green EXIT sign whose bulb invariably flickered like a votive candle. The symbolism always amused him when he processed behind the choir on Sunday. Behind were the two offices, with their own set of stairs that lead to a shared landing with those from the church. The location of the offices precluded a rose window over the altar—the only architectural flaw in the whole. At the entrance, the narthex opened out to a walkway leading to the parking lot.

In its heyday, toward the end of the nineteenth century, Stonewall Jackson Memorial Episcopal Church served as a thriving chapel of ease for local gentry. It flourished through the first half of the twentieth and then began to decline. Times changed and more fundamentalist denominations began to capture Picketsville's souls. The lure of better economic times to the east drew its major supporters away, never to return, and the faculty of the college, once the backbone of its congregation, had become increasingly humanist, Marxist, and agnostic in its approach to the hereafter. Now the church languished as a parochial mission of Saint Anne's, a large suburban parish in Roanoke.

Saint Anne's, or more accurately, its rector, Philip Bournet, took on the mission after the diocese decided to shut it down. Its previous vicar had been a seminary professor of Philip's and nearing retirement. Philip turned Stonewall Jackson Memorial into a small sinecure for him. He intended to close it as soon as his friend and former instructor retired. The vicar's fatal heart attack cut short those plans. Blake took over as vicar only because of his close friendship with Philip. Blake desperately needed a job and when he asked for a favor, Philip persuaded his congregation to extend the mission's life for a brief period.

"Two years, Blake," Philip had said. "You have two years to pull some kind of sacerdotal rabbit out of a hat. If you cannot get that church to independent status by then, it is over."

"Who has keys to the church?" the sheriff asked, drawing Blake back to the moment. They had made their way to the basement.

"What? Oh, everybody."

"What do you mean everybody?"

"Well maybe not everybody, almost everybody, Sunday school teachers, Altar Guild members, the choir, members of the Mission board, various committee chairmen, Boy Scouts, AA, and, of course, former members of all of the above…and then over the years…."

"I get the picture. Aren't you worried about being robbed?"

"We have been robbed, three times in four years. But whoever did it broke in. Apparently church folks didn't do the robbing."

"Do you know if Templeton had any enemies?"

"I have no idea. I suppose he must have, considering."

"Considering what?"

"Someone killed him. That strikes me as reasonable evidence that he had at least one enemy."

"I found this." Schwartz held out a water bottle. "Yours?"

"Looks like mine. I buy that brand by the case."

"Why is that? The water in town is considered to be the best in the state. There used to be a spa just west of here and people from all over traveled to Picketsville just to drink the water—"

"Commonwealth, you said—"

"I found this in the trash."

"Look, if this is about recycling, I'm sorry. Write me up."

Schwartz gave Blake a look that reminded him of his college football coach when he'd thrown an interception. He shrank an inch or two.

"All your bottles look like this when you're done?"

The end had been blown out.

"No. What happened to my bottle?"

"Poor man's noise suppressor, I think. You tape it to the end of your weapon...see the tape here...and here? And it muffles the report. Our man didn't want to be heard."

"You're the expert, but why a man?"

"Guns are a man's weapon. Women tend to use less violent means to kill folks—like poison, although it isn't always so. But the bottle is the clincher. Men know about bottle noise suppressors. You ask a woman how to silence a gun and if she has any idea, she'll suggest a pillow. No, we're looking for a man." Schwartz stopped at the door. "If you think of anything that might help, let me know. The bottle is just between you and me, got it?" He climbed the steps and disappeared outside.

"Right. Shouldn't that be, 'you and *I*,'" Blake said to an empty room.

Nothing in his seminary training had prepared him for a murder or its aftermath. The Book contained no appropriate liturgy; no articles in the Canons covered it. And he had until Sunday, one and a half days, to figure out what to do, find a substitute organist, and calm everyone down, including himself. The phone rang. He picked up the extension.

"Blake? What's going on up there? Dan Quarles has been on the phone to me. So has the Bishop and half the Heavenly Host."

"Murder mostly, Philip. Organist shot. I feel like I'm in the middle of an Agatha Christie novel. *Murder at the Vicarage.*"

"Do you want to meet me for lunch? We are due for a session anyway—usual place, one thirty?"

"One thirty will be fine."

Chapter Five

Rockbridge Mall briefly held the title of the best designed small mall on the east coast. That distinction lasted something like twenty minutes, as the mega-mall craze boomed. Although stripped of its title, it still remained a pleasant place to shop and dine, see a movie, or just "mall walk." Every two weeks, Philip Bournet met Blake there for lunch and reviewed Blake's progress or the lack thereof. As Rector of Saint Anne's, Philip exercised control over the mission and its activities. He did not interfere, but as the fiscally responsible agent, he needed to keep close tabs on Blake, the church, and its people.

The Admiral Maury Café was predictably nautical, with binnacles in the corners and sextants on the wall. Most of the memorabilia would probably not have been recognizable to the admiral, as he spent most of his career as a cartographer. There were, however, a few maps displayed here and there. Blake arrived first, took a booth, and ordered iced tea. Philip walked in five minutes later. In the interval between, Blake greeted three parishioners, all of whom seemed to know more about the murder than he did.

"Blake," Philip said, making the greeting sound almost like a question. He sat in the booth opposite, ordered coffee and picked up his menu. "You ordered yet?"

"No, I was waiting for you."

The waitress brought them drinks. They ordered lunch and leaned back, each waiting for the other to start. Finally, Philip said, "I knew you intended to make some personnel changes, Blake, but this is ridiculous. He couldn't have been that bad an organist."

"It's not a joking matter, Philip, this is a mess. As if the inconvenience of an ongoing police presence at the church weren't bad enough, I am already being given the 'dirty eye' by two-thirds of the congregation. This may be the last straw."

"I don't believe that."

"Philip, I think coming to Virginia may have been a mistake. I have never run into such a collection of stiff-necked people in my life. I thought my last position was a dilly. But these people…how did Tommy put up with them?"

"Tommy" referred to the Reverend Doctor Thomas Taliaferro, pronounced "Tolliver" in this part of the world, the former professor of Pastoral Theology at Virginia Theological Seminary, and Blake's immediate predecessor.

"Well, they liked him, I think. Mostly they liked Doris. You know Doris, Tommy's wife—widow?"

"Only slightly."

"Wonderful woman. Bright, sensitive, and able to make everyone in the room feel important. Tommy always said when they hired him, they really wanted Doris and so had to take him to get her. You know she sends me a copy of her poems every year for Christmas. Terrible doggerel, '*Birds tweet, Bees flit, Very sweet, Isn't it,*' that sort of thing. I haven't the heart to say anything. It's her only flaw. Anyway, Tommy had a way of overlooking unpleasantness. It was a gift. The Board would huff and puff and Tommy would smile and do whatever he planned to do anyway."

"You recommend a similar course for me?"

"Don't think so. They know why you left Philadelphia, and they are waiting for you to make a mistake. Dan Quarles as much as accused you of murder this morning."

"Me? What the—?"

"I'm exaggerating, of course, but you get my drift."

"Lord, have mercy on my soul."

"Precisely. By the way, speaking of Doris, she said Millicent Bass called and wanted to know if she had Tommy's records. I don't know why Mrs. Bass wanted to know. Probably just tidying up some loose ends."

"Records? What kind of records? LPs, CDs, that sort, or paper files?"

"Paper files. Tommy kept detailed notes of his counseling sessions, even taped some, I think. I told him not to, that it might create a problem later, but he said not to worry, they were safe. You know he was a trained and licensed psychotherapist—good at it, too. I sent him a dozen patients at one time or another. Anyway, his files are missing. He must have put them away in a safe place—attic maybe. Do me a favor and see if you can dig them out and send them to Doris. I'll give you her address."

"Sure. But what do I do now with a dead organist and a Board in open rebellion?"

"You know the rule every clergy person knows. When things seem dark and hopeless—"

"Pray?"

"No, drop back ten yards and punt."

"Philip, I said this is not a joking matter."

"No, you are right. I'm sorry. Give yourself a break. You've been their vicar for less than three months. It is still summer and people are away, occupied with other things, vacations, trips to the beach, baseball. Wait until later and you will see. Things will pick up. In the meantime, Mary Miller is a member of my congregation, and she lives up near you. I have tried to persuade her to attend Stonewall, but so far, she has refused. She visited there once in July and said she received such a chilly reception, she felt like she needed an overcoat. But, she plays the organ, has had some experience in the Methodist Church, I think. If I asked her, she might at least fill in while you get sorted out."

"That would be wonderful."

"Are you okay, Blake," Philip turned serious, "aside from the murder?"

"I suppose so. You said it yourself, though. They know about Philadelphia so I operate under a cloud. It is maddening. I have nothing to be ashamed of, I didn't do anything, and yet I feel like a juvenile delinquent visiting his probation officer every time I attend a meeting."

"I can't help you there, Blake. It's something you will just have to ride out. Leaving this church, if that's what's on your mind, will only prolong the agony."

"I know. And I owe you, Philip, for giving me the chance to stay in ministry. God must have it in for me, though."

"You're being too hard on yourself. I think he loves you and has finally given you a chance to find out what ministry is all about. If you can bring those people to an understanding of what God means when he tells us to love our neighbor, you and your 'stiff necked' congregation will have found a new life and a new calling."

Blake's face turned red during Philip's remarks.

"Don't be angry with me, Blake. You were the associate rector of a very fine, very rich, very prestigious mainline church. It had an enormous endowment, a paid choir, a two hundred and fifty thousand dollar tracker organ, stained glass windows to die for, and all the spirituality of a country club. You lived that life and it brought you down." Philip waved off Blake's beginning protest.

"No, listen to me. You did. You were the young, single, handsome man that every mother hoped her daughter would marry. You had Bishop stamped on your heel and it seemed nothing could go wrong. But in all that time, Blake, did you ever feel the Spirit moving in your life? We talked a lot over the years, and most of it concerned things, appointments, commissions, how tight you were with the Bishop. We never spoke about holiness. God put you in Picketsville so you could learn those things.

One thing is certain, that little church is not a springboard to a cardinal rectorship or a bishop's purple shirt. You will bend to his will, Blake, or you will fall from grace."

Blake looked into the very brown and very serious eyes of his friend and knew he spoke the truth. His heart sank. Truth or not, Blake had not yet prepared himself to let go of the things he believed were his and for which he had worked so hard. The thought of serving out his years in Picketsville in that oddly named church crushed him.

"It will come to you, Blake. I know you and I know that behind all that shiny-bright ecclesiastical eagerness is a deep and caring person who will make an enormous difference in the lives of hundreds of people. That is why I gave you the job, Blake. I do not need a mission. I do not even want a mission. But God does, and he wants you in it. So there you are. Ah, here's our food."

They ate in silence, Philip obviously enjoying his steak. Blake toyed with his burger and fries, his thoughts far away—in Philadelphia.

"Philip," Blake said between mouthfuls of slaw, "you believe me when I say nothing happened at Saint Katherine's, don't you?"

"You said it. You do not lie, as far as I know, so yes, I believe you. Your Bishop's letter didn't hurt, either."

"Thanks a lot."

Chapter Six

"Okay, Ike, here's where we're at." Billy Sutherlin opened his notebook and waited for a signal from Ike to begin. Ike had finished with Fisher and watched him drive away. He'd spent the next hour circling the grounds. He hadn't found much. He assigned two men to work up the victim's Toyota Tercel parked in the trees, at least he assumed that's who the car belonged to, and he taped off another set of tire tracks nearby. The lot behind the church did not seem to be used often, especially in the summer, and he guessed the tracks might be significant. Or not.

"Shoot," he said.

"Well, Miz Bass, that's the lady with the face all messed up from crying and—"

"The one who put her finger in the bloodstain?"

"Yeah. She's the church secretary and the one who found the body. She doesn't know why the victim came back to the church late Thursday night."

"Back?"

"Yeah, see they have choir practice every Thursday evening and then they all go out together. But he might've stayed behind or something. So, anyway she said this morning she aimed to get a head start on the fixing up what they do in the..." he consulted his notes, "sanctuary or is it sacristy...can't keep them straight...so she came out that door and around the corner and found him. She's pretty busted up."

"The others?"

"Well, you know my mother, course, and Mavis Bowers. She lives out by the Craddocks. I reckon she can tell you some stories about them…and then there's Grace Franks and Iris French. They all say the same thing…they came in, found the Bass woman in a state, and called you."

"What about the Reverend?"

"Well, he got here late and he don't seem to know anything. I didn't try for an alibi, what with him being a Reverend and all."

"I wouldn't be too sure about that. He's a priest, by the way. Episcopalians have priests like the Catholics. But Reverend or not, I want you to check him out. Anything else?"

"Well, that's another funny thing, Ike. The FETs gave me this here key ring."

Ike looked at the ring of keys, counted them through the plastic of the evidence bag. Five keys. He held the bag up to the light.

"You see anything interesting about these keys?" he asked and handed the bag back to Billy. His deputy took it and shifted the keys around in the bag as Ike had done. He frowned and sighed.

"Well, sir, I can't be sure if it's important or not, but it seems like all the keys is, you know, on their cut side, facing the same way except this here brass one. It looks new and is pointed the other way round."

"Any thoughts?"

Billy scratched his head. "Well, most folks don't care which way a key faces. But if this Templeton guy was, like, one of them orderly types, you know, the kind who refold their newspaper before they throw it out in the trash, or always roll their socks a certain way and, well, if he made sure all the keys faced the same way, then—"

"He was in a hurry when he put this one on, or he didn't think it would be on very long, or someone else put it on for him."

"Um, well I got two outta three there, Ike."

The remains of Waldo Templeton, neatly packaged in a blue plastic body bag, were deposited into the coroner's van. The driver and his helper slammed the rear doors shut, climbed in front, and pulled out of the parking lot. Ike watched as it turned and drove away.

"Ike," Billy said, his eyes also on the van, "about them bullet holes."

"What about them?"

"Well, I'm thinking they were small caliber, maybe .25, no more'n a .32. That usually means whoever did the shooting must have been a pro, don't you think?"

"Maybe. TV shows and books pretty much spread that notion around, but killers generally use the weapons that feel comfortable. Some pretty big time killers use some real cannons."

"Oh." Billy turned and looked disappointed. He reached for his left breast pocket and then dropped his hand. He'd quit smoking the week before, but hadn't shed the habit of reaching for the pack when he had a problem to solve.

"Well, what I meant to ask you is—assuming small caliber means a professional— how come he took two shots? One is in the shoulder and not anywhere near fatal. Then, there is the perfectly centered shot to the head."

"No telling. Too dark, or he rushed his shot, or the victim moved. My guess—the shoulder wound served as an attention getter. The shooter hits him in the arm or shoulder to spin him around, then he drills him. The second shot is either lucky or the guy is what you suspect, a pro."

Billy thought a minute and said, "I'm betting on pro."

"If you're right, there's no way we'll catch him. A hit man will be long gone by now. If he's still here, he's put together an iron clad alibi."

"Might be a she."

"Might be."

"So, besides playing the organ, who is this guy, Templeton, anyway?" Billy asked.

"We'll have to find that out first thing. Check out his ID, find out where he lived and search his place. The coroner will give us a set of prints and a dental work-up sometime Monday.

We'll run them through the County's program and see if we get a hit. Either way, we'll send them off to the Bureau, too."

"Funny about the church, him getting shot in it, I mean," Billy said.

"Maybe more important than funny. What are the chances? Churches aren't exactly the venue of choice for a shooting." Ike scuffed his toe against the gravel and turned the idea over in his mind. He believed he'd just said something significant, but couldn't think what. He hoped it would come to him later.

Ike glanced at his watch. Too late for lunch and too early for dinner. Friday afternoon and soon they'd both be caught up in the weekend craziness caused by youthful exuberance, hormones, and beer. Ike made a point to put himself in the duty rotation like any of his deputies. He'd drawn the weekend. No date tonight. He'd call Ruth anyway.

Chapter Seven

September's promise, in the southwestern corner of Virginia, is cooler weather. When that relief will arrive, however, is never certain. Ike mopped his brow and contemplated a career change in a location with a more varied climate. Someplace, anyplace, where the humidity did not compete with the temperature for top spot and summer confined its presence to a reasonable three months. The building that housed, among other things, the sheriff's office, had just been rehabbed, and a new, but erratic, air conditioning system installed.

"It's all zoned," Solly Fairmont, the town's new Maintenance Supervisor said, beaming.

Where the zones began and ended remained an unsolvable mystery to the employees captive within the walls of the Municipal Building. Sam Ryder complained for two weeks about the heat and the need to keep her computers and their myriad appendages cool. Finally she threw up her hands and purchased a small window unit, stuck its homely grill out the only window in her cell *cum* office, and closed her door. Both the door and the window were new. Bars had been replaced with studding, drywall, and door and window stock from Home Depot.

Ike settled into his chair, gritted his teeth at its squeal, and picked up the phone. He needed to talk to Ruth. Everyone in town knew he and the president of Callend College for Women were an item. The townsfolk preferred not to talk about it. They liked Ike and could forgive him this one foible, and if he wanted to hobnob with the hoity-toity folk up on the hill, well okay. Eventually, they agreed, he'd come to his senses.

He rolled his chair close to the door, kicked it shut, and winced at the ominous rattle it produced. His office had glass panels, starting halfway up, for walls. His predecessor had insisted on it. The story went around he didn't trust his deputies, afraid one of them would challenge him in an election, and he needed to keep an eye on them at all times. None of them dared to run as it turned out. But Ike took him on in the general and won in a landslide. The town's major concern since then: if Ike left, would the sheriff's office revert to its former corrupt torpor? It was a problem that worried Ike as well.

"President Harris' office," Agnes Ewalt warbled.

"Good afternoon, Agnes," Ike said. "Is your boss in?"

"Is that you, Sheriff?"

"Yes, Ma'am, it's me."

"Just a moment, I'll see if she can speak with you." Agnes Ewalt shared the townsfolk's disapproval of their relationship, only in reverse, so to speak. Ike decided if, in the unlikely event he and Ruth Harris ever married, he intended to get Agnes Ewalt pie-faced drunk, make her stand on a table and sing "I love Townies" to the tune of *I Love Paris*.

"Hi, Sheriff," Ruth said, music in her voice. "Are you behaving?"

"Serving and protecting, Ruth, serving and protecting—I'm on tonight."

"I know," she said and paused. "Ike, you're the boss. You don't have to pull shifts with the deputies. Why do you do it?"

"I can't ask them to do something I wouldn't do."

"Ike, they know that. They know you'd back them up any day, any way. You don't have to prove anything to them."

"Okay, then put it down to stubbornness. I came into the police business through the back door, sort of. I still need the experience."

"That's nonsense, Ike. You do it because no matter how much you want to convince yourself you are done living on the edge like you did in your CIA days, you still need the rush—maybe just a little one."

She had a point. He had not thought about it, but she might be right. Did he? Those days had been dangerous and heady. If Zurich hadn't happened, would he still be drifting in and out of Europe, a pawn in intelligence chess?

"Enough psychoanalysis, Doc. You up for a late date? I'm off at eleven."

"At eleven, I will be in bed, asleep, and alone. I have put in one hellish week and I have another coming. We have student transfers in, transfers out. Faculty who were spooked by the robbery business and loss of the art collection have jumped ship. I am going crazy trying to find replacements and at the same time getting classes started on Monday. Do you know anybody who can teach freshman English?"

"I met a guy today who thinks he's mastered about everything there is to know in that department. He gave me a lecture on usage."

"Really? Who?"

"His name is Blake Fisher, the Reverend Mister."

"He's the pastor or minister or whatever they call them at the church with the ridiculous name, isn't he?"

"Priest, and Stonewall Jackson is not a ridiculous name, and if I were you, my Yankee friend, I would not say so in public, not in this part of the world."

"Well really, Ike, what kind of religion are they promoting when they name a church after a slave-owning, states rights-spouting, secessionist civil war general?"

"Southern religion, honey child, and don't you forget it, unless you want a reprise of that war in your office. So, I take it tonight is a no?"

"You take it right, sorry. How did you meet Blake…what's-his-name?"

"Fisher. He had the misfortune of having his organist murdered in his church. He found it a great inconvenience."

"Murder? Who?"

"A guy named Waldo Templeton."

"Never heard of him."

"Neither has anyone else, it seems. Just another anonymous out-of-towner. You know how we feel about them."

"Well, there's your edge, Sheriff, be happy. Can you break for a bite at, say, seven?"

"Yes, where?"

"My kitchen, for starters. Then we'll just have to see."

Ike hung up and shuffled through a stack of papers on his desk. He was famous for the amount of paper he managed to accumulate on his desk and still know where everything was. He found the duty roster and looked around the outer office through the glass windows. He couldn't see Billy Sutherlin anywhere. He looked at the rack holding the radios and saw they were all in place except for the patrol teams, so Billy either had not come in or had gone missing somewhere. He stood up and stepped into the hallway looking up and down its length. No Billy. He tapped on Sam's door. His tapping resonated through the hollow core. Tap, tap. Thump, thump. He walked in.

Billy sprawled in the corner reading a magazine. Sam leaned forward in her ergonometric chair studying a flat screen monitor. Her fingers flitted sporadically across the keyboard as she searched through files for something. She stopped and waited. A message appeared on the screen and she rattled the keys some more.

"I'm almost afraid to ask, Sam, but—"

"Installing new software, Boss. I have a beta version of a fingerprint matching system. With it we can access any authorized files practically anywhere. I also have the authorizations we need. Now we don't have to wait for the State's system, the armed services, or the FBI to get around to doing our checking for us. We can do it here."

"That's good. Um, Sam?"

"Yes, sir?"

"How much did that system cost?" Ike had committed himself to the move into the latest technology, but he knew it as an area about which he knew little or nothing and each month, when the bills rolled in, he wondered if he hadn't made a mistake. His budget had started to look like the federal government's idea of spending—a big deficit.

"It's a freebie, Ike. I know a guy who wrote the thing and he wanted a representative sample of law enforcement agencies to test it. I persuaded him we represented poor and rural—a twofer. So we got the goods."

Ike started to breathe a sigh of relief and then stopped. "After the test? What will it cost then?"

"I said we were a twofer. Poor gets us a free system but—"

"Do I want to hear the but?"

"We have to really evaluate the system, not just run it. It's no biggie Ike, I can do this. I wrote a program like this in college and I can not only test it but I can write the patches if necessary. They're going to love us."

"Okay, good…Billy, why are you in here reading a magazine instead of outside watching the office?"

"Well, Ike, it's like this. Sam here said she'd teach me how to work that apparatus so I came in for a lesson, but you can see she's just lost in cyberspace there so I grabbed this magazine. It's about computers and all."

"You know Billy, I believe this may be the first time I've seen you read a magazine that didn't have a centerfold. I guess I should thank Deputy Ryder for that."

"He only came in here because it's cool," Sam said and studied another directive on the screen.

"Outside, Billy, time to go to work."

The two men left Sam with her programs, winking red and green LEDs, and manuals.

Chapter Eight

It seemed unfitting, somehow, that a man should leave this earth with nothing more in his pockets than a key ring, twenty-seven dollars plus change, a driver's license, and a library card. But that's all they found on Waldo Templeton. And the driver's license looked a little quirky. Ike turned it over and peered at the back, then again at the front. Wisconsin licenses did not cross his path very often. This one had all the characteristics of a fake—the kind you find on college campuses carried by underdrinking-age students. He had some experience with fakes, this kind and the professional ones he'd used in his other life. Over the years he had confiscated enough of them from Callend College women and their dates to fill a small filing cabinet. The library card was real.

Sam Ryder stepped out of her office, ducking her head in order to keep from bumping it on the door frame. Sam was taller than Ike by at least three inches, which put her in the stratosphere at six feet five.

"It's installed," she said. "Do you want to test it?"

"Sure. Get a set of prints and run them."

"Whose?"

"How about Billy's."

"How about yours," Billy said. "You don't want to go running my prints through that machine."

"Why not?"

"Do we have a John Doe we can try?" Sam said. "We ought to have a control. Billy we know is in there and so are you, Ike."

Ike wondered about that last part. The Agency had funny ideas about its people, even when they no longer worked for them, but he didn't want to find out this way. Maybe he'd have Sam look later, but not with anybody else around.

"We'll do Billy and a John Doe, just to be sure," he said. "I'd have you run Templeton, but we don't have his back from the coroner yet."

"How come it's always me?" Billy said. "Why not Sam here, then?"

"I already ran mine, if you must know."

"And you found out you're wanted in five states—"

"Sam, dig around in the files. There's bound to be something in them you can use."

Sam pulled open a file drawer and leafed through a stack of old cases. The original plan had been to put them on microfiche, but before the Picketsville Sheriff's Office could acquire the technology to do that, it became obsolete. Now they were waiting to be scanned into one of Sam's new databases.

"Well, here's something we can try. It's a print from a nickel bag of dope we took from a student last June. We never prosecuted and never ran the print."

"Give it a whirl. Go on, Billy. Give the nice deputy your print."

The two deputies retreated into Sam's digital den and Ike picked up the magazine Billy had brought out with him. Nobody ever accused Ike of being stupid, and he felt sure if he applied himself, he could master the intricacies of computers. He read one complete article and put the magazine down. He closed his eyes and tried to remember what he'd read and the concept embedded in it. He couldn't. He could play chess against a computer with more than moderate success. He could recite several of Shakespeare's sonnets by heart, and he'd read and understood most of Steven Hawking's *A Brief History of Time*, although the black hole bit still remained a puzzle. But when it came to computers—he knew how to turn them on and off. As for the stuff inside, the buses and the bytes, the RAMs and the ROMs, they danced away from his comprehension like fireflies in May.

"Ike, you might want to have a talk with Billy," Sam said as the two emerged from her office.

"You said you wouldn't say nothing, Sam."

"But this is a very serious matter. You'd better come clean, Billy. After all, you are a law enforcement officer—"

"Billy?"

Billy Sutherlin clenched his jaw and glared.

"He owes over forty dollars in parking tickets in Virginia Beach," Sam said triumphantly.

"You're on my list, Ryder," Billy said and flopped down in a chair and put his tooled cowboy boots up on the desk in front.

"Ike, you should see the setup she's got in there. It's like that *CSI* show. Print comes up on a screen and then zippity zap, there's a match. You know what else we should get—one of those special blue light things that show up the fingerprints and stuff."

"What special blue light things are you talking about?"

"Like they have on the TV, Ike, you've seen them. They shine this here light and fingerprints pop up all over the place and they have another that does blood."

"I've never had any problem finding blood."

"No, see it shows where the blood was at before they cleaned it up—"

"Special blue light things?"

"Yep, we need one."

"Billy, the only blue light specials I'm familiar with are at the K-Mart. You could check it out the next time you buy one of those ugly shirts." Billy scowled. Ike turned back to Sam.

"What about the other print, anything?"

"We got a hit. It belongs to a woman named Della Street. I'm not kidding, that's her name, just like the woman on the old Perry Mason TV show. She's new out of jail. She did five with time off for dealing in Philadelphia. Last known address is Johnstown, Pennsylvania. Her probation officer hasn't heard from her in four months."

"What's she doing down here?"

"If she's here—she might not be. The bag came from a student. He could have had it for weeks, bought it somewhere else and brought it down here from wherever he came from."

"Let's assume he got it locally. That way we won't get caught with our pants down if it's true. Get Essie to post whatever we can find on her. Make sure everybody's got a copy, just in case."

Ruth Harris glanced at her watch for the third time. She'd promised Ike something to eat at seven and her watch read six forty-five. Her accountant and the head of Building and Grounds wanted answers. Of course they did. So did she, but she didn't have any answers. The loss of the Dillon Art Collection had been bad enough and Dillon's donation of scholarship money a blessing, but scholarships paid student expenses, not physical plant expenses. She did not have the presence of mind, when Dillon made the offer, to build in overhead. Now she had debt in one area and a surplus in another and never the twain could meet. She shook her head.

"Gentlemen, I don't have an answer for you now. Mr. Hopkins, you will have to talk to our fiscal advisors and arrange a line of credit until we sort this thing out. Jerry, you will just have to secure the storage facility as best you can. We can't afford to rebuild the alarm system and we have no use for the building now anyway—maybe never. Nail it shut."

"Okay, I can do that, but with the temperature controls off, I can't be responsible for what happens down there."

She dismissed them and looked at her watch again. Seven.

The President's house stood only a few yards from her office and she hurried across the brick pathway to it. Ike sat on the porch in one of the school's signature rocking chairs.

"I'm sorry. Business. What am I going to do with that piece of crap in the valley?"

"I'm 10-7 at Callend College," Ike said to his shoulder and switched off his radio. "I take it the organic fertilizer you are referring to is the building that used to house parts of the Dillon Art Collection."

"That one, yes. Oh, Ike, I thought when we received the money after that disaster, we were fixed. But the money is in one pile and the debt in another."

"Dillon would renegotiate the deal."

"I can't ask."

"Can't or won't?"

"What do you mean, won't?" Ruth's back would be up in another second.

"Nothing. Not now. Let me think about it. There ought to be somebody out there who can use a super secure multimillion dollar bomb shelter."

"Who? I mean the only people who'd even think about it are right wing wackos and troglodytes."

"That's a little strong, don't you think. There must be some left wing wackos who'd be just as interested."

"As Queen Victoria is supposed to have said, 'We are not amused.'"

Ike thought a moment. Somewhere in the back of his mind a small bell began to jingle. Not loudly, and not in any compartment of his memory he could immediately identify, but it would come to him sooner or later. Whether Ruth would buy into it—another story entirely.

Chapter Nine

Sunlight slanted in through slatted blinds. The office remained cool and dark, even as an early Sunday sun blistered the pool and patio outside. He watched, a smile on his face, as his granddaughter swam laps. She turned and waved to him as she rolled over and backstroked away. He looked at the clipping faxed to him minutes before. The Saturday edition of the *Richmond Times Dispatch* gave it one column inch, only a brief description about a shooting in Picketsville, Virginia. Except for the name scrawled in the margin of the fax, he would have no idea that the dead man had anything to do with him. *Krueger*, it read. He picked up the phone, dialed, and waited for the voice on the other end.

"I assume Krueger is no longer a problem for us?" he asked.

"He made a mistake. They all do, sooner or later."

"Before he left he told me he had pictures. Can I assume they are destroyed? I don't want that weasel coming back to haunt us from beyond the grave. You have them?"

A pause.

"We're working on it. He hid them somewhere, but we think we're close."

"You know what they say about 'close,' don't you—horseshoes and hand grenades—get me that evidence or whatever he had or there'll be no business for you, now or anytime soon. You got that?"

"No problem. We'll be in touch as soon as we're done."

"You do that." He hung up and sat in the half shadows and watched his granddaughter finish her mile.

Blake stood at the back of the church and dismissed the eight o'clock congregation, the ten or twelve stalwart, old-fashioned Episcopalians who liked Jacobean English, short services, and no music. They were a dependable and largely anonymous group, a standard feature in nearly every church he'd ever served in or heard about—the Eight O'clocker.

He'd felt odd celebrating in front of the partitioned-off sanctuary. The women had managed to string a taut rope across the apse just behind the communion rail and draped some green damask over it. It reminded him of skit night at camp when he and the other campers would perform in front of sheets hung very much like that in the dining hall. The greatest hilarity at those shows invariably occurred when the boy's counselors did their skit at the end, always dressed as women—either ballet dancers or chorus girls or some variation on that theme. The sight of beefy, for most part, college athletes in tutus and lipstick always brought the house down.

The fabric, left over from another time when the congregation thought to upholster the pews, had been dragged out of the attic for the occasion. The couple who volunteered for the job left town hurriedly, no one remembered why, and the damask had been put away. Blake noticed a few moth holes here and there. Well, at least it was green, the correct color for the liturgical season. He wondered how much, if any, of it could be salvaged. He didn't have an idea what he'd do with it, but you never knew. The Sunday school's altar had been dragged up from downstairs and placed in front. The altar candles looked huge on the tiny rectangle.

He said goodbye to the last of the congregation and watched as a young woman climbed the steps, moving against the ebb tide of early worshipers. She certainly did not meet Blake's stereotype for an Eight O'clocker, and the service had ended anyway. She introduced herself rather breathlessly as Mary Miller.

Blake extended his hand to her. "I can't tell you how grateful and relieved I am to meet you," he said. "You are a life saver. I will have to thank Philip again."

Mary Miller was slim and slightly above average in height. Her face came to a gentle point at her chin, and her nose, he thought, a scant quarter of an inch too long to be genuinely attractive. It made, he thought, a sort of cute exclamation mark in the middle of her face. However, two wide and luminous eyes, the kind poets used to call limpid, offset this slight defect in her otherwise wonderful face. He could not identify her perfume, but he liked it. Blake thought her beautiful.

"I'm sorry. I hope I'm not late. I forgot the service times. I meant to call—in fact, I did before I left this morning, but, of course, you were busy and no one answered…oh dear, I hope I didn't miss a service," she said looking anxiously at the departing men and women. "You must be Blake. I'm sorry…Blake is what Philip called you. What do I call you?"

"Blake is fine. No, you are right on time. We don't have any music at the eight o'clock, and the next service isn't until ten-thirty. Here, let me show you the organ and get you settled." They walked the length of the church to where the organ stood, positioned at the right side of the chancel.

To say the organ *stood* in the church misrepresented the situation completely. *Parked* would be more appropriate. It sat there, as big as a Volkswagen and as heavy.

"It's huge." She contemplated the expanse of mahogany in front of her.

"A misadventure by the organist who preceded Waldo. Apparently he persuaded the Mission Board to dip into their savings and buy it as an investment, an exact copy of one of Virgil Fox's organs, Black Beauty, if I remember correctly, and worth a fortune."

"Wow. I can't wait to play it."

"Well don't be too sure. Virgil or no, it doesn't sound all that great. Anyway, he told them they could resell it at any time for twice what they paid for it. With no guidance from an expert, they took his advice and spent the money. The next year, organs like it began to show up in scrap heaps all over the country. Digital technology knocked out complex electronics and now, even if we wanted to sell it, no one will buy. It's not worth the cost of hauling it away. Oh, and what do I call you?"

"Mary is fine." Blake thought he saw the beginnings of a blush, but he could have been wrong.

"Three manuals and pedals, of course. Lucky for us Waldo did not lock up the organ. We never did find his key. Apparently, he had the only one, and it's missing."

Mary smiled and changed her shoes, turned on the organ, and began to play some chords. She adjusted the stops and smiled at Blake. "This has a wonderful tone and range. Even if it's not saleable, it's still a fine instrument. Why would you want to get rid of it, anyway?"

Blake hadn't thought of it that way. She had a point, and given the church's financial status, there would be no sale or purchase under any circumstances.

"Oh, here are the hymns. I guess you will have to announce them," she said.

He took the note page with the hymn numbers written on it and slipped it in his prayer book with the bulletin.

"No problem. I will leave you to your art." As he walked away, he thought, what a dorky thing to say.

Chapter Ten

The ten-thirty—Blake glanced at Mary's scrap of paper and announced the opening hymn from the back of the church. Mary looked uncertainly at him and then struck the opening chords. She played wonderfully, the choir processed, and even a few of the people in the pews joined in the singing. The liturgy unfolded predictably. Two men from the worship committee read the lessons, and Mary led them in the singing of the hymn before he read the Gospel.

He paused and studied the people as they settled themselves in preparation for his sermon. The rustle of bulletins subsided, and in a moment all eyes focused on him. They were his congregation. For better or for worse, he was married to this group of people for the foreseeable future. He wondered what he could say to them that would make them care. He looked into their faces. The regulars, the Old Liners, were all in their pews. SOFITSOP—Same Old Faces in the Same Old Places. They sat, Sunday after Sunday, in exactly the same spot—same pew. It seemed the center of the church, the spaces nearest the aisles, were filled with regulars. Some of them had been coming for decades and had staked out a proprietary claim on their places, and God help the poor visitor who had the temerity to commandeer it. Newcomers and visitors filled in at the back, or if they were very brave, the front, and along the periphery.

He remembered someone once telling him that people who failed in business tended to concentrate on the wrong things, on the negative. "Their eyes are not on the doughnut, but on the hole." Blake looked again at the stony faces centered in the middle of the church and then at the new families, the young people, and the visitors spread around the edge and made a startling discovery. He had been looking at the wrong thing. He had been looking at the hole when he should have been concentrating on the doughnut. If the church was ever to reach its potential, it would do so with new people, not with the old. They'd had years enough to move forward and failed. Now it would be up to the newcomers.

Normally, Blake would have climbed into the pulpit to preach his sermon. Today he did not. He abandoned his notes, pulpit, and routine, stepped to the front of the church and began to speak. He had no real idea what he would say, but he decided to start over and aim his remarks at the eager faces in the "doughnut," not at the frozen ones in the "hole."

"Good morning. I want to make a general comment before I say a few words about today's lessons. First, I want to tell those of you that may not have heard it already that we experienced a dreadful tragedy here Thursday night. Our organist, Waldo Templeton, was brutally murdered in the church. The fabric you see behind me is to seal off the sanctuary, which the police still insist is a crime scene. I do not have any details to tell you beyond that. I suspect many of you may be better informed than I. No funeral services have been arranged. We are still trying to find his family. Our condolences go to them, and to his many friends here." Blake glanced in the direction of the choir.

"Second, I want to welcome Ms. Mary Miller, who has graciously agreed to fill in as our organist until we can get sorted out. Mary is a parishioner at Saint Anne's, our sponsoring parish, but lives over in the Westerfield section not far from here." A smattering of applause.

"Tomorrow is, as you know, Labor Day. I want to wish you all a safe holiday. If you are traveling, be careful on the roads. It is also the traditional starting time for us to resume our regular routine. Sunday school begins next Sunday.

"Finally I want to give you a heads-up on the investigation. I am afraid the police will be in and out of the church for quite a while. Sheriff Schwartz, whom you all know, is the lead investigator, and I hope you will give him your full cooperation. I have pinned his card on the bulletin board. If you have any information that might help solve the crime, please call him.

"As you know by now, it is my practice to preach on the Gospel, but today I want to depart from that and call your attention to our second lesson. I know you just heard it, but let me reread just a few lines—'Let love be genuine. Hate what is evil, hold fast to what is good and love one another with brotherly affection.'

"That is the essence of Christian living—we turn to one another in love. I know that it is not always easy to do so. Jesus directs us to love our neighbor as ourselves, and we reply, 'You've never met my neighbor.'" A few smiles from the doughnut—nothing from the hole.

"And he goes on to say, 'and as I have loved you.' Unwarranted, unconditional love is what he is talking about, and we all know how difficult that is. We can usually manage it for our family—overlook their most glaring faults—visit them in jail...." A few more smiles.

"Paul continues, 'Live in harmony with one another. Do not be haughty but associate with the lowly, never be conceited,' and so on. Paul wrote this to the people in Rome when the newly emerging church was just taking form, evolving, you might say. And he wanted to be sure that everyone understood what being a church meant. I wonder how many of you know what it is," he said and swung his arm around to encompass the four walls.

"This is a building. It is stone and mortar and glass, but it is not a church. You look surprised. You were told it was a church. It is listed in the Yellow Pages as a church. The sign at the road says Stonewall Jackson Memorial Episcopal Church. It must be a church.

"It is not. It is a building, a building which from time to time houses a church. You are the church. Do you understand? When Paul wrote to the Church in Rome, or Corinth, or Ephesus, he did not write to an address, to a building, a place. He wrote to people. The Church in Rome consisted of many separate gatherings meeting in houses and later in the catacombs—here and there. His letter would be passed around, perhaps copied, and distributed to them. We can only guess at the number of letters he wrote that were not copied and are lost to us. But in any event those people were the Church. There were no cathedrals, no bell towers, no parish houses, just people—the Church.

"Paul wanted them to know how they were to deal with one another. 'If your enemy is hungry, feed him, if he is thirsty, give him drink….' Not an easy task, I submit, yet that is what is expected of us. We are to love our enemies. What an outrageous notion. Whose idea was that, anyway? Oh, right, umm, it was Jesus. And if we are to treat our enemies this way, what about our friends?"

He couldn't be sure, but he sensed people were shifting about in their seats. Bulletins rustled. He imagined he heard someone exhale rather more noisily than normal. He pressed on.

"I think there are two kinds of people here today. There are those of you who believe you *go* to church, and those of you who believe you *are* the Church. It is my intention, as long as I am your vicar, to persuade those in the first group to become like those in the second, to become the Church. Some of you may find that idea uncomfortable, and a few, not many, I hope, may decide this is not the place for you. But if this building were to vanish overnight, would that be the end? Would you pack up and find another building, another comfortable pew to occupy? Or would you come together and start over again?"

Eyes bright in the doughnut, flinty in the hole. Oh well, in for a penny, in for a pound.

"We need to make a decision, a commitment—this year, this month, this week, today. We need to make up our minds whether we are a Church or an address, whether we are going to conform to Paul's teaching or ignore it. To help in that, we will begin three new programs this fall." Blake was extemporizing and amazed at what he'd said. He had not thought of programs until that very moment. His notes on the pulpit contained nothing about programs, new or otherwise. Indeed, nothing of what he had said up to that point would be found in them.

"I will lead a Wednesday morning Bible study. I will ask Mary to review our music and from now on include some contemporary pieces each Sunday, and I am going to ask you to move about in the church, not walk around, no, but to sit in a different pew every Sunday. Introduce yourself to whomever you sit next to. Oh, and starting next week, I want you to wear a nametag.

"This church has been a mission for over forty years. Forty years! In that time, it has not grown. Our average Sunday attendance had remained at eighty-nine for the last twenty years. As you know, the Bishop decided to close us down a while back. Only the good graces of Saint Anne's and the friendship between Dr. Taliaferro and Philip Bournet kept it open. I have been told Saint Anne's will close us if we fail to grow in the next two years. So it is no idle threat on my part to suggest the church might not be here someday. If you are among those 'who go to church,' you can always go somewhere else. But if you are among those 'who are the Church,' you may soon face a great tragedy.

"I am calling on all of you, now, today, to decide. Shall we stay open, or shall we fold up and go away? 'Never flag in zeal, be aglow in the Spirit, and serve the Lord.' Amen."

Blake turned, but first took one last look at his congregation. As he hoped, the doughnut stayed with him and, he happily noted, a small part of the hole. But the center remained frozen and now, it appeared, angry.

The remainder of the service went smoothly enough. Mary played expertly. The choir picked up on her cues quickly and sang, without rehearsal, better than they ever had for poor Waldo. Blake followed the choir into the narthex and turned to greet his people. Out of the corner of his eye he noted some moving forward, away from him, to the door with its flickering exit sign in the front of the church. They were either leaving or going to the basement without speaking to him. He couldn't be sure, but their number seemed to be larger than usual.

The good news: instead of the usual perfunctory "G'morning, nice to see ya," or "Interesting, Reverend," people actually stopped to talk. Coffee hour promised to be something more than the painful passage it had been in the past.

"Look at the doughnut, not at the hole. Look at the doughnut, not at the hole," he repeated to himself.

Chapter Eleven

Ike stretched his full six feet two inches and yawned. Sunday morning and he'd slept in. He'd worked a double shift until two in the morning both Friday and Saturday. He did go off duty at Ruth's house Friday night for a while, and that certainly broke the tedium. What started out as a quick snack and some conversation turned into something more involved than eating, His watch had read eight-thirty when, sated in mind and body, he left her, fast asleep. He felt a little guilty about that. Not a lot, but a little.

Saturday had more than its share of problems. Callend College, now back in session, meant that the traffic from the University of Virginia and Washington and Lee, beer fueled and foolish, would keep him and his deputies hopping until the early hours of the morning. He got up slowly, showered, and shaved and headed to town.

He ate his usual breakfast at the Crossroads Diner. He didn't have to order. Flora just waved him to a stool and put coffee and the rest down without asking. Ike always ordered the same thing. He pushed his food around with his fork and recited his litany of whys—why me, why here, why did he stay, and, most important, why the Crossroads Diner every day? It served terrible food. He sighed and, as usual, left his eggs, bacon, and grits half eaten. Flora did make a decent cup of coffee, he'd give her that. The rest qualified as Southern fried dreck. He flipped open his cell phone and called his father.

"Hello," Abe Schwartz boomed into the phone, "Abe Schwartz here. That you, Ike? I got this here new caller ID gadget and it tells me who's on the line so I don't always have to answer."

"Pop, you'd talk to the devil himself if he called. You need a caller ID like Swiss cheese needs holes."

"Well, now Ike," he said, "you might be right, but it is handy sometimes, like when that two-faced Lieutenant Governor calls."

Abe, even in retirement, still wheeled and dealed in the political arena, and the Lieutenant Governor had backed out of an endorsement he'd promised one of Abe's people. Abe said he wasn't done with the son of a bitch. Unless he'd lost a step, Ike guessed the Lieutenant Governor was in for a rough patch.

"Good thing you didn't run like I wanted you to, Ike. The business is getting dirty, I tell you."

Three months ago, Abe had been furious with Ike for not taking on Bob Croft in the primary for Attorney General. Now, it seemed, all had been forgiven.

"I'm coming out to the farm, if that's all right with you."

"Fine, fine, you do that, Ike. Come for lunch. I'll have Miz Kark fix us a stuffed ham." Kosher was defined in a unique way in the Schwartz household. "Your Momma'll be tickled to see you."

Ike drove the six miles into the countryside to the farm that had been his home until he went away to college. His father never really worked the farm. He leased it out, but for his political career, "farmer" worked with the voters. Very few believed he actually farmed. For most folks in this part of the world, a Jewish farmer was as likely as a Baptist bartender, an oxymoron of enormous proportions.

Abe met him on the driveway, his expression serious.

"Now, Ike, I don't want you to worry none, but when you visit your Momma, don't be too surprised with what you see. She's been sliding lately."

"What did the doctor say?"

"Well, Ike, it's like this. Three months, six at the outside. There's nothing they can do. I asked about more chemotherapy, whether there wasn't some new treatments. He said if I wanted to, I could take her up to Boston or the Mayo out in Rochester, Minnesota, but he didn't recommend it. The cancer's everywhere, Ike. We need to start practicing our goodbyes."

Ike put his hand on his father's shoulder. He held his gaze and saw the strain in his eyes. He patted him on the shoulder and turned toward the house.

"I'll go see her now."

He crossed the porch and entered the shadowy hallway that divided the old, turn-of-the-century farmhouse in half. His mother had been moved downstairs and ensconced in what would have been the Back Parlor in another age. The blinds were drawn and the room carried the scent of disinfectant and impending death.

"Hey there, Momma. How are you doing?"

"Is that you, Isaac?" Her voice sounded reedy thin, not the strong musical voice he knew. "Crank me up a little."

"How are you?" He twisted the lever that raised the head of her hospital bed until she signaled to stop.

"Do you know what I dislike most about being a Jew?" she said. She wasn't one. She grew up a Protestant, one of a long line of politically connected, wealthy members of a fading institution, the Baltimore aristocracy. But forty-five years earlier, when she fell in love with Abe Schwartz, a hayseed politician from the Shenandoah Valley, her society family cut her off, so she had declared herself Jewish. Aside from raising her only son in the faith, that declaration was as far as she ever got in her conversion, but she insisted it was all she needed. Her ancestor, the Right Reverend William R. Whittingham, the third Episcopal Bishop of Maryland, probably still rotated in his grave.

"Strictly speaking you're not a Jew, Momma. You never converted."

"Then strictly speaking, neither are you, Isaac."

"Try telling that to all my redneck friends."

She gave him a weak smile. "What I don't like about being a Jew," she continued, "is no afterlife. When I went to school with the nuns—you didn't know we had nuns then, too, did you? They made heaven sound so good we all wanted to go right then and there. But now, I'll have to wait, and I tell you, Isaac, I am tired of waiting."

He took her hand and realized how much she had wasted away since he saw her last. He could feel the bones beneath her nearly translucent skin. "How about I talk to the new vicar at Stonewall Jackson and see if he can't find a nice comfortable spot for you on the other side of the theological aisle."

"Would you do that for me, Isaac?"

He had been joking. He looked in her eyes and saw she meant it. He did not want to think about death, but he knew she had and wanted to make some preparations.

"You don't have to tell your Poppa," she said. "I don't want to hurt his feelings."

"I won't say a word," he lied.

Chapter Twelve

Blake finished greeting people at the narthex doors and walked the length of the church to the organ. Mary looked up and smiled. She had been packing up her belongings and changing back into her street shoes. She started to put her pedal shoes and music in a plastic bag.

"You can leave them here, you know," he said. "You will be coming back, won't you?"

"Oh, yes. That is if you will have me. Was I all right?"

"You were terrific. You will spoil us with your playing. I should not speak ill of the dead, but the truth is Waldo played terribly, and as a choir director....Come downstairs when you can. We have coffee, lemonade, cookies, too, I think. I know everyone will want to meet you."

"Should I? Well then, I'll see you there in a minute."

Blake passed through the sacristy to his office, removed his vestments—surplice, cassock, and stole—and headed through the secretary's office down the back stairs to the basement. A modest crowd lingered, drinking coffee and chatting. Heads swiveled toward him and away as he entered. He saw the regulars bundled together in one corner. They sent dark looks his way from time to time. He guessed he was getting a going over.

Mary appeared at his side, her eyes following the direction of his gaze. "Who are they?"

"The Wine and Cheese Society."

"The what?"

"The people who spend time whining and saying jeeze."

Mary laughed and gave him a sidelong look. "You'd better be careful. They might hear you and really have something to say."

"After my remarks this morning, I think they may have already started."

"Well, you were pretty strong, but I liked it. Keep it up and I might have to stay permanently."

"That is an irresistible incentive. I'm convinced, but it might cost me half my congregation."

"I wouldn't want to be responsible for that. I suppose you could afford to lose the Wine and Cheese Society."

Rose Garroway marched over. He waited anxiously, half expecting an attack. Rose qualified as an old timer. She and her sister Minnie, both in their late seventies, had attended the church for at least three decades. Blake waited expectantly. Hole or doughnut, he wondered?

"When?" Rose said, her eyes fixing him with a look that could mean anything.

"Excuse me. When what?"

"When will the Bible study start? I have been waiting for something like this for years."

"Well, why not this week? Bring your Bible and we will get right at it. I suppose I should see how many others might be interested, though."

"No problem there," she said. "My sister Minnie, Mrs. Ruby, and Harold and Maxine Digeppi say they will come. You leave it to me. I'll get it organized. You just be there. What time?"

"How about eleven. That way if we want to, we can go to lunch together afterward."

"The mall. We'll go to the mall. The food court has something like fifteen different outlets. We could try them all."

Blake resumed his contemplation of the Wine and Cheese Society.

"What do you suppose they're up to?" he said, half to himself.

"That bunch?" Rose looked in the same direction. "Well, since Millie Bass is smack in the middle, it's a fair bet they are gossiping, or about to gossip, or arranging for a session when they can."

"Oh, I hope not. It is very wrong, for a church secretary especially, to do that. She has access to files and—"

"You're too late, Vicar. Millie has been the fountainhead of tittle-tattle and dirt for twenty years. She's not likely to change now. If there is a confidence to be broken or a secret to be revealed, Millie's your man—woman."

"I'll have to speak to her."

"Don't waste your breath. Nothing short of a heart attack will stop that tongue from flapping. But since my vicar told me this morning to make nice with my enemies, I guess I'll have to stop wishing for that." She marched away to assume her duties as the Wednesday Morning Bible Study Organizer.

Dan Quarles, a worried look on his, face approached him.

"Father Fisher—"

"Just plain Blake will do, Dan." Quarles stood an inch less than six feet but looked taller—like most thin men whose body proportions include shorter than normal arms. He had a broad forehead with tufts of hair sticking out at the temples. His face came to a point at his chin. His mustache made the whole look like an upside down A. Blake had been told Dan attended seminary briefly and still affected black suits and an air of piety that made Blake uncomfortable. He wondered if the clothes and attitude were a seminary leftover, or the habits of a lifetime. He smiled at his own pun.

"I just wanted to give you a heads up. Everyone is upset about your sermon. I don't know how I'm going to straighten this out."

"Who's everyone, Dan?"

"Well, everyone."

"Names, Dan. Who are upset and, more importantly, why did they tell you and not me?"

"Well, I am the chairman of the Mission Board, so naturally they would. I don't think I should name names."

"Then we are not having this conversation. I have one simple rule. If you have something to say to me, you say it to *me*. You do not go to a third party and file an anonymous complaint. Either you believe strongly enough in what you have to say to be up front about it, or you keep it to yourself."

Blake heard his words and thought they must have come from someone else. What had gotten into him? First the sermon, now he just told off Dan Quarles, the chairman of the Mission Board. Dan stood absolutely still, his jaw slowly descending toward the floor. Finally he recovered.

"Now look here, Mr. Fisher—"

"Blake."

"You need to be clear about one thing. Some of us have been here for a long time. We have put a lot of sweat and tears into this church and by golly we think we've done a pretty fair job. We will not let you, or anyone else your pal Bournet sends down here, destroy what we worked so hard to create." Quarles spun on his heel and stalked away.

Blake watched him rejoin a group of men in a corner, and then felt the white heat of scorn from their eyes as Quarles repeated their conversation. He sighed, caught sight of Mary Miller leaving, and waved a goodbye. Mary gifted him another beautiful smile.

◇◇◇

The phone rang. Blake walked to his bedroom and picked up the extension. He'd forgotten how much psychic energy Sunday mornings required. He needed a nap.

"Hello, Blake." He knew the voice but could not identify the speaker.

"Hello, who is this?"

"Oh Blake, how soon you forget. You broke my heart and now you pretend you don't know me." Blake's heart sank.

"Gloria? How did you get my number?"

"The Reverend William Smart had it in his Rolodex. Wasn't that nice of him?"

"Smart gave you my number?" Blake worked for Smart in Philadelphia, at Saint Katherine's, a lifetime ago.

"Well, not exactly. I found it on his desk when he stepped out of the office and so I just, you know, took it."

"Gloria, you have done enough. I have nothing to say to you, and you can take it as Gospel this number will be changed."

"Don't hang up, Blake. I have something important to tell you that I know you are dying to hear."

"I doubt it."

"I talked to the Picketsville sheriff's office, to your nice Mr. Schwartz. I told him everything."

"Told? You had nothing to tell, Gloria."

"Don't I? There is a difference of opinion on that. My side is borne out by the fact that I am still in Philadelphia and you are not. Who will they believe? By the way, he asked if I thought you were capable of killing. Do you want to know what I said?"

Blake felt faint. This could not be happening to him. His stomach churned. The woman had ruined him once, would she do it again? Against his better instincts, he said, "What did you tell him?"

"Oh no, Blake, it's not that easy. If you want to know, you will have to be nice to me. Not like the last time. If you want to know, you'll have to come to Philadelphia and ask me in person."

"Gloria, pray that I don't, because if come up there it will be to strangle you."

"Very good, Blake. That's what I told that nice sheriff. Goodbye."

Blake, hands shaking, put the receiver back in its cradle, and sat heavily on the bed. The early afternoon sun filtered through the blinds, casting vertical shadows on the carpet. They looked like bars on a jail cell.

"God, what are you doing to me?" he shouted.

Chapter Thirteen

Sam Ryder's space—she never thought of it as an office. Offices have desks and chairs and maybe pictures of a spouse and kids or a boyfriend or something. Sam had none of these in her life. Not yet. She believed her six feet five inches drove away most men. On a few blind dates, when she'd answered the door, the men looked up at her with an expression usually associated with someone witnessing an autopsy. One just turned and walked away, a bouquet of flowers still wrapped in plastic, clutched in his hand. She found it the next morning in the Dumpster. Sam resigned herself to being fixed up with basketball players and geeks. The former assumed that their status as pampered athletes entitled them to her sexual favors without question or preliminaries. She'd earned, among other things, a black belt in karate. The necessary application of a move involving her instep and the groin of an Associated Press All American point guard permanently ended her association with the basketball team. The geeks, on the other hand, were so intimidated by her, she grew hoarse from having to do all the talking. Her friends called her "Stork." But in her space, she reigned as queen.

The coroner had sent over a complete set of prints. They were clear and sharp, the advantage with lifting prints from a corpse. They didn't move around and blur the prints. She positioned the first fingerprint on the scanner's glass plate and started the program. If she was lucky she'd get her hit on the first try. Billy Sutherlin leaned over her shoulder.

"Lordy," he said, his breath rank from a half a loaf of garlic bread, "it's just like that *CSI* show."

"No, Billy," she said, clicking on the next button, "this is real."

"Sweet!"

Two boxes appeared on her screen. The one to the left displayed the scanned image of her print. The one on the right remained blank. Below the boxes a query menu popped up. She needed to enter the parameters she wanted to apply and the databases she wished to search.

"Ike," she said into the intercom, "how deep a scan do you want me to make?" She waited for an answer. Ike stepped through the door.

"Hey," he said, "that looks like that TV show, what's-it-called."

"*CSI*," Billy said.

Sam rolled her eyes. Ike leaned over her other shoulder, too. Tic-Tacs.

"Well, let's just try a simple program first. Do an eight-point match, local, county and state and see what we get."

Sam lifted one eyebrow. She had a sneaking suspicion Ike was flying in the dark. Eight would not be considered a simple run. She entered the parameters and clicked "next."

The right hand box opened and flashed WAIT.

"Isn't there supposed to be a bunch of fingerprints whizzing by in that other box?" Billy said.

"Like I said, Billy, this is real. To match whole prints and post them in sequence on the screen requires an enormous amount of computing power and a month to run. There's no reason to rescale and project all the no matches. Who cares about them? Now, if Ike would come up with money for a big Cray, I could do all that for you."

In a minute, the program stopped and announced, NO MATCH.

"We could go with fewer points," Ike said.

"That would be going in the wrong direction. These prints are clean and sharp. We'd only use fewer points if they weren't very good." Sam did not want to lecture her boss. She was still new to the department, having been recruited from Callend College only a few months previously. At the same time, Ike had declared her the resident expert on technical things.

"Right. Well, log on to AFIS and see if the feds have anything for us."

"This could take a while," she said.

"Okay. Well, call me if you get anything. Back to work, Billy. And Sam, what are you planning to do with all this stuff in the hall?"

"That's Templeton's computer and some discs. We picked it up when we searched his house. The place looked like he'd had it professionally cleaned. The guy was a neatnick. His cups and saucers were sorted so all the little flowers on the rim faced the same way. Amazing. It's all we found. I'll poke around in his hard drive and see what he was up to. Maybe that will tell us why he was killed."

"They should do one of them shows here," Billy said, his eyes still fixed on the flickering screen.

"What show?" Ike said.

"*CSI Miami, New York*—you know.*"

"You think *CSI Picketsville* would be a big draw in the TV ratings?"

"Shoot, yes. All them other shows are set up in big cities. They're all alike. Dudes in big old SUVs driving around shining their little flashlights in corners and good-looking babes taking pictures. But out here, it's different. They could show how folks in the country without all them fancy laboratories get the job done. Maybe Ryder here has got a friend that knows about all that stuff—like she knows about computers. Do you, Ryder?"

"You heard the man, back to work. Go away, Billy."

She reentered her parameters and turned her attention to Templeton's boxes.

She connected Templeton's computer as part of her network. It would have been easier to remove his hard drive and open it directly. The software she needed to hack into his was installed on her own drive, and she figured she needed the challenge. He had a firewall that took her less than five minutes to breach. She'd done this before. She spent the first ten minutes just opening and closing files and inventorying his software.

"Ike?" she said into the intercom. She waited while a series of snaps and crackles came back, mixed with at least one Anglo-Saxonism, and then he answered.

"You there?"

"Yes. Ike, this guy's a hacker. He's got some pretty sophisticated software on this machine. You want me to find out what he was after?"

"Sure. See if he was into blackmail."

"My thought, too."

She spent most of the next two hours following his Internet history retrieved from his hard drive. Every few minutes she jotted a note and moved on. She concluded he'd been pretty good at it. Not an expert, but pretty good. When she broke into Ibex and Crane, she frowned. Something did not feel right. She downloaded the files he'd accessed and saved them to a disc. Then, unlike Templeton, she erased her tracks into the program. It would not do for a major commercial real estate developer to discover its security had been breached by the Picketsville Sheriff's Department.

The air seemed very close and hot. The thermometer on the wall read 85°. She hadn't noticed it before, but someone had turned off her air conditioner. She walked to the window and saw a note taped to it, an official-looking reprimand. Solly Fairmont, Jolly Solly, had issues with her unauthorized air mover, it seemed. He insisted she refrain from turning the unit on as it disturbed the zone reading for her area. He said it should be removed at once. He said she should call for a technician to help with adjusting the air flow. He'd written several other things she did not bother to read. She tore the note up and switched on her window unit. It clunked and then hummed to life. For a minute or two, she stood in front of the vents letting the chilled air blow on her.

The computer running the fingerprint program beeped and MATCHED appeared on her screen underneath the print it had wedded to hers. She clicked on "details" and "print." The laser printer whined into life and a single sheet of paper swished out. She inspected it, frowned and started for the intercom, thought better of it, and walked around the corner to Ike's office. She'd finish Templeton's computer work later.

"Ike," she said, "I think we have a problem."

"What kind of a problem?"

She handed him the sheet of paper. He glanced at it and then read it through slowly.

"This is a joke, right?"

"Don't think so. That phone number looks like Quantico to me."

"They want us to hold this guy until a Special Agent Hedrick arrives to take him into custody. If he is not already in custody, we are to arrest him and hold him until this Hedrick guy arrives as he is a likely flight risk. Are these guys complete idiots? He's dead, for crying out loud. Unless they think he's an angel with wings, he isn't flying anywhere. What are they thinking about?"

Sam shrugged. "They probably missed that part. Actually they never asked for particulars, and we didn't offer any. We should call that number and tell them, but look at the sheet. It's blank except for his name which, by the way, is not Waldo Templeton."

"No surprise there."

"They didn't give us anything else except that they say there's an outstanding warrant out for his arrest," she continued.

"Okay. Get back on your computer and search for…what's his real name?"

"Walter Krueger."

"If he's wanted by the FBI, there's bound to be something on him elsewhere. I'll call this number and explain about the late Walter Krueger's unlikely prospects for flight."

She listened as Ike dialed the phone number on the sheet. He put on the speaker phone and was greeted by a robotic voice informing him that Section Chief Bullock was not available and that he should leave a message.

"This is Sheriff Ike Schwartz in Picketsville, Virginia. Please call me ASAP about Walter Krueger."

Sam retreated to her lair, leaving Ike to sort that one out.

Chapter Fourteen

Monday started out with Blake feeling like the Eighty-second Airborne had spent the night doing maneuvers on his head. Sunday boomeranged back at him—his sermon, Mary Miller, and Gloria. He looked at his watch. Eight o'clock on Labor Day morning.

He'd planned to fly to Philadelphia Sunday evening to visit his sister Irene, her husband, Bob, and his nieces and nephew. In fact he'd left Irene's phone number with Millie Bass, just in case an emergency came up. He'd called Irene at the last minute and begged off.

"Are you all right, Blake?" she'd asked.

"Fine, great, just a little under the weather. It has been a very bad couple of days."

He filled her in on the murder.

"Murder? Blake, that's awful. What will you do, I mean, did you have blood all over the place? Wow, a murder."

"Please, Irene, enough. No blood—well, a little—but the whole business seemed so matter of fact, once you got over the shock. It felt like the scene of an automobile accident, not a murder, and the local top cop heard about what happened in Philadelphia, or what he thinks happened in Philadelphia. He's a sheriff. Can you believe it? His deputies all wear Smokey the Bear hats and sound like they just stepped out of *The Dukes of Hazzard*—wee-hah! Anyway the sheriff implied Templeton, that's the dead guy's name, might have known about it, too, and might have been blackmailing me."

"Blake, nothing happened, did it? There are no grounds for blackmail."

"You know that. I know that. The police do not know that. But that is not the worst of it."

"There's more?"

"Gloria Vandergrift called me right after the sheriff left and hinted she'd talked to him. She said I should to come to Philadelphia if I wanted to know what she told him."

"You're not going to meet that…woman, are you? After what she did to you, you can't."

"No, of course not. That is another reason I think I should stay home tomorrow."

"What did you say to her, Blake?"

"I said I would strangle her."

"Good idea, bad thing to say."

"Right. I'll call you later in the week and keep you posted. Love to the kids—say hello to Bob."

Excuses made, he decided to secure his privacy. Since everyone thought he'd left town, he would let it stay that way. He parked his car in the garage and closed the doors. He returned to the house and locked up. He could get around the "everyone has a key" problem only when he stayed inside. All the doors had manual screw latches which allowed him to deadbolt from inside. All but one was painted shut, but with a knife blade, a pair of pliers, and some patience, he freed them so that they slid smoothly into their receivers. Now he was locked in and everyone else out. Blake decided he would replace at least one of them with a keyed deadbolt. The front door would do nicely. No one ever used the front door, so his Board would never notice he'd altered access to the vicarage without their permission—unless, of course, one of them tried to come in without his knowing it, and then, would they admit it?

He scrambled four eggs, fried some bacon, very crisp, and made toast and a pot of coffee. The house filled with their combined aromas. He thought about calling Mary Miller, reached for the phone, changed his mind, and went into the living room to settle in with the newspaper and breakfast.

At ten o'clock, he heard someone at the side door, no knock, just the sound of a key in the lock and the knob turning. The door groaned but did not open. A muffled thump followed, as if someone put a shoulder to it.

Blake went to a side window and peered through the blind. Millicent Bass stood on the steps, a puzzled look on her face. She stepped down to the walkway and disappeared into the basement stairwell. He heard the same sounds again. He watched her reappear at the side of the house. Would she try the front door, too? She started around the walkway toward the front of the house as a car pulled into the lot. She hastily shifted direction. Three ladies from the Altar Guild climbed out of the car chattering like schoolgirls. Millie joined them. He noticed the brown bag in her hand.

Well, he thought, what on earth did Millicent Bass want from his house badly enough to take time out on a holiday and try a break-in? Or, conversely, what did she wish to leave in his so house badly? The three ladies and Millicent drove off. He poured himself more coffee and returned to his paper.

The phone rang. Blake flinched. The caller ID indicated it came from Callend College. He felt relieved. He did not need another call from Gloria Vandergrift. The woman on the other end of the line identified herself as Ms. Ewalt and wanted to know if Mr. Fisher would be a guest at dinner that evening. She understood that it was short notice, but President Harris—

"I'd be delighted," he said, saving her the need to rationalize. Well, well, he thought. Maybe Philip had been right. Things were looking up.

An hour later, he heard noises at the door again. He decided he would slip up to the door, jerk it open, and confront Millicent. Perhaps the shock of seeing him would lead her to blurt out what she was up to. He glanced out of the blinds again. This time Sheriff Schwartz stood on the steps, a key in his hand.

Everyone has a key, including, it seemed, the police. Schwartz tried the door again and then apparently realized what it meant to be latched from the inside. He stepped away from the house. Blake watched as he circled the church and wandered off through the grassy lot toward the woods and the rear of the property. He returned five minutes later carrying a large parcel loosely wrapped in newspaper. Blake could not make it out, only that it did not seem particularly heavy. Schwartz carried the parcel to his car, opened the trunk, and put it in. As he did so, the newspapers slipped away and Blake thought he could make out the outlines of a steel box, a file box, perhaps. He thought to go out and say something to Schwartz but decided against it. He'd had enough rural police.

◇◇◇

Lee Henry folded her arms and smiled as Ike pushed through the door that served as the entrance to her salon. In any other house it would have been the family room, but she'd rigged it up with a chair, sink, and cabinets and made a living styling or cutting hair—which, depended on your gender.

"Well, look at what the cat dragged in, and on a holiday, too. How are you, Ike? You here for your semiannual haircut or is this a social call? If it's that, give me a minute and I'll just get me upstairs and slide into my black lace underwear."

Lee Henry cut hair, told stories and served as Picketsville's bawdy lady—all show, however. In fact she would have fainted dead away if Ike or any of her male customers were to respond to her approaches.

"And how are you, Lee? Any news I need to hear as the county's chief law enforcement officer?"

"Well, you heard what the blonde down at the new 99 Cent Store did when she cashed out her first customer?"

"No. What did she do?"

"Called for a price check!"

Ike smiled and took his place in the chair. "It's a haircut today, Lee. Unless you can tell me something about a guy named Waldo Templeton."

"Weird Waldo, the peeper. What do you want to know?"

"You *do* know him. Why am I not surprised? Is there anything or anybody you don't have a line on?"

"Gossip Center, that's me."

"Why 'the peeper'?"

"Well, see me and my friend, we go up to Buck Woody's on the weekends to dance and do a little drinking. And some of the kids from the colleges around here go there and we watch them and remember being young. Anyway, one night there's this ruckus on the parking lot. We got there in time to see an old Toyota peel out and the kids are all red in the face and yelling. Seems like they thought the guy in the car was this Waldo creep that they recognized as being from the uptown church, the Stonewall J., and they said they caught him peeking in the windows of a car where the couple were—you know—getting it on. He had a camera."

"He took pictures?"

"I guess so, tried to, anyway. Hey, here's one for you, Ike. This old guy had a farm with a big pond out back, fixed up nice—picnic tables, horseshoe pitch, and some peach trees. This is down in Florida, see. The pond was good for swimming, but he didn't do that no more on account of his arthritis. So, anyway, one evening he decides to go down to the pond, as he ain't been there for a while, and look her over. He grabs a five gallon bucket figuring to pick him some fruit. When he comes up to the pond, he hears voices—shouting and laughing and such. He gets closer and he sees a bunch of young women skinny dipping. When they see him, they all scootch down so only their shoulders is showing, and one of them shouts, 'We ain't coming out until you leave, old man!' The old guy looks at them for a minute and says, 'Well now, I didn't come down here to watch you ladies swim naked or make you get out of my pond naked.' He holds up the bucket and says, 'I'm here to feed the alligator.'"

Lee dissolved into a fit of laughter and Ike joined her. She had a gift. After a bad day, Lee could take you out of yourself.

"That's it on Waldo?"

"Pretty much. What's up with him?"

"He's dead. Shot twice in the sanctuary of the…what did you call it? The Stonewall J."

"Now that is peculiar, Ike. We don't do much murder business here. But then there's the toupee."

"He wore a toupee?"

"Yep. Expensive too—made in San Francisco. I peeked."

Blake felt a little guilty for enjoying all this quiet and privacy, a luxury for a clergyman. He spent an hour watching the early rounds of U. S. Open on television, got bored with power serving and wondered what professional tennis would be like if, like professional baseball, it froze its technology and only allowed wooden racquets and nylon strings. He guessed the players would just bulk up like their baseball counterparts to compensate for the reduced power. He turned it off when Andy Roddick served up an ace at over one hundred and fifty miles an hour.

He decided to search the house. He lived on the first floor. It had a bedroom, bath, and living-dining areas, the corridor to the side door, and a small utility room. Upstairs were two large bedrooms and another bath. Blake had only glanced at them when he moved in three months previously. He filled one of them with spare furniture, winter clothes, and his luggage. The other he left empty with the idea that he might eventually turn it into a library or study.

Stairs rose from the center of the house from the front door to the second floor. The house had two small dormer windows in the front but one long dormer, side to side, at the rear, which created enough space for the bedrooms and bath. He climbed the stairs and remembered Philip's request to look for Taliaferro's files. An hour and a half later, he gave up. He found no sign of the files. Worse, his gun no longer occupied its box in the closet. That could mean trouble. He wondered if he should call Schwartz. Probably not; he had enough trouble with him for one day. In the end, he called and left a message describing the pistol, a .32 caliber Colt automatic, and when he first noticed it missing. CYA.

He spent the rest of the day outlining his plan for the Wednesday Bible study. He would ask Millie to type it up and make a dozen or so copies for him in the morning. That should keep her busy while he went to the hardware store and purchased a deadbolt.

He finished by five in the evening. He tapped the papers even and laid them on the bookcase by the side door where he would see them on his way out in the morning. That is when he saw the newspaper clipping. It had fallen down behind the bookcase. Only a small corner protruded. He had missed it before. Did someone it leave it when they cleaned the house before he arrived, or had it fallen out of someone's pocket later?

The clipping bore the headline: CRIME KINGPINS STILL AT LARGE. It had been folded in four and by the look of it had been carried around in someone's wallet or purse for some time—but whose? He scanned the text only long enough to determine it had been clipped from a San Francisco paper and did not pertain to anything local. He found an envelope, put the clipping in it, and added it to the papers on the shelf.

He dressed for dinner and left the house.

He circled the church and tried to see it as his congregation must. What would he have to change about himself, he wondered, to capture their vision? Conversely, what would he have to do to persuade them to see his? He stopped his pacing. He realized he had no vision to share. He recalled his previous tenures in a half dozen churches, and recalled he had never had a vision for any church. Always, in the past, he had seen his job as merely playing out a role, filling in expectations—his, not those of his parishioners. He suspected he might have stumbled on the beginning of wisdom.

Chapter Fifteen

Essie Falco collected her purse, picked up a stack of folders, and scanned her desktop. Satisfied she hadn't forgotten anything, she waved and headed for the door. The folders she deposited on various desks for people's action the next morning.

"Essie, did that FBI honcho ever call back?" Ike shouted before she could get out the door.

"No, Sir. You want me to track him down?"

"Tomorrow, first thing, please."

The phone rang. Essie stopped and, tight lipped, checked her watch. Since her shift did not end for another two minutes, she dropped her purse and sprawled across the booking desk on her stomach, rump up, feet dangling, and arms barely reaching the extension.

"Sheriff's Office, Falco. What? It's for you, Ike," she said. "It's that Ms. Harris."

She slid off the counter, smoothed her skirt, recovered her bag, and left.

"Hi, what's up?"

"I need a favor, Ike. Please say yes."

"I'm not going to like this, am I?"

"Ike, it's just this once. I need you to fill in at dinner tonight. I have some faculty members—"

"This is a faculty do? Ruth, you know—"

"Yes, I know what you think of us. And I know you're just pig-headed enough to make my life difficult, but the Chairman of the English Department sprained his ankle and I need you to fill in."

"I don't know anything about English. Why don't you ask Blake Fisher? Did I tell you he's an expert on usage? Your crowd will just lap him up."

"You did and I already have. He's the 'guest.' You remember how these dinners work."

"You roped me in once and I swore never again. The conversations your ivory tower friends engage in make me crazy."

"Ike, this is me asking and I am desperate. Please, please, please—"

"On one condition."

"Uh oh, are we talking about carnal bribes here?"

"Well, now that you mention it, that too. But no, I had an escape route in mind. I will receive a call requiring me to leave early and you will say, 'Oh, too bad, Sheriff. Well thank you for coming' or something like that."

"Which is it? Carnal bribes or the coward's retreat?"

"Both."

"Well, I had something in mind for your birthday anyway, so okay. Will you really have a call coming?"

"Always a possibility—but for this shindig, a certainty."

"You're a hard man, Schwartz."

"You'd better hope so. Why is Fisher the 'guest' anyway? I thought he left town for the day."

"Well, I guess he plans to get back, I don't know. Anyway, you know how it works. We have our dinner and then the faculty work through a topic. I need a substitute freshman English teacher. You said he might do. I thought we'd run him through the gauntlet and see how he manages before I make the offer. Besides, it was your idea in the first place."

"Well, I'll come, but I will not engage in intellectual pillow fighting with your buddies. I will eat and mumble unintelligible redneck nonsense until they leave me alone."

"Will you promise to behave, Ike?"

"I will be mild-mannered Clark Kent. I will be your house boy. Do you remember the house boy from *Who's Afraid of Virginia Woolf?*"

"Yes, and the day you become anybody's house boy, especially mine, is the day I join the John Birch Society."

"Please, not them. I wouldn't wish that on anyone. Now the NRA—"

"Oh, right. I should posse up with those cowboys."

"Hey, there are some very nice people in the NRA."

"Name one."

"Tom Selleck."

"The actor—Magnum P.I.?"

"Great show. But I liked him in *Quigley Down Under* better. That movie had a theme even you would applaud. Anti-imperialism, racial justice, standing up for the oppressed—"

"Isn't that the movie where they ran a trailer at the end declaring no animals were killed or injured during the shooting of the movie?"

"That's the one. Since no disclaimer appeared about humans who might have been injured or killed, we can assume they were not considered important. As I said—your kind of movie."

"Give me a break. It wasn't necessary to do it for people."

"It was typical Left Coast PC."

"Enough. Will you or won't you?"

"Be good? I will. Not your house boy, but good, well pretty good, or maybe—"

"Seven o'clock sharp, and don't you dare wear your Boy Scout suit." Ruth did not like Ike's uniform.

The sheet of paper with the column of figures and letters Sam retrieved from Waldo Templeton's apartment lay on the desk beside her, begging for attention like a golden retriever—no sound, just an enormous presence. Sam drummed her fingers and stared. What were those figures? She reentered Templeton's, now Krueger's, computer and began searching through the files she'd only glanced at before—files she hadn't found interesting. The Rockbridge County assessor's office caught her eye. She went back to Krueger's Internet history. He'd hacked into their database. She followed his path to the files he'd opened. Land records, sales, and titles formed into columns, dozens of them. She moved back and forth over the cybernetic landscape provided by the assessor's office. Her instincts told her the paper and its figures were somehow linked to this site.

She pushed back from her desk and stretched. It had been a long day. Her shift ended at three. The clock on the wall read six-thirty. Sam often worked late. It never felt like an imposition. She loved her work and she would be eternally grateful to Ike Schwartz for giving her the opportunity to join the sheriff's office. She'd pursued a double major in college—Computer Science and Criminology. She dreamed of becoming a law enforcement officer, but because of her poor eyesight, she'd hedged her bet. She'd had a long love affair with all things electronic, and if she couldn't pass a physical for the FBI or a metropolitan police department, she would at least have marketable skills to flog. As it turned out, she failed four physicals for the same number of police departments and ended in a series of information technology jobs, none in law enforcement, the last at Callend College. Then she got the offer from Ike to join the sheriff's office. Ike seemed less interested in her fitness than in her ability to build computer systems and databases and, he admitted, he needed at least one female officer in a town whose major industry was an all-woman college.

Ike poked his head in the door.

"You still here, Sam?"

"Yes, Sir, I am."

"Go home."

"In a minute," she replied. Ike turned to leave.

"Ike." She still struggled with calling her boss by his first name even if everyone else did. "Do you remember when I told you about the rumors of an industrial park locating here?"

"Yeah. In fact I think the land rush may have started. My father had a pair of speculators talking to him already. And I see out-of-town cars all over the place lately. What about it?"

"I think there is something not quite right about it. I picked up the story months ago on what was supposed to be a secure site."

Sam called herself a recreational hacker. For her the challenge lay in breaking in, not taking things out. She had a rule which she obeyed, even though no one could call her on it if she didn't. At one time or another she'd managed to scan all of her bank records, her personnel file at every place she'd ever worked, and numerous other sites, even some considered top secret. She didn't leave a calling card as some of her hacker friends did. They needed that ego lift. Sam just slipped in and then slipped out leaving no footprints. She felt particularly proud of that. No one had ever traced any Internet B and E back to her.

She did break her rule one time. Her roommate married a man in the navy—one of those hurry-up weddings in Las Vegas. The wedding chapel had ninety pictures stored in its computer but wanted five hundred dollars for a CD of the set. After being skinned by a series of hidden charges, the couple had pretty much run out of money and had to pass. That night, Sam hacked into the chapel's computer and downloaded all ninety. She never did anything like that again.

Now, as the sheriff's office's computer geek, she reckoned all her wiles and sub-rosa software were kosher and that the hobby she'd once pursued knowing she risked arrest and prosecution had become her profession, and it would be others who put their pensions at risk.

"So, the anxious look on your face is there because…?"

"I've been into Krueger's machine and it is choc-a-block with attempts to confirm that rumor. He broke into Ibex and Crane. They are the developers of the project. He downloaded some files. Anyway, I went into Ibex and Crane, using his roadmap."

"And that led you to what conclusion?" Ike sounded a little peeved.

"Well, for one thing, the break-in was too easy."

"Too easy? Might it also be that you are too good?"

"No, thank you for that, but I meant too easy."

"And that is important in what way?"

"If, and I am just guessing here, but if they were going to build near Picketsville, the proposals and acreage estimates would not be posted in such a way that any moderately bright young man or woman could get at them. This information is just lying there like cheese in a mouse trap. I think they planted it on this site so that people would try to steal the data."

"To what end?"

"Disinformation. I think they intend to locate elsewhere. They let this one hang out there where anyone with a modicum of Internet skills could get it and be led into thinking Picketsville would be the site. It's a trap."

"Well, it makes some kind of sense, I guess. Go home, Sam. You can pick this up tomorrow."

"I will pretty soon. There are half a dozen files and these discs and floppies I want to look at first."

"Sam—"

"Its okay, Ike. This is like my hobby and I don't have anything on tonight. Don't worry about me. Is there anything I can do for you while I'm fiddling around in Krueger's computer?"

"Well, not while you're in the dead man's computer, but you could write a one-page manual for the rest of us on how the intercom works. I looked at the instruction book and I don't have either the time or patience to sort it out. It reads like someone translated it into English from Polish after it had been translated originally from Korean, which I expect is how it went, and I don't want to have to talk to someone in Bangladesh if I need help. I want something that says something like, for Essie, push number one, for Sam, push number two—something like that."

"No problem. It'll be on your desk in the morning."

"Great. You really are going to work late tonight?"

"It's not work, Ike."

"Can you do me another favor then? At eight-thirty or so, call me and tell me I have to come to the office immediately."

"Why do you need to come here tonight?"

"Sam, I am a patient man. I am a tolerant man. I have endured all sorts of lunatic talk in my life and survived. But, for me, listening to a small group of over-educated, over-opinionated intellectual dilettantes drives me nuts inside an hour. I'm giving them an hour and a half. Then you will rescue me and save the town the embarrassment of a multiple homicide."

"I take it you've been asked to the President's dinner party."

"That's about the size of it."

"Good luck. You have my sympathy. I'll make the call."

Chapter Sixteen

Ike parked his car on the circle that swept around the front of Callend's main building. Once out of its air conditioning, he removed his blazer and put it over his arm. The sun would set in an hour or so and the temperature would drop, but right now he succumbed to the heat and humidity. He was a big man, nearly two hundred pounds and tall. The ratio of his surface area to total volume—the law of cubes—should have worked in his favor, but it didn't. The perspiration started five yards from the car. He walked along the moss-grouted brick pathway around the building's south wing and down a gentle grade to the President's house. He inhaled the fresh scent of newly mown grass.

The architect who designed Callend's buildings in the late nineteenth century also drew up the plans for Stonewall Jackson Memorial Church. Like it, the original buildings for what was then known as the Virginia Female Academy had been constructed from local limestone. There the similarity ended. Callend's buildings stood as monuments to Victoriana while the church was a Norman jewel box. The President's house had, like the college's main building, a spacious porch which enclosed it on three sides. It also put on display Callend's famous wisteria, which laced its perimeter and, finding no more porches, doubled back, periodically sending tendrils skyward in a vain attempt to climb even higher. In the springtime, thousands of its heavy purple panicles covered the entirety of the porch and softened the chiseled limestone's stark gray. By September, however, the flowers were long gone and the leaves were beginning to brown.

He climbed the front steps and followed the sound of voices into the front hall. French doors opened out onto the porch at multiple locations. With all those entryways, Ike thought the house would make a perfect setting for an Agatha Christie play complete with charming, dark villains with names like Percy or Reginald. Men and women skulking from room to room, doing the crime, alibis intact. Loyal wives and fragile heroines in gloves, cloche hats and, of course, a big scene at the end when the sleuth would sort it all out. Never happen in real life.

He deposited his jacket on a sofa by one set of doors. The aroma of southern cooking displaced the scent of cut grass. Members of the catering crew, in dark slacks and crisp white shirts, moved quietly through the rooms. Some were setting the dining room table while others served drinks to guests on the porch. He walked to one of the sets of French doors in the large drawing room. Three men were engaged in conversation on his right as he stepped over the threshold. One man, wearing fawn slacks and a rumpled hunter green corduroy jacket with scuffed leather elbow patches and a carefully coifed gray beard and ponytail, glanced briefly in Ike's direction and held out his glass.

"Another Martini, only this time really make it really dry. All I want of the vermouth is that it be formally introduced to the gin, but they are not to become intimate—and an onion this time, not an olive. This is supposed to be a Gibson." He turned back to his companions, arm and glass still extended. A black faculty member wearing a shirt cut like a *dashiki* gave Ike a look that said, "Now you know how it feels, White Boy." Ike paused, controlled a flash of anger that painted the back of his neck red. In the last several months he'd found himself snapping at acquaintances and strangers alike, having no patience with people like this bearded twit who assumed too much. He retreated into the living room and flagged down a passing waiter.

"Here," he said, "fill this glass for the old guy with the ponytail. He wants straight gin and an onion. And can you get me a gin and tonic? I'll be out there," he pointed to a second set of doors, "with Dr. Harris."

The waiter nodded and retreated to kitchen. Ike found Ruth with four other guests, including Blake Fisher.

"There you are," she said and looked at her watch, "and on time. Sheriff, you know Doctor Fisher, I think."

"*Doctor* Fisher?" Ike said, and inspected the reedy clergyman with renewed interest.

"D. Min," Fisher said.

"Ah."

"And this is Candice Omanaka, our newest member of the Department of Dance."

Ms. Omanaka stood barely five feet tall and couldn't have weighed more than ninety pounds soaking wet. Ike wondered if she bought her clothes in the children's department and if they would have a booster seat for her at the dining room table. An unworthy thought and he suppressed a smile at the image it conjured.

Ruth also introduced Dr. Franz Weimar, Foreign Languages— German to be precise. No surprise there, and Jack Farragut, also new to the faculty and apparently pressed into dinner party duty at the last minute because of his position in the English Department. Ike sensed Jack wished he were somewhere else. They had that in common and in a different set of circumstances he might even like him. Farragut had that tall, athletic leanness usually associated with young men more at home riding surfboards than wearing mortar boards. The sort of young man the CIA used to recruit from campuses back when Ike worked for them.

They were joined a moment later by Monsignor Dunnigan. Dunnigan asked for sherry and immediately engaged Fisher in a lively discussion about the reaction in the Anglican Communion to the drift by conservative Roman Catholics toward enunciating a doctrine of Mary as co-Redemptrix. Dunnigan seemed to enjoy the discussion. Fisher's responses seemed wearily polite. Down in the southern extension of the Shenandoah Valley, excursions into arcane theology did not play well. Actually, they didn't play at all. Farragut shifted his eyes between the two men, like a man watching a tennis match, alternately confused and annoyed. Finally, he excused himself and joined the others at the opposite end of the porch. Ike went to find a waiter and another gin and tonic.

All of these activities were brought to an end when a gong reverberated through the building. Ruth collected her guests and mother-henned them into the dining room.

"Fisher," Ike said, "a word?"

"Certainly, Sheriff. What can I do for you?" The two men stepped aside to let the others pass.

"Can you make some time available for me sometime this week?"

"Do I get a choice?"

"This is not about Templeton. It's about my mother. She's not well and…I don't think she has a lot of time left. Every time the phone rings, I think this must be it."

"She's not well?"

"Cancer. Anyway, you know I'm Jewish, as is my dad. My mother 'converted,' but she was raised Episcopalian and now—"

"How's your father holding up?"

"As well as might be expected. They were a match made in heaven, I think. Whether in yours or Abe's, I'm not sure. Well, I was going to ask you to see her and…do whatever it is you do."

"Certainly."

"It's been a long time since…well, you know, and I think she feels she might not be allowed to—"

"We'll be fine."

"Thank you, Reverend."

"Blake. Reverend is not—"

"I know, I know, but as I said…okay, and if there is anything I can do to—"

"Well, now that you mention it, there is a little matter of a speeding ticket your young man, Deputy Billingsly, gave me—"

"Sorry, but you'll have to suborn a magistrate to fix that one."

"Well then, how about rescuing me from any more theological calisthenics with the good Monsignor."

"That, I can do. I'm expecting a phone call to pull me out of here. Shall the emergency it will call me to also require the services of a priest?"

"I have no doubt it shall, Sheriff. I can feel it in my bones. Someone, somewhere in the very near future is about to experience a crisis of conscience. Of course, the Church must make herself available." Fisher grinned. "You won't forget, will you, Sheriff?"

"Nope."

"Oh, one more thing. I was looking through my things and discovered something's missing."

"What?"

"A gun. I left a message at your office with a woman named Falco."

Essie, good at logging in messages, not so good at passing them on.

"What kind of gun are we talking about?"

"A .32 caliber Colt automatic."

"You own a pistol? That seems an odd thing for a minister to own."

"It was my father's."

"You father gave you a .32 Colt?"

"Yeah. I've never used it or anything. My mother didn't want it in the house so I said I'd take it. Is there a problem?"

"Nothing…it's just that a .32 Colt auto is considered a ladies' piece, you know?"

"A what? Did you say *ladies*?"

"Sorry. The figure of speech predates political correctness. In its day, it meant a pistol more appropriate for a woman to carry than a man—small caliber, short barrel, fits in a purse, and so on—not the sort of thing you'd expect a man to use. Though I did read somewhere that Pretty Boy Floyd used a .32 Colt."

"Pretty boy…who?"

"Depression era gangster…before your time. Mine too, come to think of it."

Dunnigan zeroed in on Fisher as they took their seats, intent on continuing their debate. But Blake waved him off with a smile.

"Father Dunnigan," he said, "enough theology for one night. Let's talk about more important things—food, fine wine, and who have you got in the World Series?"

Ike found a place card with his name on it and discovered he had been put at the end of the table next to the Gibson drinker. He introduced himself to Ike without betraying any sign that he had recently mistaken him for a waiter.

"Everitt Barstow," he said and extended his hand. "You must be new to the faculty. I'm Chemistry. This is Antoine Baxter," he gestured to the *dashiki* clad man, "and that is Foster Prendergast." Baxter looked a little embarrassed, and Prendergast jerked his head up and down like a chicken pecking corn.

"Antoine is head of Ethnic Studies and Prendergast is our mathematician. So you are with…?"

"The Picketsville Sheriff's Department. I'm the sheriff," Ike said and waited. The reaction was predictable and immediate. Their eyebrows, like six mismatched caterpillars, went up and then down and then reconfigured themselves into carefully crafted neutrality. Synchronized swimming had nothing on those beauties. Everitt Barstow cleared his throat and studied his water glass. Baxter made a sound somewhere between a snort and a grunt. Prendergast simply smiled and waited for more information. Ruth took her place at the head of the table opposite Ike and sat. Her guests followed suit. Ike glanced surreptitiously at his watch. He had forty-five minutes to go before he could expect a call from Sam.

Chapter Seventeen

Sam's pizza arrived and Bobby, moon eyed and needy, lingered for a few minutes. He would have spent the night if she'd let him, but she gave him a hundred-watt smile and sent him on his way. She chewed absently on her fourth slice of pizza and stared at the screen in front of her. The aroma of mozzarella and pepperoni mixed incongruously with the scent of new linoleum and jailhouse Lysol from down the hall. She studied her notes and realized Krueger's past activities would probably not produce any more useful information. Except for a few incursions into some import-export firms in San Francisco, he'd limited himself almost exclusively to Ibex and Crane. In fact, he'd visited the site several times, either to confirm his previous data gathering or to explore some more. In any event he did not succeed in going any farther into their system than the development proposal. She tried breaking all the way into it herself just to see what he'd run into. Their website was as secure as any she'd run across, and even though she did breach their wall, she realized most hackers, especially ones like Krueger, couldn't.

She finished the pizza and began to search his personal files. Her eyebrows pulled together in concentration. Her fingers flew over the keyboard. She began to retrieve deleted files. Some had been written over, but most were intact. Krueger had a large hard drive—plenty of room. He obviously had not considered the possibility his computer might some day be dissected by anyone, certainly not by the police. She restored data and tracked it back to its original location. Some of the files were huge. Pictures probably. When she was sure she had them all, she copied them to a series of discs and set them aside. The clock read eight. Too soon to call Ike. She began to open the files one at a time. The first half dozen were pictures of what she took to be local farms and roads, something to do with the development proposal she guessed. Then came a group of e-mails. Without a sense of who the recipients might be or the context of the exchange they would have to be read later.

Her second computer dinged. She'd set it up to search the Internet for information relating to Walter Krueger. Her genie program let her selectively search any and all available resources on the Internet. It would even probe some secured sites. It couldn't break in but it could read the site's indices. She'd do the breaking in. She scanned the files—there were several dozen—and hit the print icon. The laser printer whirred to life and sheets of paper began to pile up.

She turned back to her previous task, a huge file that appeared to be more photos. She rubbed her eyes, stopped, drained her Coke and stood up. Her back ached and she seriously considered quitting for the night. Enough was enough. She stretched her arms and touched the ceiling, then the floor, both with her feet flat and knees straight. She rolled her head in a circle and sat down again. She began to open the last series of pictures. The first one made her wrinkle her nose. The laser printer ceased swishing out paper. The top sheet caught her eye.

Ike's announcement resulted in a quiet fifteen minutes during which he was able to enjoy his dinner. He had no doubt he would be drawn into the conversation eventually. The food was quite good, by Picketsville standards. Molly Gilliam owned the Candlelight Inn south of Lexington and had a small catering business on the side. Her cuisine was mostly Southern, although she once made a brief foray into French and had quickly learned that unless you know how to prepare them, and are willing to eat them yourself, you should never serve snails. Garlic and butter can make almost anything palatable, but not everything. The evening was a disaster. Oddly enough, the snails had been harvested locally, thanks to an enterprising soul who'd brought the edible species to Lexington years ago, before the Department of Agriculture began to regulate what it would and would not allow into the country.

Ike had managed to get most of his prime rib disposed of when Barstow turned to him.

"So, Sheriff, would you recommend a career in law enforcement to our students?" Ike couldn't be sure if Barstow was setting him up, or if the question was sincere.

"Yes and no," he said. "It's an iffy proposition at best. Most law enforcement units are still chary about hiring women, though they do so, but there remains a deeply rooted notion that it is not a profession suitable for women. It's the same sort of prejudice you hear in the armed services and with combat soldiers."

"And you subscribe to that, I assume?" Baxter said. "How many women do you have on your force, anyway?"

"No I don't, and I have several in various capacities. One armed."

"And you give her a bullet like Andy did Barney Fife, I suppose."

"The woman can shoot the eyes out of a gnat, and drop you with one karate punch," Ike said. "No, if anybody gets the Fife bullet, it's me."

Barstow looked disappointed and tapped his glass with his knife. "It's time," he said. "The topic of the evening shall be…?"

"Racism," Omanaka said.

"No, ethnicity, Omanaka, racism is too narrow," Baxter said.

"Globalization," Prendergast offered and bobbed down for some of the few peas still on his plate.

"Scientific adventurism," Weimar offered.

"By that you mean exactly what, Franz?"

"The arrogant exploration of life in its many forms to exploit discoveries for profit. Look at the genome project, radiated grains, hormone-fed beef."

"American imperialism is my choice," Barstow said. "Sheriff, have you any thoughts on the compelling issue of the day? What concerns you most about the decay of our society?"

Ike inspected the company, read the expressions on their faces, expressions that varied from curious to supercilious. Ruth's sat tight lipped, eyes narrowed, daring him to misbehave.

"Fat men in Speedos," he said. The company fell silent. Ruth shook her head and shot him a look that, if the proverb held, would kill him. Then Jack Farragut laughed.

"My choice, too," he said. "It's symbolic of a self-absorbed but tragically uncritical society. Bravo, Sheriff." No one followed his lead, and the table fell silent again.

"Dr. Harris," Barstow said. "As our hostess, we leave the choice to you."

"I will give our good Sheriff one more chance," she said. Ike heard the steel in her voice. "I happen to know he can do better." Ruth glared at Ike. He thought a minute, realized Sam's call would be coming soon, and therefore relief was on its way.

"The loss of common courtesy, civility and tolerance for contrary views," he said.

"Explain," Barstow said.

"Look, when you asked us to come up with topics, each of you selected one that was divisive by its very nature. Each called for choosing up sides—to make assumptions about people, to categorize them into right thinkers and wrong thinkers—stereotyping them and forcing them to one or the other side of your issue. You are either for, or you are against. You affirm a woman's right to choose or you don't. Those, thus affirmed, classify those who aren't as the enemy, as Conservative or Liberal. If, for example, I were to come down on more than one issue in that camp, I will be labeled as part of the Great Right Wing Conspiracy—or the great Left Wing—"

"You are not a believer in conspiracies, I take it?" Barstow interrupted. He had the look of a deer hunter who had an eight-point buck in his crosshairs.

"I believe people conspire. I believe conspiracies exist, but except for those with no moral implications, they generally don't stand the test of time."

"You don't believe there were any shots fired from the grassy knoll?"

"I have no information there were or were not."

"You really believe Lee Harvey Oswald acted alone? The sheriff of Picketsville speaks. In your position as Picketsville's chief law enforcement officer, you have access to information to support that, no doubt?" Barstow had crossed the line and everyone at the table knew it. And in fact, at one time Ike did have access to that very information.

"I believe the probability that Oswald acted alone is no more or less likely than the probability that there were shooters on the knoll," Ike said. He could feel the heat on his neck. There was an embarrassed silence. Then everyone tried to talk at once. Ike raised his hand.

"You see how it is," Ike continued. "As you just demonstrated, we polarize our issues and force everyone into camps. Once in them, members then tend to separate themselves even farther as the debate continues. At least one president, among others, said, 'Those who are not for us, are against us.' He was quoting Lenin, I think, although I doubt he realized it at the time.

"If we all hold to that premise, eventually we create a polarized society and eventually a society of 'haters,' people who despise this president or the one before him, or the one aiming to get elected next. Opponents become objects of disdain and we pull farther and farther apart, pointing self-righteous, accusatory, and sanctimonious fingers at one another."

"And then," Fisher interrupted, "any deviation we make from the strict guidelines of the right or left leaves those of us in the middle with no place to go, but certain that however we vote, we will end up supporting one extreme or the other, but not for the reasons they will attach to the victory. Why, people ask, do the voting percentages often hover in the low thirty percent range? Because the middle can't, in good conscience, bring themselves to endorse either extreme."

Ike decided he would have to reassess his take on Fisher. "When you say something like 'scientific adventurism,' Doctor Weimar," Ike continued, "you introduce a whole new trigger phrase that requires us to scorn anyone promoting a policy your label implies wrong. Do you see?"

"Well, I think it's a bit *Über menschen* of you to use that kind of judgmental language, Sheriff. After all who are you to—"

"Ah, now you get it. Who indeed? My point exactly."

Ike faced two rows of angry stares. He wasn't sure if Ruth was with him or against him. He picked up his dinner knife and pointed it at Barstow.

"When I arrived this evening, Doctor Barstow, you barely glanced at me, but since I was wearing dark slacks and a white shirt, you mistook me for a waiter. You handed me your glass assuming I would fetch you a drink. I hope you don't mind my saying this, but your tone of voice was patronizing. Baxter made the same mistake, but thought it was only fitting that I, as a white man, should have to put up with some of the white privilege arrogance African-Americans have endured for centuries. He's probably right in that, but it's beside the point."

"I have no—"

"Doctor Harris, on the other hand, requested I not wear my uniform tonight. She feared that it typecast me in some people's minds. Everyone has seen so many Hollywood versions of smarmy southern sheriffs with their mirrored sunglasses and rampant big-otry, that there could never be any real dialogue with me. When I introduced myself to you, that was the reaction I got."

Dunnigan broke in. "Nicely put, Ike. When I first arrived in this part of the country, not that long ago, I should add, I was told there were three religions—Jews, Christians, and Catholics—"

"Keep pressing the doctrine of Mary as co-redeemer, and they'll be right," Fisher muttered.

Dunnigan scowled. "As I was saying, I heard that when I first arrived in this part of the world and still do. Now as to that—"

"We are straying from the task at hand," Barstow said, trying to reassert his control over the discussion. He fidgeted and looked distressed. Farragut half stood and leaned over the table so that he could see him.

"Doctor Barstow," he said, "I am new here. I come from the Midwest, from the University of Illinois. Out there we tend to be a little more forgiving of other people's views, but the sheriff is right. We have a society characterized by language that is either abusive or downright toxic. We sit here in this ivory tower covered by—what is that vine?"

"Virginia creeper," Prendergast said.

"Wisteria," Barstow corrected.

"Wisteria, creeper, whatever, and we opine about the state of a world with which many of us have little or no contact. We read books, specialty journals and all the correct newspapers. We discuss issues *ad nauseum*, but we almost never engage. Monsignor Dunnigan, you spent an interminable twenty minutes discussing an incompressible theological issue with Fisher here. I have no doubt that among theological types, it is a burning issue, perhaps an issue defining the faith position of many in the future as Fisher seems to imply, but do you really think the public cares a rat's rear end about it? People are engaged in the realities of life while we sit here in academic cotton wool and suppose we've been assigned the task of defining our culture."

Ike's phone chirruped.

"It's okay, Sam. I can manage this," he murmured. Having found an ally, he was ready to launch into a full-scale attack. Fisher stood and looked eagerly at Ike.

"Ike," Sam said. "This isn't a rescue call. I have some things you need to see. Maybe they could wait, but since you asked.... Anyway I think you should skip dessert and get down here." She must have heard the raised voices in the background. "What's going on up there?"

"The wonders of intellectual engagement," he said and hung up. He looked at Ruth as innocently as he could. She returned his gaze, still tight lipped and annoyed.

"This is the real thing, Ruth, I promise." She looked doubtful.

"Gentlemen and ladies," he said. Omanaka's lips thinned in disapproval at the word *ladies.* "I have an emergency concerning, I believe, your murder victim, Doctor Fisher. I have to leave. Oh, and I wonder if you could assist me. It seems there is a crisis of…ah—"

"Conscience. Of course, Sheriff, happy to be of assistance, Sorry, Doctor Harris, duty calls."

Ruth looked from one to the other and at the shambles Ike had made of her intellectual soiree and shook her head. Finally she gave them a rueful smile and waved them out the door.

"Thank you for coming. We will try to carry on without you. You were saying, Doctor Farragut…?"

"The use of polemic never…."

Chapter Eighteen

When the two men reached the porch and fresh air, Fisher said, "Sheriff, I'll try to see your mother tomorrow. That's if that's okay and your father doesn't object."

"He won't. He understands and, more importantly, he loves her enough that he only wants what will make her happy."

"Tomorrow then. I'll call first."

Ike reached the office ten minutes later. The doors were locked but he could see lights and hear the air conditioner's hum coming from Sam's area. He let himself in. Sam was seated in the same position as when he left hours before, bent over a series of papers on her desk. Her computer screens cast a blue-green glow in the room and the printer seemed to have gone berserk. Reams of papers spilled out and piled up in the finish tray. The air carried a hint of pizza.

"What have you got?" he said and pulled up a chair. Sam handed him a sheaf of glossy prints.

"Brace yourself," she said. "This guy is not your average church organist—or maybe he is. I haven't been to church in a long time and things may have changed since my confirmation."

Ike looked at the pictures. They were not, strictly speaking, salacious. Candid shots and some that might have passed as either amateur attempts at studio art or gritty porn. Most seemed taken through windows of cars or houses, and all with a telescopic lens.

"Where—?"

"They were on Krueger's hard drive. He'd deleted them, but you know deleting only means that the directory no longer lists them. They are not really deleted until the drive fills and they are overwritten by new material. He was careless."

"Just as well. What do you suppose he was up to? I mean besides creating some awkward porn. And who are these other people?"

"No clue, but here is something else. It's a blank legal document conveying part ownership of property to him. He had something in mind. The pictures might have been a means to force people to sign. There are pictures of property around the valley as well."

Ike scanned the rest of the pictures. "Things are getting complicated. Why am I not surprised? We need to know more about Krueger and what he was up to first."

"My guess," Sam said, "is the deed transfers had something to do with Ibex and Crane's development deal."

"It would give him an ownership position in zoning meetings and a means of exerting a little more pressure on the developer, maybe extracting a little more money. But somebody wanted him dead. That doesn't jibe with a real estate scam."

"Blackmail does."

"Yeah. We'll have to wait and see about that. What did you find out about him on the Internet?"

"Well if it's the same guy, he's been missing for nearly eight months. The press alleges he had some kind of position with the San Francisco mob, and just as the FBI moved in to crack down on them, he faded. If I read this stuff right, the FBI is hot on his trail or something…a warrant outstanding for his arrest, maybe, and not for producing pictures of naked ladies, couples caught in the act, and middle-aged men standing in front of stretch limos. The warrant thing is a little vague."

"Okay. Let's see what the Bureau tells us, if and when Chief Bullock finally returns my call. Now, I want you to pack this in and go home. You have the early shift tomorrow. Check in with me about nine."

Sam began backing out of the programs on her two machines. She set aside the material she had not yet explored. Ike turned to leave.

"Ike," she said, "do you have a problem with my air conditioner?"

"No, why?"

"Jolly Solly says I have to get rid of it."

"Tell him to talk to me."

"Thanks."

Ruth saw the last of her guests to the door and returned to the dining room.

The dinner had ended shortly after Ike and Fisher left. Barstow's concept of an intellectual discourse among his peers had degenerated into a verbal free-for-all. Jack Farragut took the bit in his teeth and played havoc with Barstow's carefully orchestrated evening. Omanaka, at one point, tried to throw *crème brûlée* on poor Franz Weimar. Well, she did not actually throw it. She got so excited at Baxter's insistence on defining racism his way, she slapped the table. Her hand accidentally hit the end of her spoon and the offending bit of custard sailed across the table at Weimar. Ruth didn't know whether to laugh or cry—at the way the evening had gone. Ike, on the other hand, was another matter entirely.

She left the caterers to clean up and retreated to her study. The phone beckoned. She dialed and caught Ike as he was leaving his office. So he really did go to work. Wonder of wonders.

"If you had been wearing your Boy Scout suit with your cop belt tonight, I would have pulled your gun and shot you, Sheriff."

"Duty belt, not cop belt. Sometimes it's called web gear but that's mostly Army or personnel who have fabric gear attached to a web belt. So, I did what, exactly, to warrant a bullet?"

"Web gear? That sounds like something I need to surf the Internet. I'm sticking with cop belt and you know perfectly well what you did. You destroyed my dinner party."

"Actually web gear *is* a term for Internet surfing. It's duty belt, whether you like it or not. I thought the evening went very well. Excellent food, beautiful hostess…can I say host*ess* and not host *person* and stay in your good graces? We had a very stimulating debate over the great issues. New voices were heard and a good time was had by all."

"Bullshit. Just host will do and the Speedo thing was good, I have to admit. What was Fisher's crisis?"

"Dunnigan."

"I thought so. He's a pain in the…what do you call it?"

"*Toukas.* He can be. You still want Fisher on your faculty?"

"No, I guess not."

"Because?"

"He's more about religion than english lit. He's the product of white privilege and a rich kid's education, but that doesn't qualify him to teach at a college level. And then there's the church and state business—"

"You don't mean you're afraid someone will call in the ACLU on you."

"No, but—well it's just not worth the hassle, potential or real. I thought Jack Farragut did well."

"He's a stud."

"Are you up to sneaking back here for a night cap?"

"A night cap?" Ike looked at his watch. "A little late for that."

"An all night cap, then."

"Can I wear my duty belt?"

"As long as you don't get some kinky ideas about hand-cuffs."

"Never crossed my mind."

"Fifteen minutes, and no funny business. Oh, but if you want to wear your Speedo—"

Ike laughed. "Madam President, I will do nearly anything for you but I draw the line at Speedos."

"Well, Sheriff, there is hope for us after all. At last we've found something we both agree on."

Chapter Nineteen

Ruth rolled over, propped herself up on one elbow and nudged Ike.

"Ike, what's happening to you?"

"What?"

"You are testy and short tempered and…I don't know, but you're not yourself lately."

"Are you still angry at me about dinner?"

"No, I guess not. That was classic Schwartz. No, I mean other times. I know you have a temper. I ought to. You certainly gave me a dose of it when we first met, but except when people really push your buttons, you are a very nice man. But lately you're snapping at people for trivial reasons."

"It's noticeable?"

"Not bad, Ike, I'm just worried it will get worse. I thought if I said something, you might try to figure out why."

"I don't know. I could call the shrink I saw at the Phipps Clinic after…." He let the sentence trail off.

"After your wife was killed. Is that what you can't say?" He rolled on his back. He didn't want to go where she seemed bound to take him. He inhaled her scent, a nice earthy female aroma mingled with rumpled sheets and the last of late-blooming roses wafting in through the open window.

"Ike?"

"Maybe," he said and squeezed his eyes shut.

"You know what I think?"

"What?"

"I think you spent all those years after she died feeling guilty and angry. Then, when you found out there was nothing you could have done to prevent her death, you thought you were finished. But you're not."

"Why not? It's over and that's that."

"You've never grieved for her, Ike, never really said goodbye. You were too busy trying to bury the whole thing. Your friend, Charlie, had to force the details out of you and you found out you had been betrayed. Now you need to finish the process."

"Eloise is dead. You and I are alive. That's enough."

"No, it's not enough. I'm not talking Kübler-Ross necessarily, but you need to do something. Have you shed a tear for her? Have you visited her grave? There are things you need to do. Until you face up to that loss…look, I am not jealous or clingy, but I am fond of you, Schwartz, more than fond, if you must know. I don't want to wait around in second place while you carry her around forever."

Ike touched her thigh. Not a request for anything, just for comfort, for making sure she was there. He sighed. She was right, of course. There would be no peace until he closed the books on that part of his life.

"Next week," he said. "I will go to the cemetery next week sometime." He paused. "Would you come with me?" She lay still. He listened to her breathe, watched the rise and fall of her breast.

"Maybe next Tuesday or Wednesday, Ike, and late afternoon. I have meetings and, you know, academic busywork to do. And I will have to deal with poor old Barstow's ruffled feathers. Next week, yes."

"Okay, Wednesday, say four, four-thirty?" It could be a start—a start that might lead somewhere else. He wondered if she realized where that might be and if, in the end, she would be willing to go.

"Four it is—and Ike?"

"Yeah?"

"Not to worry. I'm a grown-up woman. I know what might be. I'll deal with that when I have to, if I have to."

He smiled.

Tuesday morning started out with the threat of rain. It would be a relief from Indian summer. Blake had enough heat and humidity for one year. He ate, showered, dressed, and crossed the parking lot to the church. Millicent was already ensconced at her desk.

"Good morning," she said. Her face looked like she had been sucking lemons. "I heard some talk about what you said in church Sunday, Mr. Fisher."

"Did you? I am not surprised, so did I. Well, you know what they say about pleasing everybody…comes with the territory, I guess. Did you have a pleasant holiday?"

"Yes, very nice. How was your trip to Philadelphia?"

"I didn't go. I spent the day at home reading and getting this ready." The look on Millicent's face was worth a month's salary.

"But I thought—"

"Had dinner up at the college, too. Any news about poor Waldo—family, funeral?"

"No. You were at home? No one came to see you."

"Now, that's the funny thing. I could have sworn someone came to the door while I looked for Dr. Taliaferro's old files upstairs. I thought I heard someone, but when I came down there was nobody there."

"Dr. Taliaferro's files?" Her eyes flickered momentarily.

"Yes. Philip asked me to look for them. By the way, I have a few things I would like for you to do for me this morning." He waved the sheaf of papers in front of her. He handed her his outline and explained what he wanted her to do. She seemed considerably more docile than usual, and he guessed he had given her a scare, or maybe two. Why would his interest in Taliaferro's files upset her?

"Fifteen copies, Millie. Oh, by the way, is there a key to my desk?"

"There is a box in the closet with keys in it. If there is a key to the desk, it's in there." She attacked her keyboard furiously.

Blake found the box. It looked like it once held recipes. Images of cakes and pies were silk screened on its top and sides. He took it into his office and dumped the keys on his desk. There were about forty of them. Most looked like door keys and were stamped with an M or a W, depending on which way he held the key. He sorted the keys into piles, ones that looked like candidates for the desk, the M/W keys, and all the others.

"Millie," he called through the office door, "what are all these keys marked M or W?"

"M, for master. They are old church keys. We changed the locks fifteen years ago and those are the old keys."

"These keys are anywhere between twenty and thirty years old? Why didn't you just throw them away?"

"No one told me to."

He took the pile of M keys and dropped them into his wastebasket with a clatter. He then worked his way through the pile of possible desk keys. None worked.

"How about the rest of these keys?" he asked.

"I don't know exactly. They are just there."

"Has anyone needed a key, or reported one missing, anything like that?"

"No."

"Well, I guess I can dump them too." He scooped up the keys and was about to drop them into the wastebasket with the others when she appeared in the door, her face now anxious.

"Don't," she almost shouted, "I...I think one of them locks my desk. I'd like to look for it."

"Certainly, here." He put the keys back in the box and handed it to her. What on earth had gotten into Millicent Bass, he wondered? He heard the sound of keys falling on her desk and then, one by one, into her wastepaper basket, then the rattle of the keyboard as she resumed her typing.

"You find it?" he asked.

"Yes, yes I did, thank you."

Satisfied she would be occupied for the rest of the morning, he walked out, telling her he would be back in a half hour and that he had an errand he needed to run. The errand involved the hardware store and a deadbolt, but she did not need to know about that. She was still typing when he returned.

Millie left at noon. Blake sat quietly and closed his eyes. He realized that his prayer life had disappeared into a black hole. Except for the few supplications said in desperate moments, he was reduced to reciting a few careless prayers in the morning when he read his Daily Office and occasionally, when he wanted to talk to himself but felt more pious if he included God in the conversation, not as a participant, naturally, but as an observer.

"God," he said, "I am in a mess here. I know I need to get myself straightened out and I know I need to include you in the process. The problem is—I don't know how to do that. I have never needed your help before. When the business in Philadelphia happened, I thought you were playing a cruel joke on me and I got angry. I guess I've been that way ever since. Now, I am really in a spot and I need to...."

What did he need to do? He paused and tried hard to accept the thing he desperately did not want to face. He could work this all out. He had always come out on top. How was this any different? He felt afraid, but of what?

"What am I afraid of?" he said aloud.

Of change. You are afraid to change.

"I'm talking to myself, now. Okay, I need to change. Change what?" He sat in silence. Neither he, nor this other self, had anything more to add. He waited.

"Okay, God, I need to change. Show me how."

Well, that's a start, I suppose. What is your heart telling you?

Did he say that? Or did the words come from somewhere, or someone else? He shook his head and waited for more, but nothing came. He wanted more but at the same time feared he might get it. He did not relish the idea of words being put in his mouth, even by God.

However, he did feel a little better. He did not know why, but he did. And he felt very hungry. Lunch. He would come back to this later. He walked through Millie's office and glanced at her desk. He paused and looked again. Her desk did not have a lock. He looked more closely and wondered if he had heard her correctly. No lock. He drove to the Pizza Hut.

Blake took a corner table and waited to be served. Millicent Bass, he noticed, sat in a booth with three other women. She, that is to say they, were so deep in conversation, they had not seen him come in. Grace Franks and Sylvia Parks were in a booth behind them. Millie and her cronies seemed unaware of their presence as well. He watched as Grace and Sylvia stood to leave. Grace looked stricken, as though her pasta had declared war on her digestive system. Sylvia patted Grace on the shoulder and sent a venomous look in Millie's direction. They marched out without saying anything to Millie or the other women, who remained so wrapped up in chatter they did not even notice their departure.

Very curious, he thought.

Chapter Twenty

Lunch finished, he drove back to the vicarage. He hoped to get the deadbolt in place quickly before he called on the sheriff's mother. It turned out to be bit more complicated than he'd expected. The thumb latch worked like a deadbolt, but the mounting in the door was different. He had to drill a new, larger hole in the door, reset the striker plate in the jamb, and enlarge the track for the bolt. He had nearly finished when Lanny Markowitz rounded the corner.

"Vicar? Problem?"

"You caught me, Lanny. I thought I could get this done without anyone from the Board finding out."

"Why would you care? After Sunday, it's pretty clear you don't much care what any of us think, or know."

"Excuse me?"

"Vicar, I came over here to talk to you. Someone needs to sit down and have some face time with you, and Quarles hasn't the guts, so I will do it."

"I guess you'd better come inside, then. First, though, would you mind holding this key-set against the door while I run these bolts into place? Thanks."

Blake tightened the bolts, tried the key, and satisfied he now had some privacy, picked up his tools and gestured for Lanny to enter.

"Deadbolt, Lanny. People have been wandering through here without my say-so or knowledge. I know the house belongs to the church, but while I am Vicar, I expect folks to respect my privacy. If someone wants to come in, they can knock, ask, and show me some common courtesy. What is it you wanted to tell me?"

"It's that attitude, Vicar. You seem to think that because Bournet put you here without any input from us you can say and do anything you want. You need to remember that we are the Board and we are in charge of the church."

"Wrong, Lanny, you are the Board. That part is true, but you do not pay my salary, Saint Anne's does. Your job is advisory only. Are you here to give me advice?"

"We never had any trouble with Taliaferro or the guy before him. How come you are trying to change us?"

Change. There was that word again.

"Are you afraid of change, Lanny? Most people are. I am—you too?"

"Let me be straight with you, Fisher. We know all about what you did to that woman in Philadelphia. We know you are on a short string here and any screw up and you're toast, so we expect you to toe the line, not make waves. Most of us are happy with the way things are, thank you."

Blake thought he heard a minuscule hesitation in *most of us*. "I see. You do understand that if this congregation is not ready to become an independent congregation in less than two years, the game is up? This beautiful church will be closed?"

"That's what they said before, but it didn't happen. We'll find another church to sponsor us."

"Not this time. Philip Bournet took this mission over against the advice and wishes of the Bishop. No one else will. It's me or nobody, Lanny."

Lanny's face turned a beet red. He started to say something and changed his mind.

"Look, Lanny, you're right. We need to have it out, but not the way you think. You said you knew about what happened in Philadelphia. Let me tell you, so that you understand—nothing happened in Philadelphia. An accusation was made, but nothing happened. It simply is not true. In spite of that fact, I had to leave. That is the way things work for clergy. Even the hint of scandal, however far-fetched, and we take the hit."

"I don't believe you. We received letters from people up there that say otherwise."

"Letters from whom? Not from the Bishop, not from Bill Smart, not from anyone who would know—just letters from people who want to believe the worst about clergy in general and me in particular. Do you want to see the Bishop's letter again? I have copies." Blake walked to the small desk in the corner and retrieved a file. "Letters, Lanny, from the Bishop, from Smart, and from rectors of four other churches reporting the same behavior by the same woman in question in their churches. You want more?"

Lanny stood an inch or two shorter than Blake. Had he been taller but proportioned the same, he might have made a success as a professional athlete. He'd tried, but except for a season in Class A ball, it hadn't happened. He had one of those flat Slavic faces that you used to see on patriotic Russian posters—men and women sitting on tractors staring at the horizon or helmeted and armed, looking determined. That was back when it was still the USSR. He scanned the letters and then read them more carefully.

"How come we never saw these? Why are you even here?"

"About the first—I don't know. They were sent to you. Look at the bottom of that cover letter, 'cc: the Mission Board, Stonewall Jackson Memorial Episcopal Church, Picketsville, Virginia'. Somebody got them."

"We never saw these, I swear. And how can something like this happen?"

"Lanny, you are a school teacher, right? Suppose a girl in your class accused you of some kind of misconduct. Even if it was a lie, what would happen to you?"

"There'd be a hearing and hopefully, I would be cleared and....Oh, I see, even if I was exonerated, I would be reassigned to another school or district probably."

"Would you try to clear your name? After all, people would say, 'Where there's smoke there's fire,' wouldn't they? Would you sue?"

"No, I guess not. A friend of mine had that happen to him. By the time the lawyers got done digging around in his past, he would have been better off if he had really done something to the girl. No, no suit."

"You see my point, then?"

"I'm sorry, Vicar. I have been thinking some pretty bad things about you. We all have, I'm afraid. The only letters we had were the other ones. They were the only ones in the file we received."

"Who compiled the files?"

"I'm not sure. I guess Millie or Dan Quarles or Grace and Bob Franks—maybe all four."

The two men stared at each other, then, embarrassed, looked away.

"What now, Lanny? Are we going to stay enemies or can we work together?"

"I have to think this through, but yeah, we can work together, as long as you understand, most of us like things the way they are."

"No problem, as long as you understand it's my job to change your mind."

Lanny left with a puzzled look on his face. Blake called Mary Miller—no answer. He walked to the front door and admired his handiwork one more time.

◇◇◇

Blake found the Schwartz place easily. The house sat back from the road and on a little rise. It reminded him of the farmhouses in Bucks County where he grew up. He parked and walked toward the front steps. An old man, but unmistakably Ike's father, met him on the porch.

"You're the padre from the stone church," he said and held out his hand. "Abe Schwartz, pleased to meetcha."

"Blake Fisher. I hope this is not going to—"

"No indeed, Son. We're all God's children—that's what I believe. My old granddaddy would have boxed my ears if he heard me say it, but times change. Come on in. The missus is expecting you."

Blake spent an hour with Mrs. Schwartz. When he came out, he wasn't sure who had ministered to whom.

"She's an amazing lady," he said. Abe smiled.

"Ain't she though."

"She knows—"

"Oh, yeah. She knows. We all do. We don't talk about it much, but we know."

"How about you, Mr. Schwartz, are you okay?"

"Abe. You call me Abe. Everybody does." Blake waited. "Been married near fifty years. Imagine that. Now I ask you, Padre, ain't that something to hold on to forever. You have any idea how long it's going to take me to run out of memories? I'll be gone myself 'fore that happens. No sir, we're okay fine."

Blake left the farm lost in thought. This is what they taught him in Pastoral Care classes, what they meant when they said visiting the dying was sacramental. All those years he'd served in ordained ministry and this was the first time he'd really experienced what it was all about. He shook his head.

Chapter Twenty-one

Billy Sutherlin scratched his head. Someone had taken the chair from the duty desk and he couldn't figure out where or how to sit.

"Ike," he called, "there ain't no chair out here. What's up with that?"

Ike stepped out of his glass cage—his office—and inspected the room.

"It's not anywhere? Did you check with Sam? She might have borrowed it." Billy walked down the corridor to Sam's space and peeked in.

"Nope, in fact, she's ticked off big time because somebody took her air cooler."

"Ike," Sam said, rounding the corner, "that idiot Fairmont took my air conditioner."

"Essie, get Fairmont over here, now," Ike said. The door swung open as if ordered, but not for Solly Fairmont. Instead, a very tall man who might as well have worn a sign saying "Hi, I'm from the FBI," complete with blue suit, white shirt and red tie, ducked through the door. Sam's jaw dropped. She looked him straight in the eye.

"Hello," he said.

"Hey," she replied and turned a bright red.

"You are?" Ike said.

"Hedrick, Special Agent Karl Hedrick. I've come to collect my prisoner. Didn't you get our message?"

"My office," Ike said and tilted his head toward the door. "Deputy Ryder will join us. Sam, are you with us?"

"Oh, right…do you need anything?"

"Bring the files you have on Krueger, but hold the glossies for now." She paused, squinted, understood, and went to her office.

"This way, Special Agent Hedrick," Ike said and ushered him into his office. Sam scurried in behind them.

"Now then, about your man…we have a problem."

"You lost him? Listen, we need to know if something like that—"

"We didn't lose him. We have him—on ice, you could say."

"So what's the problem?"

"He's dead."

"You killed him? Damn. I told the chief we needed to get here sooner. What did your guys do to him?"

"Special Agent Hedrick," Ike said patiently, "this is not a chapter from *First Blood* and Krueger is not Rambo. If your boss had taken the time or demonstrated a little inter-agency courtesy, you could have saved yourself a trip. But because you guys up there in Quantico think the folks out in the country are not worthy of your time, you blew a day and wasted my afternoon."

"Look," Hedrick began, "I don't know what this is all about but we sent you a directive to hold that man until we could come and get him. Now you say he's dead. What am I supposed to think?"

"Well to begin with, the operative words are, *supposed to think*. You didn't and aren't. You or your boss—what's his name, Bullock—knew too little and assumed too much so you ignored my call."

"What do you mean, assumed?"

"You all assumed we had a man in custody. What we had was a corpse. Krueger was found shot to death. He was known around here as Waldo Templeton. Nobody seemed to know anything more about him except he played the organ badly and some thought him 'creepy.' We had a murder to solve. So we ran his prints. You all picked up on that and then, instead of calling to find out the particulars, sent that imperious note dictating what we should do. This is my jurisdiction, Hedrick, and if you want something, you ask. You don't demand."

"We're not going to get into a pissing match here, are we, Sheriff?"

"Stop right there, Sonny." Hedrick flinched at *Sonny.* "There are a few things you need to know. In the first place, the fact we operate with limited budgets and resources out here in the country does not mean we are incompetent. Our unsolved crime rate is very low. I have four cold cases which, by the way, represents less than one percent of our total. How many do you have? Second, we deal with everything from murder to drug busts to major thefts, and we get the job done. We do it. Sometimes we get help but most times we just go and do it. Third, no one in this department wears funny sunglasses and talks like Boss Hogg, and finally, you are out of your depth here."

Hedrick started to say something and thought better of it.

"You know, Hedrick, there is an important lesson here. With all the hoopla in Washington about reorganizing of the intelligence community, you all are missing a major point. All those plans and schemes address vertical rearrangements. Who will be top dog? Will he or she get budgetary authority and access to the president? Who reports to whom and you know what? It won't amount to a hill of beans unless the horizontal part is fixed. Now this is just my take on the situation, but I think that unless and until you people learn to respect and communicate with people like me, nothing will change. If information has to run up the ladder and then back down, we will always be behind the curve. Your boss needed to return my telephone call. Why didn't he?" Ike sat back in his chair, winced at the squeal it made, and waited for the FBI man to reply.

"I don't know…he…I don't know. You're right, I guess, but—"

"The conventional wisdom in the Bureau is, don't expect too much from the hicks in the sticks."

"Well, I wouldn't put it that way."

"No, of course you wouldn't. Rubes, yokels, maybe—look, you strike me as a bright guy. You are young and have a career ahead of you. If you are going to be a Special Agent for the foreseeable future, then start to change the way you and all the young guys up there react to local police. Some of us are good at what we do, some not. But you need to know the difference before you waltz into an office like this and make demands. Do you still want your 'prisoner,' or can we move ahead and share some information?"

"So, what happened?"

"Sam?"

"The man known as Waldo Templeton, AKA Walter Krueger, was found shot to death in the Stonewall Jackson Memorial Episcopal Church Friday morning by a Millicent Bass, the church secretary. Cause of death, a .32 caliber bullet wound to the head. A second, but not lethal, wound was found in his left shoulder, no exit wound. The coroner puts the death at any time between nine pm and midnight. Choir practice ends about nine."

"Could one of the choir members have done it?"

"We're checking. We ran his prints—you know all about that—and we are now attempting to determine a motive—anything. Our search of the Internet revealed that Krueger was of particular interest to the FBI."

"How did he get in the church?"

"How? Templeton had a key. We don't know about the killer."

"You check out all the other key holders?"

"Everyone has a key," Ike and Sam said together.

Sam continued her recital. "It appears he had something to do with the San Francisco mob, your people were after him, and if you wanted him for a witness, it's too late. Someone got to him first. We're hoping you can help us."

"Anything to add, Hedrick?" Ike asked. Hedrick looked upset.

"Not now. Mind if I make a phone call?"

"In a minute. First, I want to ask you a question. Except that he played the organ there once a week, can you think of any reason why this guy would be shot twice in a church in Picketsville, Virginia?"

Hedrick paused, just for the briefest of moments, "No," he said.

Ike saw the flicker in his eyes, heard the lie. A song his father used to sing popped into his head—*your lips tell me no, no, but there's yes, yes in your eyes.* What was this guy holding back? And why?

"You're absolutely sure?"

"No idea, Sheriff."

"Bullshit, Special Agent Hedrick. As I said, unless and until…."

Chapter Twenty-two

Agnes Ewalt ushered Ike into Ruth's office.

"He's here," she muttered, turned on her heel and left.

Ike turned and watched her leave the room. "I don't think Agnes likes me very much," he said as the door clicked shut.

"She thinks you are beneath me—socially that is."

"And sometimes recreationally."

"That worries her, too. So, here you are, as Agnes said. Question—why?"

"Bad afternoon with the Federal Bureau of Investigation and I need to unload on somebody. If I buy you a drink out of the stash you keep in your filing cabinet, can it be you?"

"Help yourself but use a paper cup. Agnes may pop in here any time and she's a practicing Baptist."

Ike slid open the file drawer built into the base of a mahogany bookcase and lifted out a bottle. "I guess that explains the sour look I get every time I show up."

"It explains some of the looks—not all."

"The other times are—"

"She is just naturally that way. 'Weaned on pickles,' as my dear old grandmother used to say."

Ike poured himself an inch and a half of Maker's Mark and raised an inquiring eyebrow at her.

"Very light. Put some water with it," she said.

They drank in silence. Maker's Mark was usually out of Ike's price range and the thought of drinking on the College's dime had him feeling better already. He flopped down in one of the two crewelwork wing chairs with a groan and stretched out his legs.

"Tell me something, Sheriff, what is it about my people you find so annoying? I mean, at my dinner you promised to behave and then you—"

"You *are* still angry about the dinner."

"Not exactly, but I've been thinking about you and Barstow."

"The old guy with the ponytail."

"One of my more important faculty members."

"Ah. By faculty, you mean that collection of highly educated elitists you keep on your payroll?"

"What makes them elitists and worthy of your disdain? You are, after all, a product of the same system that produced them. Harvard and Yale Law pretty much put you in their league, wouldn't you say?"

"God forbid. Look, I only tried to steer the conversation along somewhat pleasanter lines."

She pivoted her leather desk chair back and forth, her toes barely touching the carpet guard, and inspected her cup. "Cardboard, even plastic coated, doesn't do justice to the booze, does it?"

"I've had worse. You were saying?"

"Okay, Fat Guys in Speedos—good move, but pleasanter? I mean how do you figure that?"

"Let's just say my idea of unpleasant is sanctimonious blather from the intelligentsia."

"Look, they're my bread and butter. If you and I are going to have anything more than the equivalent of going steady like a couple of high school kids, we have to come to an understanding about them."

"Do you know the only known physiological difference between intelligent people and everyone else?"

She put her elbows on her desk pad and cupped her chin in her hands. "I give up. What, bigger brains?"

"No, intelligent people have more zinc and copper in their hair."

"Where'd you hear that?"

"Internet."

"Oh, right. You are tapped into the ultimate source of information for a generation unwilling or unable to do real research."

"That's the place."

"Sheesh. You don't like my faculty even if they have all that copper and zinc?"

"Two of your guys were bald, but Barstow's ponytail is probably worth melting down."

"I have money problems. Gold is what I'm looking for in a man's hair—the Golden Fleece. You have any gold in that mop of yours?"

"No, but Abe probably does. Forensics people tell me that metals and drugs usually end up in a person's hair. Abe takes some kind of gold-based medication for his arthritis. We could ask."

"Never mind. So, what's the problem with my faculty?"

Ike stood and paced, punctuating his sentences in the air with his forefinger. "It's not that they're faculty, or that they're any more or less opinionated than the average guy on the streets of Picketsville. God knows. I listen to idiotic redneck philosophy all day long. No, it's just that faculty, as the educated class, if you will, have a responsibility to remain objective. And they don't."

"Don't?"

"No, they don't. Their problem, the problem of most intellectuals, is they think they have been ordained by a God they do not believe in to design programs that do not concern them that affect the lives of people they do not respect."

"Wow, all that? Come on, Schwartz, you can do better than an aphorism that sounds like something lifted from H. L. Mencken."

"Not Mencken. He was one of them. They read him, you know, the way sophomores read Nostradamus—as if he were a great social prophet instead of a bright, cynical guy with a column to sell."

"Okay, you sound like Spiro Agnew, then."

"Better." He sat down again, this time in the second wing-back chair. "Agnew's one of Abe's favorite bad guys, but he's ancient history. How'd you—?"

"I'm a history professor, remember, and besides I was raised by parents who could have been poster children for middle-class liberalism. Maybe we should get them together, my folks and yours. My guess is they have more in common than we do."

"Probably. That bodes well if we can move past a going steady, high school relationship."

"Don't push it. And Mencken isn't exactly contemporary, either."

"No, not for mortals. But for liberal thinkers—"

"Ah, now I get it. That's where this is leading, isn't it? It's Liberal versus Conservative and you're the voice of conservatism."

"It's Political Correctness versus Common Sense."

"I knew it," Ruth crowed and sat up straight. "You are the spokesperson of the righteous right."

"Spokes*man*. And not right or left, just tired of the posturing by both."

"Admit it, Schwartz, you just hate liberals."

"I don't hate them, but rich ones, especially those in legislatures and Congress, do scare me."

"Scare you? Why?"

"Because their wealth insulates them from the consequences of their actions."

"And rich conservatives in legislatures and Congress aren't insulated?"

"On the contrary, they are usually the beneficiaries of their actions. More venal, but easier to track."

Ruth bit her lip. She hated it when Ike was in one of his "I don't care if you piss in my eye, just don't tell me it's rain" moods. No matter how determined she was to shred his arguments, he inevitably staked out the moral high ground and left her mired in a rhetorical rut. She spun her chair so her back was to him and studied the expensively bound volumes on her credenza.

"You know something, Schwartz? You are all show and no go. Peel away all that smart-ass Mr. Right and you are a caring sensitive man who, if push got to shove, would come down on the side of compassion and liberality. And you don't fool me for a moment."

Ike sipped from his paper cup and hid a smile. "Fooling you is not an occupation I would wish on anyone, but as for your faculty—"

"Enough already with the faculty....Okay, here's one for you," she said, hoping to move the discussion to an area where she had the edge. "What do bulletproof vests, fire escapes, windshield wipers, and laser printers all have in common?"

"They were all invented by women."

"How'd you know that?"

"Saw it on the Internet."

"Shit. I think I need another one of these," she said and lifted her cup over her shoulder. "This is going to be a long evening."

"What will Agnes say?"

Chapter Twenty-three

Blake jerked awake. He'd overslept. He made some wheat toast, reheated the previous day's coffee in the microwave, and gulped it all down as he dashed out the door and rushed to the church to set up for the first meeting of the Wednesday Bible Study. He placed a television set and VCR on a cart and arranged twenty chairs in rows facing the set. Twenty seemed optimistic. He put five away and frowned at the arrangement. In truth, he had no idea how many, if any, people would show. A commitment made at a church coffee hour was about as trustworthy as a teenager with a credit card. At ten minutes to eleven, Rose and her sister arrived, followed a few minutes later by the Digeppis, Dorothy Sutherlin, Sylvia Parks and eight others—fourteen plus himself. Good call. When everyone settled down, Blake announced they were going to watch a video. The group stirred and smiled and scrunched down in their chairs, getting comfortable in their TV posture. He hit the play button and the credits for *Godspell* materialized on the screen. He studied the expressions on their faces as the group watched—expressions that ranged from enjoyment, to mild disapproval, to looks he guessed were a combination of pleasure and guilt—guilt for enjoying something that might otherwise be construed as disrespectful or irreligious.

When it ended, he turned up the lights and asked what they thought. The comments were vague and accompanied with looks of generalized confusion.

"Okay," he said, sensing their discomfort. "I'm sorry that took so long. I showed this video for a reason. It represents one person's idea of how the gospel of Matthew should be seen and understood. It is, however, only a particular person's view. That's important. I could have shown you *Jesus Christ Superstar, The Last Temptation of Christ, The Ten Commandments, The Greatest Story Ever Told, Ben Hur,* or any of the hundreds of films made over the years. I chose this one because it is joyful, stays pretty close to the gospel narrative, and does not introduce or suggest ideas contrary to what the church teaches. I can't say that about most of the others, including some of the well-known Hollywood epics like *The Chalice* or *The Robe.* I won't even discuss Victor Mature as Sampson. But the point is—each of them, for better or for worse, presents one person's vision of the story.

"I want you to think about the gospels for a minute. They are living documents. Even though they were written almost two thousand years ago about events that happened earlier than that, they are as alive and as current for us today as they were for those who saw and heard them then, or for those eyewitnesses who were party to the events themselves.

"Each of us sees the gospel through the lens of our own experience. The longer we live, usually, the greater our experience and the richer and deeper the story becomes."

"He's talking about us," Rose said and gave Minnie a nudge.

"That is not to say," Blake continued, "that young people cannot have experiences that can enrich the vision. I know some people in their late teens with life experiences equal to any octogenarian. Whatever our age or experience may be, when we read the gospels, we necessarily bring our own lives into the story. And the gospel becomes personal and relevant. I hope you will do that. It is important in helping us to understand the narrative and it is equally important in helping us to understand each other—a necessary first step in building a true faith community."

He paused and waited for a reaction. Everyone sat quietly, faces expectant.

"Okay, here's the second part. We will start with the Gospel of Matthew, the same as the video. I would like you to bring your own Bible to our sessions and in as many different translations as you can manage. And I expect you to talk, to share how the Book speaks to you. To let the rest of us look through your lens, so to speak. Do not wait for me. I have no intention of doing a teaching session. I will read what the scholars have to say. I will check commentaries and articles, but you will be responsible for most of the talking, not me."

Smiles and frowns.

"You mean we have to read the Book before we come, and be prepared to tell everyone else what we think God meant?" Sylvia Parks asked.

"That is a very nice summing up, Sylvia."

Blake understood Sylvia had practiced law briefly, but gave it up to raise her family. By the time her children were old enough to allow her to return to the law, her husband had built his personal fortune to the point where she no longer needed a career. She and her husband reportedly spent winters in the south of France, Hilton Head or one of the many playgrounds frequented by the rich. Sylvia had only recently joined the church but had thrown herself into volunteer work. She and her husband rented a place near Floyd, outside Roanoke, but she made the long commute up to Picketsville for church. Blake wondered about that, but was happy to have her as a parishioner. He guessed she had her reasons. In a small church, you couldn't be too particular. Besides, she was part of the doughnut.

Time and money had been kind to Sylvia. She dressed simply, but Blake guessed she paid large sums to dressmakers to achieve simplicity. Slender without being thin, she wore her hair parted in the middle and had let it go gray. It flowed naturally in a silver shower to her shoulders, interrupted only by dark streaks over both temples that created a dashing, almost devilish, look. Her outfits ran to silver, grays and blacks, usually accessorized with a pearl choker or a high-necked silk blouse. Basic black and pearls—the uniform of a superannuated debutante, but

Blake doubted she had ever waltzed with any acne-cursed Ivy Leaguer. Hers was an acquired sophistication. He believed even her speech had undergone a major modification. She spoke with the carefully modulated tone people associate with newsreaders and actors. He supposed that somewhere, deep down, lurked an accent from her past—New York, New Jersey, maybe south Boston—and if she ever became stressed or excited, he guessed she would bawl like Eliza Doolittle.

"Is everyone here perfectly clear about what we will be doing next Wednesday?" he asked the group. Heads nodded. Blake closed the meeting with a prayer and they broke for lunch.

"The mall," Rose announced. "I wanted to go to Nathan's for a loaded hot dog, but Minnie said she needed something a little healthier, so we are meeting at Panda Express." The group filed out, most to their cars, and then to the mall. A few begged off and went home. The video had run well over an hour and with his remarks, two hours had passed since he started. Blake checked his office for messages. Millie had already left for the day. He locked up and followed the others to the mall.

Most of the group settled at small tables in the great foyer around which the several vendors had their stalls. Blake joined Rose, Minnie, and a young woman whose name he could only remember as Kathy. Rose turned to him and said, "Vicar, I need a word with you." Blake nodded. "It's about that secretary of yours." Blake turned and faced her. "She is an unreconstructed guttersnipe, a mean-spirited harridan, and worst of all, a terrible gossip."

"Rose, really," Minnie said, alarmed.

"I get so angry, sometimes. The people in this church know what the Bass woman is. They have all been the subject of her nasty tongue and yet nobody has been willing to call her on it."

"Not even you?" Blake asked.

Rose looked embarrassed. "No, not even me. Look, for most of the time, her talk was just petty. The kind of thing you expect from someone from an unhappy home. Lately, however, it has become very personal and about things in people's lives they did not know anyone knew. I tell you, it's got poor Grace Franks beside herself. You've got to rein her in before she really hurts someone, or someone hurts her."

"You think that's possible? Someone might hurt her? I will speak to her, Rose, but I need the right moment."

"Well, make it soon before someone shoots the…that woman."

Chapter Twenty-four

Blake spent the rest of the afternoon making calls and hospital visits in and around Lexington, and because it was nearly seven, decided to eat in the hospital cafeteria instead of going straight home. Sheriff Schwartz was sitting in his black and white waiting for him when he pulled into his driveway.

"Sheriff, to what do I owe the honor?"

"Brought you some news about your dead organist I thought you'd like to hear."

"You've caught the killer?"

"No, and not likely to, either."

"That does not sound like good news. Maybe you'd better come in."

They walked around to the front door and Blake unlocked the newly installed deadbolt and the door latch. He turned on some lights and gestured for the sheriff to sit. He went into the kitchen and put on a pot of coffee and returned.

"So, the killer's still at large. That it?"

"Yes and no. We matched the victim's fingerprints, but instead of Waldo Templeton, we got a Walter Krueger. That's all the FBI will tell us. I don't know why. Everybody has a history somewhere. We checked his driver's license, for example—fake."

"And you concluded from that?"

"Feds know something and aren't willing to share. I'm working on a way around that but....Anyway, when the FBI saw his prints they hopped down here to pick him up."

"They wanted the body?"

"No, they made a mistake. They wanted him."

"So you think it was a hit? That's what you call them, right?"

"A hit? Well, why not?"

"And you think his killer blew in from out of town—a professional 'hit man' or something like that?"

"That's about it. Either way it's not quite off my blotter and not quite on the feds', but knowing those birds, they'll do what they can to catch the guy. Then they'll turn him, and hide him away somewhere. You want me to put in a word for you if he can play the organ?"

"No, thanks anyway. So, why are you telling me all this?"

"In a minute. There's a problem."

"Oh please, what now?"

"Where were you Monday, before the dinner?"

"Here at home, alone."

"Alone? So nobody can verify you were here at all?"

"I didn't say that. Actually, I do have a witness of a sort—you."

"Me? I didn't see you all day."

"No, but I saw you. You were here at this house at about one o'clock in the afternoon. You tried to break in, as a matter of fact." Blake smiled and watched with delight as Schwartz's face turned red. It started on his neck and crept up to the roots of his hair. "You must have realized I was home because you, unlike my other visitor and potential 'B and E,' gave up after one door. Now, if I know all that, I must have been here, right?"

"Okay, you were here. I thought so. It seemed unlikely you'd be in Philadelphia and get back in time for dinner at the college. A really smooth operator could have arranged it, but not you. Anyway, I had to check."

"Thanks a lot, and why did you have to check?"

"We had a complaint from Philadelphia. A woman said you were stalking her."

"Gloria Vandergrift. Is there no end to this?"

"Police didn't seem too excited but they wanted to be sure."

"Nice. But that doesn't tell me why you were trying to get in the house Monday. If you had succeeded and found any evidence that implicated me, would it would be inadmissible in court?"

"You think so? You watch too much television."

"Okay, you would have 'found' it later with a real search warrant. It's nice to know the police are straightforward in their duties."

"Sarcasm does not become you, but just to be clear, my job is to put the bad guys away. The way the criminal justice system has evolved lately, it's getting harder and harder to do that, so now we do what we have to do."

"Okay. But you still haven't told me why you wanted to get in here. I mean, if you had knocked I would have invited you in. *Knock and it shall be opened to you, seek and ye shall find*—and all that."

"At first, I thought you were out of town. That's what the Bass woman told me. I wanted to check Krueger's keys against your door. Then I found something out back and decided I would check it first."

"You are a very suspicious man, if I may say so, Sheriff."

"Goes with the territory—keeps food on the table and me alive to enjoy it."

"So what did you find?"

"I'll get it. It probably belongs to the church and you'll want it back."

Schwartz went outside and returned a moment later with a gray, steel file box.

Blake inspected the box. It had apparently been forced open, but the latch seemed intact. Inside were three file folders. He looked at them. They contained letters to Taliaferro and some counseling notes.

"This all there was?" he asked.

"That's the lot."

"Well, now I know what happened to Taliaferro's files. I've been looking all over for them."

"How do you suppose that box got back there?"

"I expect someone mistakenly put this box outside near the trashcans after Taliaferro died. The kids in the neighborhood use our parking lot for a skate park. They also use our trashcans for various tricks they do, and my guess is they found this box, opened it out of curiosity, and then, finding nothing of interest, tossed the files in the trash. When they were done, they pitched it into the bushes."

"Makes sense. Well, so long, Reverend. By the way, the gun that killed Krueger was a .32, probably a small automatic. I hate to say this, but that puts you on the suspect list. Just a heads up. You have a lawyer?"

"No. You think I need one?"

"Everyone needs a lawyer. That's why we have so many. Ask the American Bar Association. You said you had another attempt by someone to break in?"

"Yeah. My secretary, Mrs. Bass, tried."

"What did she want?"

"No idea. I left her outside."

"Something screwy there. She thought you were away, same as I. She wanted something. I wonder what."

"No clue. Good night, Sheriff," Blake said, but he had a sinking feeling he had not seen the last of Schwartz.

Chapter Twenty-five

The next morning, Blake carried Schwartz's box and its contents to his office. Millie Bass had not yet arrived. He put the box in the middle of his desk, opened it, and withdrew the few remaining files. He put them in a manila envelope, dug out Doris Taliaferro's address, found an old-fashioned balance beam postage scale and weighed it. A search of Millie's desk turned up her cache of stamps. He figured two dollars would more than cover the postage. He took three fifty-cent stamps, to which he added two thirty-fours left over from one of the Post Office Department's postage increases, and stuck them on the package. He was about to close the drawer when he saw the key. It was buried in a jumble of paperclips. It looked familiar, like one of the keys he had sorted through Tuesday morning. But then, every key looked pretty much like every other key when you got right down to it. On a hunch, he carried it back into his office and after he put the stamped and addressed package in his briefcase, tried the key in the steel box's lock. It worked. He had the lid back down when Millie arrived. She stood in the door with her mouth open as if to say something but no sound came out.

"Good morning, Millie. You look like you've seen a ghost. Guess what I found."

"Dr. Taliaferro's files," she croaked. "Where…I mean what…?"

Blake decided not to tell her how he came across the box. Who knew what kind of story she would invent and spread around the neighborhood?

"Was there…were the files…are they…?"

"All taken care of," he said and gestured vaguely at his brief-case. It was not exactly the truth, but close enough.

"Then, that's it."

"I guess. Say, I found the key to the box in your drawer. Lucky, huh?"

"Oh, yes…I…that is, we, Dr. Taliaferro and I kept an extra key in the drawer. He sometimes misplaced his, and then he'd need it. So, you've taken care of the files?" she repeated.

"I guess so. Unless there is something you know that I should. No? Well, since the box is in pretty good condition, I think I will use it. I have some files of my own I need to move. I'll store them in this box. I kept all my old sermon notes, I don't know why. I guess I haven't the heart to throw them away. I should, but I keep thinking I might need them some day. I can put them in here and free up some drawer space."

He jerked open his lower drawer and removed fifteen inches of notes and squeezed them in the box. He locked it and lifted it into his crowded closet. It did not fit.

"Millie," he shouted through the half opened door, "is there any room in the big closet out there? This box won't fit in here."

Millie rounded the corner, saw Blake's predicament and turned back to the large closet in her office that held office supplies. She made some shelf space by removing two reams of copy paper that took up nearly a foot of shelf. There was at least twenty-four inches between it and the shelf above, and the closet was a standard twenty-two inches deep. Blake slid the box in and placed one ream of paper on top, the other, on edge, in front.

"You can't even tell it's there. Thanks, Millie." She grunted a response.

Millie wanted to say something, but she was seething. She'd searched high and low for those files. She'd scoured the church attic, the basement closets, and even the vicarage, twice. All for nothing, and now this…this man stumbles onto them and puts the files away. She sat drumming her fist softly on the mouse pad until she'd calmed down. In fact, she knew most of the juicier items anyway, and guessed it would not be long before this new vicar would start keeping records, too—that is, if he lasted. And after the uproar he caused Sunday, that did not seem too likely.

And then, she still had copies of those letters from Philadelphia buried with the other letters, the ones from the clergy up there. She could retrieve either set anytime she liked, put them in their proper file if, for example, the issue ever came up about why they had not been distributed before. She had a copy of the cover letter that indicated she did her part. How they got lost in the transmission would remain a great mystery.

She thumped the mouse pad some more and listened as he shifted around in his chair in the next room, then watched as the door between the offices swung shut. The light blinked on the phone. He was making a call. Well, she thought, let's just see what this is all about, and picked up the receiver.

He had Bournet on the line.

"Philip? I think we are in the clear. The police found out our murdered organist skipped out of San Francisco with information about organized crime up there. They think the mob found him and some hit man flew in to do the shooting."

"Good news for you, then. Must be a relief."

"It is. By the way, thank you for Mary Miller. She is a delight."

"Isn't she wonderful? Betsy said you two were made for each other. She has high hopes." Betsy Bournet prided herself in matchmaking.

"Philip, please, you are not trying to marry me off, are you?"

"Not me, Betsy."

"Well tell her she is premature. Mary is delightful, but right now all I can say is, I think she is a lovely person and I hope to see more of her. That's it. Tell Betsy. It will make her feel better, and maybe help her resist the temptation to push any harder."

"I'll do that," Philip chuckled.

Millie quietly returned the receiver to its cradle. She had what she needed. She pulled open a file drawer and recovered a packet of the damning letters from Philadelphia and put them in an envelope.

"Let's see what the beautiful Ms. Miller thinks of him when she reads these," she muttered.

By hanging up, and because she was angry, she missed the significance of the first part of the conversation, the information that might have changed a great number of things in her unhappy life.

Life had not always been hard for her. Thirty years before, Millie Carney married a graduate of the Naval Academy in one of the dozen or so ceremonies performed in the Academy chapel immediately after the graduation exercises. A year later she suspected her husband of cheating. She did not know it for a fact, but there were hastily ended conversations, and then she found some unexplained long-distance phone calls on their bill, calls to her best friend, Darlene.

After fretting about it for a month, she confronted her husband, who denied any wrongdoing. The calls, he told her, were about his possible assignment to Turkey. Darlene, he said, had been there and he wanted to know more about the country—that was all. Millie did not believe him.

Millie stewed over what she believed to be their affair. She tried following her husband on the nights he said he had to work late, but he never budged from his office. It was all she could do to get home before he did. Finally she decided to do something and put an end to it. Darlene worked in Naval Intelligence. She found some old Polaroid pictures taken when she and Darlene went on a singles cruise years before. Unlike Millie, Darlene had always been a risk taker. One night, in a moment of alcohol-fueled exuberance, she decided to dance on the top of a table for some of the young men, during the course of which, her top fell off. The picture made her look completely wanton, even though a split-second later she had recovered her top and modesty, and run red-faced from the room.

Millie mailed the picture anonymously to Darlene's boss. Darlene was fired. Millie gloated. Her husband found out what she had done and left her. Two years later, he married Darlene, confirming Millie's worst suspicions. Since that time she lived in her private world of victimhood, repeating and embellishing her story, the cause of her unhappiness, to anyone who would listen.

Blake spent the afternoon reading and rereading the Sunday lessons. He worked on his notes until five-thirty and then left to fix himself a light supper. While he ate his omelet he heard cars arriving. Thursday and choir practice—Mary Miller would be there. He wondered if he were somehow reverting to adolescence. He gulped down his meal and stalled around—watched the end of the news. Finally he caved in and left the house and crossed the parking lot to sit in on choir practice. It was, after all, Mary's first meeting with the choir, and she might need some help. At least that is what he told himself.

He went through his office and opened the door between it and the sacristy, and the sacristy door as well, so that he could hear but not be seen. The rehearsal seemed to be in full swing as he settled in his chair. He could not be sure which sounded better to him, the music, or Mary's voice. He decided Betsy Bournet knew what she was talking about. Finally, he could not resist the temptation to go into the church, and he walked into the nave.

The choir barely noticed him as it swung full-voiced into a cantata of some complexity. Blake was stunned. The choir had never sung anything more difficult than the simple harmonies in the hymnal and an occasional descant, and then not very well. Mary had brought them a light year away from the dull fare they usually dished up on a Sunday. When they finished, Blake applauded. Mary blushed, and most of the choir smiled in appreciation.

"Join us," Lanny Markowitz said.

"You do not want me to sing, Lanny, I promise you. A cow overdue for milking sounds better." Amid laughter they broke up and drifted out the door. Blake sidled over to Mary.

"Can I buy you a cup of coffee and dessert?" he asked. "I know it's a 'school night' but—"

"Actually, I am starving. I came here straight from work and haven't eaten anything since ten o'clock this morning."

"Neither have I," he lied. "I'll buy you dinner."

"I'll join you, but I will pay, if it is all the same with you."

They arranged to meet at the local Friendly's. He helped Lanny lock up and drove to the restaurant. Mary had a booth and he joined her. Most of the other choir members were there, too, ordering ice cream.

"They have a tradition," Mary said, "of meeting after choir practice for dessert—not all of them but the, ah, nicer ones." She lowered her eyes in embarrassment at the last remark. "I shouldn't have said that. I am sure they are all nice."

"Of course they are, and Osama Bin Laden is just misunderstood. Have you ordered? I think I will follow your choir and have dessert."

"I thought you said you hadn't eaten. You should have something more than dessert."

"I lied. I wanted an excuse to be with you. Sorry."

Mary blushed again. He guessed if Betsy Bournet had her way, he would be responsible for a lot of blushes in the future.

The waitress sauntered over to their booth, snapped her gum, and took their orders. While they waited, they talked. He had to ignore the stares and smirks on the faces of the choir members. Lanny caught his eye and gave him a thumbs up. Mary asked about the murder investigation and he told her about Schwartz's discovery that Templeton was, in fact, a mobster from San Francisco.

"Wow," she said, "how exciting. It's like a movie." Her eyes danced at the thought. "Credits roll…a plane, sunset behind it, drops in for a landing," she began. Blake watched as she flattened her hand and brought it in for a landing next to her mashed potatoes. "Brrrt, brrt," she said, making the sounds of airplane wheels touching down on the tarmac. "Door opens and a man wearing aviator sunglasses gets off and retrieves his luggage. No one knows, but it has a secret compartment."

"Naturally, everyone who wears aviator sunglasses—he ought to have a trench coat, too—all those guys have secret compartments in their luggage. I'm thinking about getting one myself," Blake added.

"Hush." She gave him a stern look. "This is my movie. He checks into a cheap motel in Picketsville—"

"There are no motels in Picketsville, cheap or otherwise."

"He checks into a motel out on the highway…satisfied? And he opens the bag. The secret compartment has a big gun, one of those big shiny ones, you know, like Clint Eastwood had in that movie?"

"A three fifty-seven magnum."

"That's the one, a three fifty-seven magnet." Blake did not correct her. He liked magnet better anyway. "He drives to Stonewall Jackson Church, sneaks up the stairs. Waldo is playing the organ—Bach, I think—deedle dee, dum, dum, dah. He doesn't see the killer. Waldo…what was his real name, do you know?"

"Walter. Walter Krueger."

"Walter/Waldo turns and stares at the man. He takes off his aviator sunglasses and says, 'That's right, Walter/Waldo, it's me.' Then, blam! He shoots poor Walter/Waldo. 'Arrgh' says Walter/Waldo and he falls down dead."

"Very dramatic. One problem, Walter/Waldo was killed behind the altar, not at the organ."

"Oh well, then Aviator Glasses sneaks up the stairs through your office, where he pauses to admire your diplomas. He is a man with academic aspirations. And then he skulks into the sanctuary, where he lurks, an evil presence, waiting for his victim. Walter/Waldo plays Bach, deedle dee…"

"I get the picture. How does he get into the offices? The doors are locked."

"He's a crook. He can pick a lock, can't he?"

"Sure, but what is Walter/Waldo doing in the church at that time? Choir practice would have ended long before then. And how would the bad guy know? Wouldn't he need to follow him around, find out his habits, things like that?"

"You are deliberately trying to ruin my movie," she said with a pout.

"Sorry. How about this. Aviator Glasses is on the airplane. He is studying some pictures. We zoom in and see they are pictures of Walter/Waldo. The plane lands."

"Brrt, brrt," Mary added.

"Exactly. He books into a motel nearby and then drives his rental to Picketsville. He parks in front of Walter/Waldo's house and waits. His victim drives up, unaware of the danger that lurks in the shadows. Headlights go out. He gets out of his car. Aviator Glasses follows Walter/Waldo to the front door. He turns. He's terrified. Aviator Glasses says, 'That's right, Walter/Waldo, its me' and—"

"Blam!" she finished. "You're right, that makes more sense." She finished her dinner and got up to leave. "But that's not what happened." Blake speared the check.

"My treat," he said.

"No way," she protested.

"Just this time. You can pay the next time."

"Who said anything about a next time?"

"Tomorrow night, dinner and a movie, how about it?"

"Oh I see, you want me to spring for the expensive meal."

"Dutch," he said.

"What time?"

"Seven?"

"No good. Pick me up at seven-thirty."

Blake watched her leave. He poured himself another coffee and stared at his placemat. He turned his thoughts from Mary and their "movie." His eyebrows knit in a frown. It did make more sense—that was the problem. It did not happen that way.

Chapter Twenty-six

Mary picked up her mail and quickly sorted through it. Anything without a first-class stamp went into the wastepaper basket with the fliers and junk mail. The rest she dropped, unopened, in the pile on the little desk by her front door. Mary had a rule. Neither telephones nor mail would manage her life. She did not have an answering machine. She did once, and found that it obligated her to make calls she did not want to make. The messages were on the machine and it would be rude not to return the call. By getting rid of the machine, she got rid of the obligation as well. She didn't have to respond to a message she never received.

She also refused to answer calls while she ate. She rejected the tyranny of the telephone. She managed her mail in the same way. She sorted it quickly when it arrived, discarded most of it, and saved the rest for Sunday afternoon when she would open each piece, read it carefully and, if necessary, frame a reply which she would write on the spot. She found that only in this way could she keep up with her correspondence and pay her bills in a timely manner. She gathered her bag and keys, and left for work.

Lanny Markowitz and Dan Quarles met every other week for lunch. They used the time to set the Mission Board's agenda and discuss problems. The Jack Pines Inn had a clientele drawn primarily from locals. Its location far off the main road all but assured that no one except locals could find it even if they called for directions. Dan had served as chairman of the Mission Board for more years than Lanny could remember. Lanny, on the other hand, had only been on for two. Because no one else would accept the responsibility, he also agreed to be vice-chairman.

Dan sat and pulled out his handkerchief, which he dipped into his water glass, and proceeded to wipe the Formica table. The Jack Pines Inn was not known for its food or ambiance. Satisfied that the table met his standard of hygiene, he turned to Lanny.

"So what are we going to do about the Vicar?"

"Fisher? What's the problem?"

"You heard him Sunday. People are angry."

"Nuts, people are always hot over one thing or another. I say let him go. If he fails, we don't have a problem because he'll be gone. If he succeeds, we don't have a problem either. No, the real problem is Millie Bass, if you ask me. We need to fire her."

The waitress brought their sandwiches. She put a cracked iced tea pitcher down next to them and left.

Lanny toyed with his food. He had been eating here for a long time but never noticed the food before.

"We can't fire Mrs. Bass," Dan said. "Why, half the congregation would be furious if we did."

"Dan, I know your wife is a friend of Millie's, one of her inner circle, so you don't have a completely unbiased view. I do. Bass is a disaster. She spreads gossip and rumors like candy on Halloween. Her stories are mean and hurtful. It didn't used to be that way. It used to be just idle gossip—but not any more. And she is a liar."

"Now wait just a minute, that's going pretty far."

"No, it isn't. There is something you don't know. I didn't know about it, either, until Tuesday. You remember those packets we got when Fisher was hired. They all had those letters from people in Philadelphia in them, you remember."

"Of course, I do. I helped put them together."

"You did?"

"Yes. So what?"

"How many letters were included, do you remember?"

"I don't know. Three or four, maybe five. All bad, I remember that—except for Bournet's."

"Did you know there were other letters sent to the church from clergy in Philadelphia, the Bishop and some others?"

"There were no other letters, Lanny."

"There were. I've seen them, or copies anyway, and they all say 'cc: Stonewall Jackson Mission Board' at the bottom."

"We never got any letters like that."

"No, we didn't, but Millie did. She got them and she buried them. The only good letter we saw came from Bournet that said he had every confidence in Fisher and so on. We have been treating this guy like a leper with halitosis for nearly three months because we didn't know the truth—the truth we would have known if Millie Bass had put the good letters in the packets."

"That's a pretty strong accusation, Lanny. I don't know."

"Dan, I am not a big Fisher fan, you know that. But we have done him a disservice and we need to make it right. Nearly every one of the old-timers thinks Fisher is some kind of monster. Millie Bass did that to him, and we need to fix it. I don't know about you, but most of the time when I find myself opposing him, I'm not thinking about what he's saying, but what I believed he did. I bet most of us are in the same boat. It has to stop. We have to set the record straight, and Millie Bass has to go before she poisons the well beyond hope."

Dan licked his lips, looked out the window, and then inspected the contents of his soup bowl as if he thought he would see reason in the dregs of cream of broccoli. Lanny stood up, his food uneaten. He dropped three dollars on the table and left.

"If you won't do it, I will," he said over his shoulder as he left. He thought he heard a plaintive "Oh, dear," but he could not be sure.

Blake pulled up in front of Mary Miller's town house at seven twenty-five. He decided waiting five minutes would be the tactful thing to do. He got out of his car and inspected the chrysanthemums that lined the walk. The yard was tiny but Mary had made the most of it. There were mums and dahlias, some asters about to bloom, and some sort of ground cover he could not identify. His inspection took about fifteen seconds, and then he changed his mind about arriving early and rang her bell. She opened the door immediately. He guessed she had been just inside watching and waiting. He walked her to the car. She opened her own door before he could, and slid gracefully in, no mean accomplishment. Blake drove a small, and very low, sports car. Mary had somehow folded her long legs in without a hitch.

The ride to the mall passed without much in the way of conversation. He had the top down and the wind noise prevented any but the most perfunctory talk.

He'd made reservations at L'Escoffier, a restaurant with pretensions and a name more French than its cuisine. It differed very little from the other eateries in the area—the odd collection of unconnected memorabilia tacked to the walls near the ceiling, and a menu that featured basic beef, seafood, and chicken dishes, only the fries were *pommes frites*, and the entrees, *boeuf, pêche, et poulet.*

Later, Blake could not remember what he had ordered or how it tasted. His whole attention was focused on Mary. She, on the other hand, seemed to enjoy her food immensely. She ate, sampled his, and chattered on about any of a dozen subjects. Blake listened, fascinated.

After they finished their coffee and paid their half of the bill, they strolled around the corner to the multiplex theater. They discovered the movie offerings were all either R-rated or one of those moronic kid flicks designed to fill theaters at the end of summer. Blake suggested a walk instead, window-shopping and people watching. They strolled along the several wings, stopping now and then, to admire or critique some item. In front of Classique—The Store for Women, Blake paused.

"Look at that gown," he said. The manikin in the window was draped in a black beaded cocktail dress. The neckline was scooped, but not too low, and it had spaghetti straps.

"You like that?" she asked.

"It's really pretty," he said. "It would look wonderful on you."

"You don't think it's too...slinky?"

"I have a theory about clothes," he said. "Clothes make the man, but women make the clothes. I mean you can take a derelict off the street, clean him up, put him in a pinstripe suit, and pass him off as a banker. But you put a dumpy woman in that dress and she's a dumpy woman in a beaded dress. Put a fast woman in it, and it becomes, as you so delicately put it, slinky. On you, it would be elegant."

He got the blush he expected. They passed Victoria's Secret.

"We'll just move right along," she said. "Eyes front."

At Radio Shack, Blake stopped to look at cell phones.

"You don't have one, do you?" he asked.

"No, and I don't want one."

"You are so hard to reach," he said, "I am ready to buy one for you."

"Please don't. I treasure my privacy. I wish I didn't have the regular phone. I would get rid of it if I could."

"You are a very funny lady."

"Funny like in Ha Ha, or funny like in Gaga?"

She paused in front of the jewelry store. The window had been arranged to show off a collection of diamond engagement rings. *End of Summer Sale*, announced a big sign in the window.

"I almost had an engagement ring once." She gave him a sidelong look.

"Really?" he said and felt a small and quite unjustified pang of jealousy.

"Yep. About as big as that one in the middle." She pointed to a diamond that had to be at least two carats.

"It's none of my business," he said, "but what happened?"

"Oh, we had a disagreement about housing. He wanted me to move in with him before we got married to 'see if it would work.' I told him that at that moment, it was clear to me it wouldn't, and gave the ring back. I never even got it out of the box."

"I'm speechless."

"That's a nice change," she said and smiled.

They walked some more. Finally they made a turn and realized they were back where they had started.

"Sorry about the movie," they both said at the same time and laughed.

"Tomorrow?" he asked.

"No, I can't. And Sunday you work and will be tired." He began to protest and then changed his mind. He did not need to rush.

"Monday night. What would you like to do Monday?"

"Would you take me to the theater? I love stage productions. There's a road company doing *Cats* in Roanoke. Could we go there?"

"Sure, consider it done. Would you like to eat first?"

"Sure."

He drove her home. The street seemed darker than he remembered it. Then he saw that her streetlight was out. He parked, got out, and opened the door for her.

"You know, I thought there was something familiar about your address. Templeton lived near here, didn't he?"

"Yes," she said. He could not see her expression in the darkness. She averted her head and hurried to the door.

"Did you know him?" he persisted.

"Blake, I have to go in now. I had a wonderful time."

"You didn't answer. Did you know him?"

"Oh yeah, I knew him," she said and let herself in the house.

"You never told me you knew Templeton."

The door shut and Blake found himself alone on the doorstep.

Chapter Twenty-seven

"I'm not going," Grace Franks screeched. Her eyes had become red rimmed and flecks of dried saliva filled the lines at the corners of her mouth. Her voice climbed a half octave. "I hate those people. They're evil."

"Keep your voice down, Grace. You want the whole neighborhood to hear you?"

"I don't care. I will not go to that church anymore. It's full of hypocrites and—"

"Give it a rest, Grace, we're going. Get in the car. I'll be late for choir."

"Then go without me. Go on. Get in the car and go."

"I've had enough of this, you hear? Will you get a grip? You sound like you're nuts."

"Maybe I am. If I am, it's because you are making me crazy, you and your…girlfriends."

"Me? *My* girlfriends? That's rich…pot calling the kettle black, I say. How many times do I have to tell you, Grace? There aren't any girlfriends."

"You say."

He unclenched his fist. He'd been doing that a lot lately, and she wondered how much longer it would be before he smacked her. *To the moon, Alice!*

He shook his head and left the kitchen to finish dressing. She sat with her head in her hands. She hated him, she knew that, but she could not do anything about it. Even if she tried, they knew. Everybody knew. They would come right to her first.

"You still here?" he said, knotting his tie. "It's time to go."

"I said I am not going."

"Either you get in the car or I'll—"

"You would, wouldn't you?" She followed him out to the driveway and got in the car. They drove to church. He chewed on the stub end of an unlit cigar and talked about the garden and how he wanted her to water it the next day. He droned on, but she was not listening. She was thinking about guns.

Her father had lots of them. Her father had been a colonel in the army and kept guns from the service—souvenirs—Japanese, German and nineteen fifties vintage Russian weapons from his tour in Korea. He had a big collection of them, handguns, rifles, shotguns, and even some illegal automatic weapons. He tried to teach her how to shoot when she was six. The noise scared her so much she cried all the way home. But she had mastered them eventually. Her father kept dragging her back to the range until she forced herself to learn out of a sense of survival. Now she thought about those guns and especially the one she thought of as hers. She thought what his face would like if she reached into her purse and aimed it at his stupid cigar. The thought made her smile.

"What's so funny," he said.

"You are."

By ten o'clock the temperature had inched up ten degrees. Stonewall Jackson would stay cool inside, but outside on the parking lot, the heat rose off the asphalt and made you hurry to the church's cool gloom.

Blake waited near the end of the parking lot, standing first on one foot and then the other. The asphalt burned through the thin leather of his loafers. He had prepared a surprise for Mary. The day before, he had carefully lettered a sign and mounted it next to his own. Mary now had a reserved parking place near the rear door. He wanted to catch her as she drove in and guide her to the place. The sun beat down on him and he wished he had at least taken off his robes after the eight o'clock service. Now he did not dare for fear he would miss her, so he stood in the parking lot arrayed in his full regalia and felt the perspiration trickle down his back.

Finally, her car pulled into the lot. He waved frantically, signaling her to come to him. She hesitated and then drove slowly forward. He backed up and directed her into the spot like a ground crewman at the airport, bringing his hands together slowly as she edged to a stop. He stepped aside so she could see his sign. She grinned and shook her head.

"People are going to start talking," she said.

"Let them," he replied. "That is nothing more than I would do for anyone on the staff. See, even Millie Bass has a spot."

"Did Waldo Templeton have a reserved spot, too?"

"Well, no, but he would have if I'd thought about it."

She smiled at him. "You must be boiling in that outfit," she said. "Get back inside before you melt."

Blake stood at the crossing at the front of the church between the two rows of pews. The altar area had been restored, the damask curtain removed and, except for a few traces of bloodstains, everything seemed to be back to normal. He thought there might be a sermon in there somewhere, but not today. He bowed his head and prayed, looked up and scanned the congregation.

"Good morning," he said. There were fewer people in the "hole" he thought, but maybe a few more in the "doughnut." Call it even.

He began his sermon slowly. The second lesson for the day was from Philippians. He needed some time to get from "at the name of Jesus every knee shall bow and every tongue confess, that Jesus Christ is Lord," to the Ten Commandments. It was not an easy transition, and he wondered if he had made a mistake not to just select the appropriate lessons instead of sticking to the lectionary.

He spoke slowly, pausing to make a point here and there. He measured his audience. They were attentive; even the "hole" seemed to be listening. Finally he said, "Bow to what? No, bow to whom? If Jesus is Lord, what obligation does that place on us? What does he expect of us, day by day? John's gospel tells us he says, 'If you love me, you will keep my commandments.' So how about, for starters, we keep God's Law."

Not a great segue, but he had learned long ago that very few people listened for things like that anyway. They took the message as delivered and rarely noticed the rhetoric. Once on his topic, he rolled on. He ticked off each of the commandments, one by one. Most of them he simply summarized and briefly described. After each he paused and intoned, "Can we say, in the privacy of our hearts, I have kept this commandment?"

He spent a little more time on honoring one's father and mother. There were a handful of teenagers slouched in the back of the church and he thought he might make a point or two with them.

"Can we say, in the privacy of our hearts, I have kept this commandment?"

He stopped again on the Seventh Commandment. He knew he probably should not. He did not know why, but felt compelled to do so. "Adultery," he heralded, and watched as adults squirmed, and the teenagers sat up and took notice. Good. Now they were all listening.

Epiphanies are a sometime thing. They come in all sizes and at odd and often inconvenient moments. He'd been in Picketsville for a little over three months, all of them prejudiced by the dark clouds of his personal disappointment. As he spoke the words, at that precise moment, he realized with painful clarity that much of the distance between him and his congregation was of his own making—the residue of his unhappiness. He smiled and turned back to the people. *Time to lighten up, Fisher.*

"You have no doubt heard what Moses said to Aaron at the foot of Mount Sinai. No? Ah. Well, he comes down from the heights and says, 'Aaron, I've been talking to You Know Who'—

to speak God's name was forbidden, you understand—'about His commandments and I have good news and I have bad news.' And Aaron says, 'So, what's the good news?' and Moses says, 'I got him down to ten.' Aaron says, 'Great, and the bad news?' Moses says, 'Adultery is still in.'"

Blake waited. Had he gone too far? A few tentative smiles, a chuckle in the rear. Not loud but genuine. He counted several disapproving scowls among the smiles. *Too soon to tell a joke? Well, they might as well get used to it. It's definitely time to lighten up.*

"I told the story to illustrate a point," he went on. "Many people would very much like this commandment to go away. Adultery has become the lifestyle of modern America. Daytime television, soap operas, even primetime is saturated with adulterous relationships…relationships that often seem as complex as strands of DNA. Movies, books, everywhere you turn, adultery, not fidelity, illicit sex, not chastity, is the standard. Indeed the institution of marriage has been systematically and thoroughly trivialized by our culture and its leaders."

He scanned his congregation again.

"If the statistics are correct, at least half of you here today have had, or are now engaged in, a relationship of that sort." He stopped and looked at the people. Stony, icy, and shocked silence greeted him. Then, for reasons he never understood, even years later, added, "And you know who you are.…Again, can we say, in the privacy of our hearts, I have kept this commandment?"

He had started pacing at the fourth commandment, and now, as he pivoted to walk to his left, he caught sight of Grace Franks. She had a look on her face that could only be described as dumbfounded. She rose and left the church.

Blake moved on through eight and then jumped directly to ten. He quickly polished off Covetousness. He paused and surveyed his congregation once again.

"I skipped the ninth commandment, because that is the one I want to discuss at length today. 'Thou shalt not bear false witness against thy neighbor.' Most of us think this law has something to do with testimony given in court, with perjury. And in some ways it does. Perjury is a felony in most courts, and the penalties can be very severe. In the first century, they could be even more so. The rule was as follows—if you bore false witness, that is, if you gave untrue testimony in a trial, and the person was subsequently acquitted and your story deemed false, you received the punishment the accused would have received had he been found guilty. You understand? If it was a capital crime, you got stoned to death, not him or her, but you.

"But the commandment has a much deeper application. Remember, God gave it to Moses, for the people in the wilderness. These were nomads living in tents, cheek by jowl. Any behavior that separated them or lessened their mutual affection and harmony could be catastrophic. Think about all of the commandments. Aren't they actually designed to keep people at peace? What effect would theft or adultery have on the social equilibrium of a tribe living on the edge in the desert?

"This commandment is one of those strictures. Bearing false witness in that context is what today we call gossip."

There, he said it. It might have been his imagination, but he felt the air crackle. Feet shuffled. People coughed nervously. A few heads turned to steal a look at Millie Bass. She sat stock still, her lips pursed and eyes squeezed together as if she were trying to read an eye chart without her glasses. Whatever goodwill his story about Moses had created seemed to have drained out of his listeners.

"I daresay there is not one of us in the room that has not broken this commandment at least once this week. You know how it goes. We hear something about Miss A. We pass it along and the story gets more elaborate and negative with each telling until we are part of a chain that has contributed to the character assassination of another human being. And the problem is, we cannot take it back. Once the words are out of our mouth, they have a life of their own. They pass from lip to ear, and twenty years later they are still alive in someone's memory waiting for a reason to wander off again.

"Did you know," he continued, "the root word for gossip and gospel is the same? Isn't that interesting? And it should tell us something. Stories that uplift and speak to the truth ultimately come from God. Those that do the reverse are the work of the Devil. I want us to search our hearts this morning. When was the last time we yielded to the temptation to gossip? How will we resist it the next time?

"I'll close with this. In my opinion, more people have gone to Hell for breaking this commandment than the other nine put together. Can we say, in the privacy of our hearts, I have kept this commandment?"

He stopped. You could hear the proverbial pin drop. Finally a voice in the back said, "Amen." It sounded like Rose Garroway.

Chapter Twenty-eight

Coffee hour slipped by quietly. Some of the congregation skipped it altogether. The few who remained seemed subdued. Rose Garroway and most of the Wednesday Morning Bible Study came over. Rose handed Blake some punch.

"You look like you could use a drink, cowboy. We are here to offer to be your posse, your bodyguards, if you need us."

"Well, I appreciate that, Ma'am, you betcha. I'll call you if I need you."

Mary stopped by on her way out. He confirmed their date for the next evening. He told her he had orchestra seat tickets. She asked if that was good. He said it was. Sylvia Parks joined him at the coffee pot.

"Feel like the Lone Ranger?" she asked in her smooth, cultivated voice. "Don't worry. You said what two thirds of the people in this church have been thinking for at least a decade, only they didn't think it had anything to do with them. Let us hope the worst of them heard you and change their ways. Besides, the Moses story—that was good."

"Maybe I should have quit then, while I was ahead."

One by one people drifted away. Blake took a last look around and went home. He ate two hot dogs, drank a quart of milk, and slept until seven o'clock when the phone rang.

It took him a moment to figure out where he was. The lights were out and the blinds drawn. He struggled in that not fully awake, not quite asleep state where reality is distorted, time slides and memory fails. For a moment he thought he must have slept through the night and it was seven in the morning. It would be his day off. He woke up a bit and reset his mental clock. The phone kept ringing.

"Okay, okay," he said and cleared his throat. His voice sounded like Louis Armstrong's singing. He stumbled to the phone in the half-light and answered.

"Blake?" Mary said. Her voice sounded strange and far away.

"Um, hi," he said collecting himself. He cleared his throat again.

"I cannot see you any more."

"What?"

"I said I cannot see you any more. I found out what you did to that woman in Philadelphia. I cannot think how I ever allowed myself to…how I missed that in you."

"Mary, nothing happened. What do you mean you just learned, I—"

"I do my mail on Sundays. Someone sent me an envelope and it had letters in it, Blake, about you and that woman. How could you?"

"Who sent you…? Mary, those letters are lies. Mary, please don't hang up, it's not true."

"Denying them is what I'd expect. You will need to find a new organist, too," she said, ignoring him. "I cannot play for you any more, either."

"Mary, listen. If you don't believe me call Philip. He knows the truth. You trust Philip, don't you? Or call Lanny Markowitz, I'll give you his number. I have it here somewhere, wait, he knows, too. There are other letters, real ones you need to see."

The line went dead.

He slammed his fist on the table. Letters. Who sent them? Where did they come from? He knew. Lanny said only three people had any possible access to the letters, and the first in line was Millie Bass. Where else? She'd held back the good letters and forwarded the bad ones. She had to be the one who sent them to Mary. He did not even bother to think why. Millie Bass did not need a reason.

He called Lanny.

"Lanny, do me a favor will you? Call Mary Miller and tell her about the letters I showed you. I think Millie Bass sent her copies of the bad ones, and she just quit."

"Well, I'll call right now, but you know, I had a meeting with Dan last Friday and we, or I guess I, decided—"

"I'm going to fire her, Lanny. Tomorrow is her last day."

"That's what I wanted to tell you, we decided—"

"You cannot talk me out of it, Lanny. I don't care how many people get upset and leave the church. Good riddance. She's history."

"Your call, Vicar. I'll support you."

"You will?"

"One hundred percent."

"And you'll call Mary?"

"Absolutely, right away. We can't afford to lose her—you maybe, Millie definitely, but not Mary. Just kidding, Vicar, I'll call right now."

Blake sat on the edge of his bed. Cannot lose her—me maybe, but not her. Lanny had no idea how right he was. Blake hung his head.

Chapter Twenty-nine

Blake usually looked forward to Mondays. He'd spend the time with the Sunday paper he'd saved, maybe playing golf, or catching up on his reading. Mondays were good times. Not today. For the second Monday in a row, he woke up tired and miserable. He dragged himself out of bed and made a pot of coffee and a plate full of toast. He smeared peanut butter on the lot, poured his coffee, and slumped in a chair in the living room.

He would fire Millie Bass this morning. The thought made him feel a little better. He rushed through his Daily Office, skipped the Psalms, and barely skimmed the lessons. He promised God he would make it up to him later. At nine o'clock he left the house and walked to the office. Millie's car was not in its spot. He waited until nine thirty and called her home. No answer. He looked at her calendar. It indicated she had a dentist appointment that morning. Had she told him about that? He could not remember. He would have to fire her tomorrow.

He swallowed his disappointment and went back home. Now what? He decided to drive to Roanoke and see Philip. He would know what to do.

Sally, Philip's secretary, greeted him as he entered the office area.

"Is Himself in?" he asked, he hoped with a measure of light-heartedness.

"Sorry, Mr. Fisher, he's in Richmond at some kind of emergency meeting. I don't expect him back until late. Can I give him a message if he calls?"

Blake considered the offer and declined. He would try some other day.

His day off. Blake decided to make the best of it. He would be a tourist and explore the city. He had to cancel his theater tickets anyway. He wandered around, window-shopping and exploring. At noon he detected the aroma of kebabs and followed his nose to a small restaurant that specialized in Near Eastern food. He ordered kebabs and Greek beer and ate out on the sidewalk where he could watch people as they scurried past.

He found the theater and cancelled his tickets. He shook his head and reaffirmed his decision to fire Millie Bass. First thing tomorrow. He stuffed the credit receipts in his pocket and headed back to his car, a good forty-minute walk away. As he passed an office supply house, a box in the window caught his eye. It was the twin of the one Taliaferro used—the one that now held his old sermon notes. On an impulse, he went in. There were three more boxes shelved at the back of the store. He inspected each in turn. The keys caught his eye first. He removed one set. There were two identical keys on a ring. Most locks came with two keys. He frowned and pulled out his key ring. The key to his box had the same lands and grooves but was steel. The keys to the store's boxes were brass.

His next stop was a hardware store. He walked back to the key duplicating machine and showed his key to the clerk, who confirmed it was a copy, not an original. He had a copy made, thanked the man and hurried to his car. Now he had it. The key he found in Millie's drawer had to be a copy. If the box came with two keys, would not Taliaferro have given her the second key if he wanted to protect himself? Why make a copy? Taliaferro might have lost one, or kept his own backup at home and a third with Millie, but Blake bet he hadn't. Records of such a sensitive nature would not have been placed in harm's way with someone like Millie Bass. No, somehow she got hold of the key and made a copy. Taliaferro's files must have been a goldmine for her.

The enormity of the situation only hit him when he turned onto old Route 11 and headed toward the church. A breach of privacy, the invasion of psychological counseling sessions, if discovered, could lead to a major scandal and possibly to lawsuits that could break the church and possibly the Diocese.

And where were those files now? He did not believe for a second they were in a sanitary landfill somewhere. Someone had them, and he was pretty sure he knew who. Tomorrow, he would have it out with Millie and then try to do some damage control. He gritted his teeth. What else could go wrong?

As it turned out, Special Agent Hedrick never left town. He took a room at the Magnolia Motel. Ike knew that because Dorothy Sutherlin heard it from Mavis Bowers, whose nephew's wife worked there part-time as a bookkeeper. Dorothy told Billy and Billy told Ike. He could not have retrieved that information faster if it had been posted on the Internet. Why did Hedrick do that?

Well, at least, Sam seemed happy. Ike watched as the she and Hedrick stalked gracefully down the street like a pair of giraffes. Sam had signed out and the two of them were on their way to lunch, necks bent toward one another as they talked. Ike wondered if he was about to lose his new deputy so soon. And if so, who would manage all the equipment she'd assembled? As much as he hoped, for Sam's sake, that Hedrick was staying in town because he had leave time coming and decided to spend it in Picketsville with her, he knew something else held the FBI man in town. Certainly the boys in Washington hadn't decided to open a field office in Picketsville. Since he couldn't pry the reason out of Hedrick, he figured he'd have to figure a way around him. Two calls to Langley and he had the phone number he needed.

"Hello?" A woman's voice. A young woman.

"Hi, I'm trying to locate Harry Grafton. Is he there?" Silence. "Hello, are you still there?"

"Who's calling?" she said. Nervous.

"Ike Schwartz, Sheriff Ike Schwartz, Picketsville, Virginia."

"Oh. Hi there, Sheriff, how are you? This is Jennifer. Do you remember me?"

Jennifer Ames. He remembered. "Are you with…is Harry there?"

"Yes, I'll get him."

Well, well. Old Harry landed on his feet big time. Jennifer was young, rich, and smart. Lucky Harry.

"Sheriff?" Grafton sounded reserved, careful. "What's up?"

"I need a favor."

"Um, what kind of favor are we talking about here. You know I'm with the Agency now?"

"Oh yeah. Look, it's nothing that can compromise you or what we both know about the art thing, okay?"

"Well…excuse me…what Jen? Yeah, I know…I owe him one, I know…Sorry Sheriff, you were saying?"

"More than one, Harry, but I'll take this one for now. Look, I'm being stonewalled by your former associates in the Bureau. I ask a question about a homicide we have here, a man named Walter Krueger. I can't get a straight answer from the Bureau and now we find out they've been after him for months. I need to know why they dummied up. And why is one of their people squatting in my town for no apparent reason."

"How can I help?"

"Give me a name. Someone who can tell me why Special Agent Hedrick is hanging around town and what he's after. Why was Walter Krueger shot twice in the local church? In short, what the hell is going on? There must be somebody in the Bureau I can talk to."

"I don't keep in touch anymore. Not much. I guess you can figure out why. Look, give me a day. I'll check around and get back to you."

"Fair enough. Call me if you have anything. Are you and the girl I found in the motel...?"

"Jennifer. Yes, you could say that. It's looking good but I still have some baggage from before, and then, there are my kids. I'm not sure I should ask her to take that on."

Ike heard the woman say something like "I love them, Harry." He had no idea what Grafton was talking about. He just remembered a frightened hostage who helped him cover for Grafton, the Bureau castoff, so he could redeem himself with another agency.

"Thanks, and good luck."

Sam wondered if, at last, her luck, her life might have changed. All those years as the Stork, the geek, the lady jock—a giant freak in a world of normal-sized people—were over. Karl Hedrick was her size, maybe an inch taller, but where she had the pale skin and green eyes you'd expect with true redheads, his glowed a lovely café au lait. And she felt something might be there between them, but....

"Karl, why are you still here?" she asked, not entirely sure she really wanted to hear the answer, so much depended on it. She sipped her tea. Patricia's English Tea Room, Picketsville's only nod in the direction of refinement, was nearly empty. Five older women in purple dresses and red hats, looking like a college of female Cardinals, occupied a table in the corner and were absorbed in self-generated hilarity.

Karl folded his napkin, eyes down, avoiding hers. A single rose in a blue bud vase competed unsuccessfully against his coffee's aroma.

"Karl?"

"I have leave time accrued and I thought you and I might...."

He didn't finish the sentence. She waited, wanting to believe, afraid her heart was about to be broken.

"Karl, I am a Phi Beta Kappa from Michigan State Please...."

"It's the truth," he said and lifted his gaze to meet hers. "But not all of the truth. Okay?"

"What's true? What part?"

"I'm still here because you…we…you know. But the other part is I asked to be here. I am not using leave time. But I would if I had to. That's what I told Chief Bullock and he said, okay, I should stay. It's the Krueger business. It's not as simple as it seems and…anyway, I'm the Agent in Place for now so…."

"You would have stayed anyway?"

"If they let me, yes. Leave is not something you just take, but yes."

She smiled an enormous smile, a smile that lighted the entire room and even caused a brief, a very brief, pause in the raucous laughter among the Red Hats.

"That's good," she said. "That's really good."

Blake drove up to his house and braked hard in a shower of gravel. He walked to the church and let himself in. He needed to see if Millie had ever come in, and if so, check for messages and mail. The offices were just as he had left them that morning. He slid one closet door open and shut—no sign of any activity at all.

His kebabs started talking to him. He loved Jordanian food but now regretted the choice. He went outside, crossed the parking lot to his house, and let himself in. The light on his answering machine blinked an S.O.S. at him.

"Later," he said. "You will have to get in line and wait your turn to screw up the rest of my day."

He wrote a list of people to call. The Mission Board needed to be called. Did they have a lawyer? Did he? Schwartz said he needed one and only half meant it. Now he really did, but not for the reasons Schwartz gave. Would Sylvia Parks take him on as a client? He added her to the list. Philip had to be told. He could be liable too, as could his vestry. He was sure they had an attorney. Philip would know what to do about the Bishop. Who else? He started to hum *Santa Claus Is Coming to Town.* He was making a list and checking it. The tune was entirely too cheerful. He did not feel cheerful and stopped.

He could not think of anyone or anything else to add. He just hoped he could contain the problem before it went public. The first thing he had to do was find the files. He ran his hand through his hair and listened to his stomach growl. The kebabs had made their peace with his gastro-intestinal system and now he was hungry.

He went to the kitchen, muttering to the answering machine, "Not yet. I'm not ready for you yet."

He found some cold pizza in the refrigerator. He heated up a cup of coffee in the microwave and sat at the dining room table to eat. His mother would kill him if she knew how he ate. He chewed the cold cheese and pepperoni and tried to think.

By nine o'clock he had managed to acquire some semblance of calm. He realized he had done everything he could. The Mission Board had their monthly meeting the next evening. He would bring it up to them then. What he learned at the meeting would determine if he needed to call Sylvia. In the meantime he would see about the files. He would confront Millie in the morning and get her to surrender them. The threat of jail and lawsuits ought to be enough to get her to cough them up.

The answering machine winked at him.

"Okay, okay, I'm coming, talk to me."

The first message was from his bank. His checks were ready. Great. He had been in the area nearly three months and finally he had checks with his name and address on them.

The second message was his sister Irene wanting to know how he was, and if everything had worked out all right. Oh, ducky. Everything is just terrific.

The third was Mary.

"Blake," she said in a little voice that he guessed meant she was crying. "I am so sorry. I talked to Lanny Markowitz and to Philip. I am so sorry." A pause. "I should not have done that to you without at least hearing your side of the story. I guess I didn't think your sermon had anything to do with me. Maybe if I had listened….I know you probably don't want to, and I don't blame you if you don't, but would you please call me?"

He paused the machine. Rewound it and played the message again. He felt twenty pounds lighter. He would indeed call.

The last message brought him back to earth.

"So, she told you," a voice muttered. "That's bad enough. Why did you have to tell the world? What kind of minister are you? You are supposed to help people, not hurt them." The voice was husky. It sounded like a woman, but he could not be sure. It might be a teenager playing a joke, an "I saw what you did" kind of joke. "Well," the message continued. "I'll settle with her, and you could be next."

He momentarily forgot about Mary and played the message over and over. Take care of whom? The message made no sense. He sat back and tried to think. Had he heard that voice before? There was something familiar about it, but he might be imagining things. He started to rewind the tape and then, remembering Mary's call, decided to save it. He ejected the tape and put it away. He spent the next five minutes rooting through the closet looking for a fresh cassette.

He reached for the phone just as the flare of headlights swept across his window and stopped him. He heard a car door slam and a moment later a knock at the side door. Now what?

Ike Schwartz stood on the stoop.

"You have a lawyer, Reverend?" Schwartz said.

"What? You know, it's funny you should ask, Sheriff. I was just thinking about you and lawyers just now. What brings you here, on an otherwise disastrous Monday, asking me about attorneys?"

Schwartz ignored him and circled the room.

"Can you account for your whereabouts from say quarter to eleven this morning to three this afternoon?"

Blake thought a moment.

"I have you again, Sheriff. Yes, I can." He didn't know if Schwartz was pleased or disappointed. "I went to Saint Anne's Church in Roanoke this morning. I got there at about eleven. I took old Route 11 instead of the interstate. It would take me at least forty-five minutes to an hour to drive there, I think you would agree, so that meant I had to leave here at, say ten-twenty. The secretary there saw me and will verify when I was there. I spent the day, most of it, in the city. I have proof. Here is my lunch receipt. Kebabs. Note the time stamp. Here is a credit slip for some theater tickets I had to cancel. Again, please note the time. I was there, not here. I have a receipt for a key I had made…time stamp. Do you need more? I parked in a garage and the ticket will—"

Schwartz held up his hand and inspected the ticket and credit slip.

"Okay," he said.

"Okay? Is that all you're going to say to me? Okay? Aren't you going to tell me why you are here at least? Why you think I need a lawyer, and why I need to account for my movements today?"

"Millicent Bass," he said.

"What about Mrs. Bass?"

"She's dead."

"Dead?"

"Murdered."

"Murdered? When? Oh, I see, today sometime between eleven this morning and three this afternoon, right? And naturally, the first person you thought of was me, the murderous vicar, the Philadelphia Ripper, right?"

"Actually no, Reverend. But I wanted to get you out of the way. I have to ask."

"Okay. You want to fill me in on the details? I've got to make an accounting of this to my Board and congregation. My God, poor Millie."

"A neighbor called about noon. Said Mrs. Bass didn't show up for a luncheon engagement. Essie, that's our dispatcher, told her missing lunches were not a police matter. The caller said, she knew that, but Mrs. Bass also missed her dentist appointment. No idea how she knew that—I'll have to ask. Anyway, she said she went to her house and saw Bass' Buick in the driveway but when she knocked, no one came to the door. Our dispatcher sent a car around. Officers banged on all the doors. One opened by itself—don't give me that look, it did—so they call out, no answer, and go in. The place has been trashed and she's on the floor. Somebody shot her."

"What do you mean, the place was trashed?"

"Whoever killed her, tossed her house. Drawers pulled out and dumped on the floor, closets emptied, desk rifled. The place is a mess. We figure she must have stepped out for a minute, maybe started for the dentist, forgot something and came back to find some guy robbing her house. Then he bumped her off."

"That would mean that the killer knew she had a dentist's appointment and would be gone long enough to pull the robbery."

"Or maybe he knew she worked all morning for you. Either way, you're right, he knew her routine."

"What if he or she, whoever, was not there to rob her, but was looking for something?"

"What would they be looking for?"

"Dr. Taliaferro's files. The ones that used to be in the box you found in the back lot, remember?"

"I thought you said kids dumped them in the trash."

"I said I thought they might have. I don't think so anymore."

Blake filled him in on his discovery of the keys and what he thought they meant. He mentioned Philip's earlier request to find the files. He told him about Millie's habitual gossiping and the reactions to it.

"She must have gotten hold of those files to use in her dishing the dirt sessions. Someone found out and went to get them from her. She walks in, and the person is caught red-handed, he panics and shoots her."

"Pretty drastic, don't you think?" Schwartz said, one eyebrow arched. "Why not just confront her and demand the files, threaten to expose her if she didn't. Why shoot her?"

"I don't know. Maybe this will help." Blake retrieved the message tape from his desk drawer. He replaced the tape in the machine and fast-forwarded it to the last message. Schwartz listened carefully, asked to hear it again.

"You recognize the voice?" he asked.

"No, not really. It sounds vaguely familiar, but no, I don't."

"Can I have this?"

"You can borrow it. I want it back, though. There are other messages on that tape."

"I'll make a copy of this last bit, and give it back tomorrow." He got up to leave.

"Can I look at Millie's house? I want to be sure the files aren't there."

"I can't let you in a crime scene. There are rules, and if you did find something it could compromise the chain of evidence."

"Yeah, right. I guess you watch too much television, too, Sheriff. Besides, I would just be there to identify and claim church property."

"Okay, tomorrow, seven a.m., but no funny business."

He left. Blake looked at the clock. Quarter to twelve, too late to call Mary. And seven in the morning would be too early. He shook his head in frustration. Even in death, Millie Bass could ruin his day.

Chapter Thirty

Sunlight crept through the pines making long slender shadows from their trunks. Hardly anyone would be up this early. Grace Franks loved the early morning when the air still retained some of the night's coolness and quiet. She twisted a piece of paper and lit it with her butane lighter. It caught and flared. She dropped it into the burn barrel and watched as the rest of the papers lying in the bottom caught and slowly, one by one, curled, turned black, and crumbled into ashes. She stood over her fire, acrid smoke swirling around her head, occasionally stirring the contents of the barrel. She raised her arms. From a distance, with her high cheekbones and tan skin, she looked like one of the witches from *Macbeth* or a perhaps a slim, pagan priestess officiating at a fire ritual. Morning was a good time to burn things.

Burn barrels were a thing of the past, illegal even. Young people whose memories didn't include a time when trash was a personal responsibility, not a municipal entitlement, had moved into her neighborhood. They built fancy houses, ran water mains and forced her to cap her well—outsiders and pushy Baby Boomers, or were they Xers? She could never keep them straight. And now there were the Millennials—the M generation. She qualified as a Boomer but had never felt a part of her generation.

Her new neighbors did not approve of her and her barrel. They zealously recycled. They worried about the deer population, the ecology, the ozone layer and generally made a nuisance of themselves. They thought the smoke from Grace's barrel polluted the air, represented a health hazard, or caused global warming. So now a truck picked up her trash twice a week, a service for which she had to pay a monthly assessment. But Grace still preferred burning things, especially things she did not trust to the trash truck or its nosey crew.

Mary stared at the phone. Her eyes, accented by dark smudges, were red from crying. She had not slept. She sat huddled in her pajamas, hugging herself, her robe pulled tight over her shoulders. She watched the sunlight seep through her kitchen window and creep across the tile floor toward her feet.

At midnight, she had acknowledged he would not call, but she waited anyway. Now, at six thirty in the morning, her hopes rose a bit. He might call. If he had gotten home late, he wouldn't have, but maybe this morning....

She sipped her coffee and watched the minutes tick away. He was not going to call, that day or ever, she decided. She went upstairs to shower and repair her face. She had to get ready for work.

Blake met Schwartz at Millie's house at exactly seven. Schwartz handed him his tape.

"Did you call her?" he asked.

"Who?"

"The lady on the tape, the one who apologized and asked you to call her. Did you?"

"No, it was too late last night and too early this morning. I'll try later."

The sheriff stared at him, hands on his hips, and shook his head. "Reverend, you are clueless," he said. "For all your education and cultured clerical empathy, you careen through life without a scrap of common sense when it comes to women, which, by the way, we already knew from your antics in Philadelphia. But I had no idea that on top of cluelessness, you were also stupid."

Blake felt his face getting red.

"Look, I'm not stupid, it's just that—"

"That woman was on her knees to you. My guess is she sat by that telephone all night, and would have taken a call from you at three in the morning. She was in tears. Do you have any idea what it cost her to make that call?"

Blake started to say something but Schwartz put up his hand and waved off his protest.

"Call her."

He walked back to his car and retrieved his cell phone and called. No answer.

"No answer," he said.

"What a jerk," Schwartz muttered, but Blake heard him and his face reddened further. They let themselves into Millie Bass' house.

As Schwartz said, it had been trashed. Papers were scattered all over the floor. Drawers were pulled out from cabinets and dressers and their contents tossed every which way. The kitchen was worse. Whoever shot Millie had opened canisters and dumped the contents on the floor. Napkins, silverware, and groceries were scattered everywhere. Room by room, Blake took in the chaos. He pivoted around, searching for anything that might look like a file folder. In what must have been a den, he found a pile of manila folders. Their labels, however, indicated they were personal files, photographs, bills and dozens of travel brochures, but no sign of Dr. Taliaferro's notes.

"If he was after the files, he must have gotten them," Blake said. His heart sank. Millie's death was bad enough, but to know the files were still floating around out there somewhere made the day overwhelmingly bleak.

"Satisfied, Reverend?"

"I guess. Say, could you possibly call me Blake? Besides the bad grammar, I really don't like being called Reverend, Rev. or any variation on it."

"And you would call me Ike?"

"Well, yeah…."

"I'll think about it."

Blake returned to his car and drove back to the church. He programmed Mary's number into speed-dial and called every five minutes from then on.

Chapter Thirty-one

Grace watched sadly as the last embers of her fire died down. She did not mourn the loss of her fire. She just did not want to go back into the house, and the fire served as an excuse to stay outdoors. Her gaze wandered across to the yard next door. She watched Donald Jenkins' backside appear in the patio door. He backed out carefully, easing a wheelchair over the small rise created by the doorsill, and then wheeled his wife, Betty, onto the patio. Grace could hear him murmuring to her as he maneuvered the chair into the small gazebo at the edge of the terrace.

He looked up and waved to Grace. She waved back.

"How are you, Betty?" she called.

Betty had ALS, Lou Gehrig's disease. She had been getting worse for years. Donald had taken early retirement and devoted his days to caring for her. Everyone said he was a saint. Betty struggled to lift her head and gave Grace a weak smile. There was a flutter at her wrist that Grace took for a wave. Poor woman. Donald stood behind Betty and held up his right hand with all five fingers spread and raised his eyebrows. Grace shook her head. He shrugged his shoulders and looked disappointed.

Blake climbed the short flight of stairs to Millie's office. Not her office anymore. He would have to find another secretary. Funny thing about that, a day ago he had looked forward to replacing her. Today the thought hung over him like a dark cloud. At the top of the stairs, he glanced to his left and froze, one foot in midair. The office looked like Millie's house. Papers were strewn everywhere, her desk drawers emptied and the contents of the supply closet dumped on the floor.

The office had been in order the previous evening. He stepped carefully over the mess and peeked into his office. It looked the same. He stared at the supply closet. Anything missing? He let his eyes wander over the emptied and disordered shelves. Then he saw, or more accurately, he did not see—Taliaferro's box was missing. Who would want to steal his old sermon notes?

He called Schwartz and told him what he found and that the space had been neat as a pin the day before.

"And don't ask me if I have a lawyer," he snapped.

"Wasn't planning to, that goes without saying. No, what I want is for you get into your house and lock the door. I'll come fetch you as soon as I get there."

"What? Why should I do that?"

"Well, I'm thinking about that message on your machine. It seems pretty clear that someone is after those files. He or she obviously didn't get them and will assume that if they were not at Bass', and not in the office, you know where they are. He'll come looking for them and you don't want to be there when he does. The guy has a gun, remember?"

"I'll be fine right here. I'll just lock up and…he's got a key, doesn't he."

"Everybody has a key."

"I'll wait for you in the house."

"You do that. You can call that lady while you wait."

"Call the lady…? Oh, yeah, I'll do that. Oh, and Sheriff…?"

"Yeah?"

"You'd need a court order to do it, but what do you think about putting a tap on the phones? If I get another call, you might be able to trace it or at least identify the caller."

Schwartz grunted something and agreed.

Blake locked the church and strode quickly toward his house, keys in hand. Then he remembered he had not locked the deadbolt on his front door. The killer could be waiting for him in the house. He hesitated halfway across the parking lot. He thought he would be safe outside. Suppose the killer had a rifle? He heard his phone ring. He decided to make a dash for it and raced the rest of the way to the house, went in and picked up the phone.

"Hello," he barked, his eyes frantically scanning the room, ears alert for suspicious sounds.

"Blake?" The voice sounded small and frightened.

"Mary? I am so glad you called. I have been trying to reach you all day," he said more softly, and sank into an armchair, all thoughts of killers, guns, and ambush evaporated.

"You have, really?"

"Really, truly."

He was still on the phone when Schwartz slipped into the room, service revolver held two-handed.

"The door was wide open, I thought maybe…." He stopped talking when he saw the grin on Blake's face. "That the lady?"

Blake nodded.

"What a jerk," he said, but this time more kindly.

Chapter Thirty-two

Ike slipped out to the college for lunch. Ruth insisted he eat with her in the cafeteria.

"People are talking enough, Schwartz. I need to make you a little more public if I want to keep the private part."

"I see. I think."

She pushed a gift-wrapped box across the table at him.

"What's this?"

"A gift."

"It's a box. Thank you. I can use a nice box."

"Don't start, Schwartz. Why is it men can't just say 'thank you,' or 'wow,' like normal people. Why are you all so bad at showing gratitude?"

"Sorry. We're no good at accepting compliments or help. It's a guy thing. Keep up the good work, Ruth. You'll make me a 'sensitive man' yet. Whatever happened to Phil Donahue, anyway?"

"Just open the box, smartass. Donahue's being bronzed and set up in NOW headquarters' lobby."

He chuckled, fumbled with the ribbon, and opened the box.

"What is it?"

"Time to ditch the Old Spice, Sheriff, move into the new millennium. Join the now generation. It's Hugo Boss."

"But I like Old Spice. My father uses it. It's our annual birthday present to each other."

"I'll bet your grandfather used it, too."

"Bay Rum, I think. Old Spice came later. This is going to break the old man's heart." He twisted off the cap and sniffed. "Whoo. Just a dab, I take it."

"The stuff costs, Ike. A dab is about right."

"I can slosh on Old Spice."

"That's the problem. Sometimes I think you were born in another century."

"I *was* born in another century. So were you."

"You know what I mean."

He put the box aside and thought a moment. "What's your take on the Reverend?"

"Fisher? He's okay, I guess. Not my sort, I'm afraid."

"Why, not your sort?"

"I'm uncomfortable in the presence of public virtue and piety. He's a little too good to be true. There has to be something wrong with him. Why is he here? He looks like he belongs on Wall Street."

"He had some difficulties in Philadelphia."

"Oh? What kind of…what did you say…difficulties?"

"I checked. Someone hung a frame around him…the kind that ruins clergymen's lives."

"You sure it was a frame? Priests and sex…lethal combination. What did he do?"

"You weren't listening. He didn't do anything."

"Where there's smoke—"

"Come on, Ruth, that's a knee jerk reaction from the agnostic left. You, of all people, ought to reserve judgment. You folks tend to be modernists and humanists and tolerant of practically anything or anyone except someone like Fisher who wears his religion on his sleeve, or in his case, on his collar, I guess. You see the religion, not the man, and are eager to believe anything negative about him."

"That's not fair. You know as well as I that the papers are full of one messy bit after another among his genre and there're government regs limiting the extent religion can play on campuses, so we naturally—"

"It's not court rulings or media coverage. It's an intellectual bias that lumps any display of, in this instance, Christian faith, with wrong thinking. Actually you all are far more tolerant of nearly every other faith group, their peculiarities and practices notwithstanding, than Christians, did you know that?"

"Rabbi Schwartz speaks. Is that it? Look, religion is just religion."

"Not quite. There are shades of discrimination. I bet if a Native American group wanted to build a sweat lodge or someone else wanted to start a program in Hinduism or Buddhism, or maybe invite Tich Nat Hanh to your campus, you all wouldn't bat an eyelash. But if a fundamentalist from Lynchburg asked to run a Bible study during lunch hour, you'd send him packing."

"Schwartz, you are impossible. Impossible and contrary. Hugo Boss is wasted on you."

"Hugo Boss is wasted on ninety percent of the male population. It's right up there with fat guys in Speedos. Speedos are the Hugo Boss of swim trunks. No, I just think you should give Fisher a chance, that's all. By the way, I may have a tenant for your vacant bomb shelter slash art storage facility."

"Really? Who?"

"Not yet, but I've been talking around, calling some people I know. I'll tell you when it's a little more definite."

"You'll have to run any proposal through my Finance Department. If they okay it, it's a done deal. I'm in no position to turn down anything short of the Mafia."

"The Mafia—right."

She scrutinized his face. "Why do I suddenly feel really uneasy?"

Chapter Thirty-three

Blake seated himself at the head of the table. At five minutes to eight all but one of the Mission Board members were assembled. Dan Quarles pulled at his mustache. He seemed lost in worried thought. The others read over a hastily put together agenda. It did not tell them much: Item one, Vicar's Report; item two, Treasurer's Report; item three, New Business; item four, Old Business. Marge Burk stared at the sheet and frowned. The rest merely glanced at it and busied themselves with coffee cups, scratch pads, or glancing occasionally at Blake and murmuring. He counted heads. Everyone present except Bob Franks. They waited. At eight ten, he asked if Bob had said anything about being late. Dan came out of his reverie with a start.

"Sorry, Vicar," he said. "Lost my train of thought. Yes, Bob called this morning and said he was taking Grace to the beach for a few days. He said they had some business to attend to or something like that. Grace hasn't been herself lately."

"Slipped out of gear again, probably," Tom Graham muttered.

"That's not a very nice thing to say," Amy Brandt said.

"I am not a very nice man," Graham answered. Amy's face turned a bright red.

Amy had been appointed to the Board as an afterthought. She was a "twofer." The board lacked any representation from the newer families and, apart from Marge Burk, had no women. Except for Amy, the board was composed almost exclusively of "old-timers." She attended meetings faithfully but contributed very little. Blake thought of her as their token airhead—nice, honest, but not all there. He looked forward to the day when the terms of this current board would end and he could find replacements for them. That would not happen for a year and a half, unfortunately. In the meantime, he had to work with this group.

"She got caught at her burn barrel again, I'll bet. Every couple of weeks she goes out and torches a pile of trash. Neighbors call the police and Bob has to calm them down and then take care of Grace," Lanny said. He and the Franks lived in the same community.

"Well, in that case," Blake said, "I guess we can get started. You all know, of course, about Millie Bass."

Silence and five blank stares.

"Do I take your silence to mean you have not heard about Millie?"

"You fired her, Vicar. Well, I guess we knew that was coming," Lanny said and nodded his head in approval.

"Fired? Look here, Vicar, don't you think you are being a little precipitous?" Dan said. "We are the board and it seems to me that we should have been appraised of the—"

"Put a sock in it, Danny," Marge said. "If the vicar wants to sack Millie, he can. I'm glad I won't be in your shoes, Vicar, when the rest of the congregation finds out. They'll crucify you." She seemed almost pleased at the prospect.

"Stop it," Blake said angrily. "You really don't know? What kind of people are you? Didn't any one of you know Millie at all?"

"We knew she hooked out of work yesterday while you were away on your day off," Dan said, and added, "and again today."

"And you didn't think to call to find out if anything might be wrong, if she was sick or anything?" Blake held on to his temper, eyes boring into each one of them.

"Why should we?" Graham said, inspecting his fingernails. "She was a difficult woman with a sharp tongue and a mean disposition. Why should I worry about her?"

"Graham, you are absolutely right—you are not a very nice man," Blake snapped. "So none of you know?"

"You didn't fire her?" Dan asked as if he dared not hope for a reprieve from what might become a major upheaval.

"No, Dan, I did not." A look of relief spread across Quarles' face.

"She is dead, people—murdered yesterday around noon—over twenty-four hours ago. Twenty-four hours, and not one of you knew, or cared to know, anything about her. A woman who served this mission for twenty years dies and the leadership, that's you, is so distant and indifferent that it doesn't even know?"

The Board sat in stunned silence as Blake filled them in on the circumstances surrounding Millie's death. He announced a funeral service had been arranged for Friday and he expected them all to be there. A few protested and then looked away in embarrassment.

Blake put his elbows on the table and supported his chin with the heels of his hand. He let the silence build and then dropped his bombshell.

"There's more," he said quietly. "It appears that Millie had, or her killer thought she had, Dr. Taliaferro's files."

Dan Quarles exhaled so suddenly he sprayed most of the contents of his coffee cup on the table in front of him.

"I don't know what the connection is," Blake continued, "but I do know this—Millie had been reading them. I suppose, to add a little substance to her rumor mongering. You understand the significance of what I am telling you? Those files are still out there somewhere."

A subdued Tom Graham said, "If any of his counselees finds out we were responsible for the loss of those files, and if they fall into the wrong hands, if a breach of confidentiality can be traced back to us, we could be sued."

"Sued?" Marge Burks yelped. "What could they get? The church is broke." Marge had the dubious job of treasurer and ought to know.

"Stonewall Jackson can be sued, Saint Anne's can be sued, the Bishop can be sued, for crying out loud, and we, the board, can be sued as individuals. We are not bonded, remember? We decided we did not want to 'waste the money,' I think you said at the time purchasing a bond came up, Marge. If a jury finds even the hint of negligence, we can be held individually liable as well."

"Dan, problem?" Blake said. Dan absently mopped at the coffee spill, his face livid.

"I'm fine," he rasped. "Must be something I ate. If you will excuse me...." He stood and weaved his way to the door and disappeared. They listened as the outside door slammed shut.

"He left," Marge said. "How can he walk out of here at a time like this?"

"I think he was one of Taliaferro's patients, or counselees, or whatever you call them. Maybe he's worried about someone reading his files," Lanny said.

"Maybe he is calling his lawyer," Graham added and looked distressed. Blake knew that Tom Graham had money, a lot of it. Of all the Board members, he had the most at risk.

"What do we do now, Vicar?" asked Lanny.

"I think if we can retrieve the files and get them sealed again, and if we can keep this 'in the family,' we have a chance of getting out of this mess. I have asked Sheriff Schwartz to help us, and...praying wouldn't hurt."

They sat in silence and Blake watched as the phenomenon of "foxhole faith" set in. Men in foxholes with bullets whizzing over their heads turned to God when nothing else could make them even acknowledge even the possibility of a Creator.

"Okay," he said after a minute or two. "That's about it. I will keep you all informed, and, please, what we have talked about tonight cannot leave this room. Not unless you want to face a judge. Lanny, will you call Dan and make sure he's all right? Anything else?"

"Oh, one thing, Vicar. I know it doesn't seem very important now, but I said I would ask," Amy piped up. "Mary Miller wants Waldo's keys to the organ."

"I don't have them," he said. "Did you say keys—plural, keys, not key?"

"Yeah, he had a little key ring and there were two keys on it. One opened the organ."

"What did the other one do, Amy?"

"No idea. But there were two little keys on a ring and he always had them. Mary wants to be able to lock up the organ. Kids have been getting into it."

"I'll look for a duplicate and ask the police if they were with Waldo's things." He dismissed them with a prayer and sent them on their way considerably more subdued and quieter than usual.

Two keys.

Chapter Thirty-four

Harry Grafton called Ike at six in the morning on his home line. Ike didn't have to ask how Grafton got it. The Agency has its own phone book.

"Sorry to wake you, Sheriff. Call this number," Grafton said. He recited the number. Ike thanked him, hung up and dialed the number. The person on the other end picked up immediately.

"This is Ike Schwartz. Harry Grafton said I could call you."

"Harry's a good man. He got screwed over by my guys and he said you helped him out. That so?"

"Something like that. Right time and place...that sort of thing."

"Okay. You don't know me and you never will. By the way, you are not the most popular guy in the Bureau, Sheriff. You've rubbed a lot of people the wrong way up here."

"I missed the Dale Carnegie session on how to make friends with FBI agents."

"Obviously. Well, here's the situation. Krueger had been placed in the Witness Protection Program. Somehow we lost him—slipped the net. Big suits downtown are afraid you'll find that out and cause further embarrassment to the Bureau. Will you?"

"You guys aren't my enemies. You just get in the way sometimes. Look, I have a job to do. I don't want to do it and have to play games with the people you send down here at the same time. Cooperate with me—I cooperate with you. Simple."

"Right. Understood. Just to let you know, we all aren't that way. Maybe we'll have a chance to work a case together someday."

"I hope not. No offense, but I'm not looking for more high-profile crime in my town."

"Okay. Moving right along, Section Chief Bullock has his you-know-whats in a vise with the big dogs upstairs for letting it happen. Special Agent Hedrick is now the Agent in Place. He's supposed to grab your killer and bring him in. He will do whatever he has to do to find out where you are and get there first. That's it. I gotta go. Good luck."

Ike held the phone and stared out the window. After a while, a friendly voice told him what to do if he wanted to make a call. He hung up. Poor Sam.

◇◇◇

Sylvia Parks' Mercedes drove up and parked as Blake turned the corner and headed to the church. She waited for him by the office door.

"I heard about Millie," she said. "Terrible. She was not one of my favorite people, you know, but she did not deserve that."

They climbed the stairs to the offices and Sylvia surveyed the riot of papers and material on the floor. She raised an inquisitive eyebrow.

"The police think whoever killed Millie was looking for something. Her house looked worse than this."

"Any idea what they were looking for?"

He thought a minute. Should he say anything? He had ordered the Board to leave the news about the files in the room. Should he be the one to take the news out? Finally he said, "Can I retain you as my attorney?"

"Me? You're kidding. What do you need a lawyer for, Blake? What did you do?"

"Answer my question first."

"Well, I am in good standing with the bar, so I could. You're serious, aren't you?"

"Serious as a heart attack."

"Okay, give me a dollar."

"What?"

"A dollar. I cannot be your attorney unless you pay me a retainer or sign an agreement to do so. Give me a dollar."

Blake dug a crumpled dollar bill from his wallet and handed it to her.

"Anything I say to you now is covered under lawyer-client confidentiality?"

"Yes."

He told her about the missing files and his suspicions that Millie had read them and probably had them in her possessions and that they were now missing. Sylvia listened patiently, a small frown on her otherwise smooth forehead, and said she guessed if the news got out, a lot of people would need a lawyer. She volunteered to serve as the church's attorney as well, until some other arrangements were made.

"And, just to be sure, as your attorney, you don't have the files?"

"No."

"And you have no information as to their whereabouts?"

"None."

She frowned. He couldn't be sure if she didn't believe him or if the thought of the files in the wrong hands was more serious than even he'd imagined.

"Well, that will have to do for now," she said and brightened.

Relieved, he thanked her and then, as an afterthought, asked why she was waiting for him in the first place.

"Well, I told you I heard about Millie. I figured I could come in and help out, answer the phone, type a little, you know. I had no idea I would be needed any other way. Good thing I came."

The two of them began to gather up the papers and files that were scattered all over the floor. Blake concentrated on his office and Sylvia tried to make sense out of the chaos in Millie's. It would be months before any sort of order was restored to the files. They were interrupted by the arrival of Ike Schwartz. He stood at the top of the stairs and watched them for a moment before either saw him.

"Ah, Sheriff Schwartz," Blake said. "I'm glad you are here. This is Sylvia Parks, my attorney. You don't need to ask any more. Have you brought news?"

"I came by to say it was all right to clean up the mess, but I see you didn't wait. Also, to tell you we lifted some pretty clean prints from some of the papers, especially the two packets of paper."

Schwartz followed Blake into his office and sat on the one spare chair.

"And they belong to…?"

"Don't know. Unless we fingerprint your entire congregation, we may never know. On the other hand, if our investigation turns up a list of suspects, the prints may help us narrow it down."

"You know, Sheriff, there is one thing I don't understand."

"Just one?"

"Well, no, several, but one right now. Why did it take so long for all this to happen?" He saw the puzzlement in Schwartz's eyes. "Look, Taliaferro died four months ago. Those files must have been in Millie's hands probably as long. So why did someone come after them now? Surely, with her tongue wagging, the fact she had them would be obvious to anyone familiar with at least their own files. Why now?"

"That's an excellent question. I guess she must have said something recently that let the cat out of the bag. Or maybe the killer just found out about the files."

"Or something happened recently that set him off."

"Correct. Anything happen in the church that might qualify? You make a big announcement or start a big project…maybe preach a sermon?"

"No, nothing like that. Except for Waldo getting shot, nothing dramatic has happened in this church for forty years."

Blake glanced at the mess on his floor. Several dozen keys lay scattered by his upturned wastepaper basket. Keys.

"Sheriff," he said, as he scooped up the keys, "did you happen to find any keys on Templeton when you did whatever you do?"

"Keys? Yes, one big key ring, house keys, car keys, that kind of thing."

"How about a small key ring with two keys, two small keys. We are missing the organ keys. We can't lock it up and the kids are beginning to use it as a noise maker."

"I don't remember a small key ring. Keys on separate rings always beg the question."

While he spoke, Blake sorted through the pile of keys again. There were no small keys that looked like they might fit the organ lock. He went into the secretary's office and scooped up the rest from the floor. He sorted out the best prospects, as he had Wednesday. None fit the organ.

"Maybe he left them at his house. He must have had at least a duplicate set. Do you suppose we could look at his house?"

"We searched it already."

"But not for keys. No one has been by there since?"

"No. The place is sealed. By this afternoon, the FBI will assume jurisdiction and shut us out. Then we'll need a court order to get in."

"No, that's not true," Sylvia said. Hearing *court order* must have perked up her antennae, and she slipped into the office. "Waldo is dead. He forfeits his rights to protection against unlawful search and seizure. He is the victim, not the perpetrator. His house is, therefore, an extension of the crime scene and accessible by the police without a warrant or order. Unless and until the FBI stops us, it's still your case."

"Some lawyer you got there, Reverend. So you're saying we can just go in?"

"In the pursuit of an investigation, yes."

"We aren't the investigating authority anymore."

"Doesn't matter. If you have reason to believe there are circumstances that materially alter the course of the investigation, you can enter the premises."

"What circumstances would that be?"

"The organ keys are missing."

"That would do?"

"You have anything better?"

Schwartz stared at his shoes and frowned. "I'll meet you here this afternoon at five o'clock. Wait, it will have to be later. I have to go somewhere first. Reverend, bring your lawyer. My gut says one of us is going to need her."

Chapter Thirty-five

As uninformed as the Mission Board seemed to be the night before, by eleven o'clock the next morning, when the Bible study assembled, it appeared everyone knew about the murder. When Blake joined them, Rose Garroway was in full voice. All the contempt she once held for Millicent poured out in a torrent. She had an appreciative and supporting audience and soon others joined in, adding their resentment to Rose's. Blake sat quietly and listened. He heard in their anger the echo of his own.

Millicent Bass had wounded him twice. She'd substituted innuendo letters in the Board's packet for exculpatory ones, and then sent the same damning letters to Mary. Because of the first, most of the leadership, and many others, he supposed, thought of him as unfit and certainly undesirable as their minister. And for a while, Mary must have, too.

Millie, Rose opined, had become a destructive force and had received a form of divine judgment. Her words were hard and unforgiving. Finally, Blake held up his hand.

"Rose, stop, enough. The woman is dead. Nothing we say now can change who she was. On the other hand, the things we do say now reflect on us, not on her."

The group fell silent. Rose reddened and looked unhappy.

"You know I have as much reason to dislike her as anyone in this room, maybe more." He told them about the letters. Amazed expressions lit several faces. The regulars, like Rose, nodded as if to say, "I thought so." The newer members looked shocked.

"I figured something like that happened," Rose said, "Didn't I, Minnie?" Her sister let her eyes leave the knitting in her lap long enough to nod and smile.

"There are a lot of people who need to hear that story, Vicar. That woman...."

"No more, Rose. It's time to let her rest in peace." He waved off the protests and said, "Millicent Bass lived her life as a lonely and unhappy woman. Because of it, or in addition to it—I am not sure which—she developed a destructive habit. If she had not been so lonely, she might not have become a world-class gossip. But her habit of snooping and telling became a way to develop friendships and a kind of perverted happiness. I imagine it started out innocently enough—she knew something no one else knew and she shared it, harmless gossip, I expect most of us would call it. Somewhere along the way, someone or something twisted her around and set her on the path she took." He looked into the skeptical faces of his audience.

"Listen, did anyone have their arm twisted? Was anyone forced to listen? At one time or another, each of you participated in it, first or second hand. Did you say anything? Did you walk away? The truth is—we were all her co-dependants. We promoted it. I suppose some even encouraged it. If gossip is what killed her, then we all stand accused of aiding and abetting."

The room stayed silent for a long time. Finally, Rose said, "Don't you just hate it when your clergyman turns out to be a Christian?" and the women laughed, relieved. Blake joined them and then said, "You know Millie's funeral is Friday. I don't think very many people will come, and that is a shame."

"We can't do much about that," Rose said. "As ye sow, so shall ye reap—"

"That may be true. But then, I think you all should be thinking about what you were sowing here just a few minutes ago. I think it is about time we started sowing good seed. You don't want a group like this picking the meat off your bones when your time comes."

He watched as the frowns turned into embarrassed smiles.

"Here's what I want you to do. Call your friends and get them to the funeral. I don't care if they moan and groan. And then, I want you all to do the eulogies. I want each of you to find something nice to say about Millie at her funeral."

"So that someone, not exactly our nearest and dearest, will do the same for us someday?" Minnie asked.

"Perhaps. It's more along the lines of loving your enemy, Minnie."

"I think it would be easier to find an ice cube in Hell than to find something positive about Millicent Bass," Sylvia snorted.

"I'll tell you something else," Blake said. "Our anger and contempt for her is not healthy. It is in our own best interest to get rid of it, or we will carry it to our grave, and the dark force that led Millie to wander down the path she took will remain in our hearts, and the Devil will have won after all. We will purge our demons faster and more completely with an act of love than with an act made in anger. Remember what I told you Sunday? That the root for the word gossip and the root for the word gospel is the same? A story that edifies is God's word. A story that destroys is the Devil's. Unfortunately, discerning the difference between the two is sometimes very hard. We need to remember that all of us tread very close to that line most of the time. So Friday, try to show some mercy on one who crossed it."

The meeting ended and they adjourned to the mall for lunch. Blake begged off. He said he had arrangements to make for the funeral. There were a few other things on his mind as well.

Most municipal graveyards are designed to provide a sense of peace for visitors, mourners, and the curious. Picketsville's Memorial Park was no exception. Located on a hillside west of town and planted with trees representing every local variety, it offered visitors both an arboretum and a stunning view of the Blue Ridge Mountains to the east. Behind, to the west, a state park established a permanent buffer against any possible commercial or residential encroachment and provided a soft, evergreen backdrop.

Eloise Schwartz, nee McNamara, occupied a small plot in the corner close by a small copse of dogwoods. Picketsville may have had its detractors, those who found its size or rustic culture wanting, its people backward and its vision limited, but whatever drawbacks it may or may not have had, its cemetery belied them all. It always struck Ike as ironic that the town's chief critics were concentrated at the college, since most of what they decried fell to them to provide. Ike parked the car and sat for a moment behind the wheel. Ruth stared straight ahead.

"This is the first time I've been out here," Ruth said, her voice hushed. "It's beautiful."

He opened the door and walked around to open hers. On any other day, she would have opened her own door and, if he had tried to be male and gallant, given him a quick lecture. But not today. Not lately, in fact. He opened the door and she stepped out.

"No headstones?" Ruth was raised in the antique northeast where churches were routinely photogenic and had charming, movie set graveyards surrounding them.

"I brought her here, because she had no family," he said. "Her parents were killed in an automobile accident when she turned eighteen. She has a brother on disability from Desert Storm. He drinks most of it. There was no one else, so I brought her here."

They walked along a gravel path to Eloise's corner and sat on a stone bench. In spite of the afternoon sun, the bench felt cool on the backs of their legs. Eloise had a plaque set flush with the earth six feet from them. There was a place to put flowers, but Ike had not thought to bring any. He wished he had. He vowed he would the next time he came. On an impulse, he stood and collected some wildflowers that had crept past the cut line into the lawn. He laid them on the sod at a point he guessed would be above her heart.

They sat in silence for a long time. What could he say? Honeysuckle surrounded the place, clinging to shrubs and low trees, its tendrils reaching out toward the open grass. If the mowing crew did not stay on top of it, it would soon cover the place and in a year the cemetery would disappear beneath a mountain of tangled stems. It was a sobering thought. The cloying sweet scent filled the still, warm air. Somewhere two blue-jays argued. Nature is never silent. Humans may think they are the purveyors of noise and when they quiet down, the world is silent, but they are wrong. Insects, birds and small living things buzz, click and sing twenty-four hours a day. It is ears that do not hear that create silence.

Ike, elbows on knees, lowered his chin into his cupped hands. Ruth sat perfectly still, waiting. When his shoulders began to shake, she put her arm around him. He leaned on her shoulder. They stayed there that way for twenty minutes.

"Thanks," is all he said, and led her back to the car.

"Anytime."

The trip back to town seemed shorter than it had coming out.

◇◇◇

The boys walked slowly through the back lot kicking the tall grass, heads down and faces puckered in concentration. They walked slowly back and forth, searching but not finding. Finally one of them saw Blake standing in the parking lot and strolled over, trying to look laid-back and cool.

"Say, Mister," he said, "have you seen our box?"

Blake inspected the boy. He could have been anywhere between twelve and fifteen. He carried a skateboard under his arm. Blake noticed they all had them. The others stopped walking and watched their companion from a distance, straining to hear what he said.

"What kind of box? Maybe a gray steel one with papers inside?"

"Yeah. We found it by them steps," the boy said, pointing at the church's basement entrance. His tone indicated no concern that he and his friends might have taken something that belonged to someone else. "We figured it was, like, trash and we could use it to make a ramp."

"What happened to the papers inside it?"

"We left them in there. Only a couple of old folders anyway."

"You didn't see a lot of folders? Just two or three?"

"Yeah, just the ones like I said."

Blake searched the boy's eyes. Did he tell the truth or did he want to cover up the fact he and his friends took the box and tossed the files?

"When did you find the box?"

"Like in May or June. I don't know for sure. While ago."

"Not more recently than that? Three weeks, not three months ago?"

"No sir, you can ask anybody. We kept it out in the field there covered with old newspapers."

"Well, as a matter of fact, we did find it, and since it belongs to the church, we kept it. Maybe I can find you another box." He saw the doubt and disappointment register in the boy's eyes.

"You go to church?"

"Nah. Nothing doing in church has anything to do with me."

"How about your folks?"

"They tried this one once, but said it was, you know, like, totally cold."

"Cold? You mean unfriendly?"

"Yeah, that way."

"But you do like the church's parking lot. Something there for you."

"Well the other guy, the one who was in charge before you, said it was okay to skate and do our tricks here if there wasn't nobody around. Be better if you paved the rest of the lot, though."

"Pave it?"

"Some ramps and a half-pipe, that'd be, like awesome."

Blake did not know what a half-pipe was but guessed it would, indeed, be very awesome, or awful. He'd have to think about that. The boy walked away to explain to his friends what had happened to their ramp prop.

Sylvia Parks and then Schwartz drove up a moment later. He looked at his watch. Five forty-five. Close enough. Sylvia alighted from her Mercedes SUV at the same time the sheriff slid out of his standard government-issue Crown Vic. She began talking in full stride. "Krueger, I assume, must be Waldo in another life. I will pursue that later, but I have something else to tell you first, Sheriff," She dug a sheaf of papers from her purse. "This is a court order authorizing us to 'enter, inspect and remove as appropriate any and all such church property as may be found on or about the premises known as'...etcetera, etcetera."

"How did you manage that?"

"It happens that Attorney General Croft is my son-in-law, and Judge Landis, who signed this rag, is my husband's old college roommate. It's a small world, don't you think?"

Schwartz stood motionless in the parking lot, staring at her, eyes hard. Blake shifted his gaze between the two of them. He sensed Schwartz had something on his mind but had no idea what it might be.

"You look shocked," she said, her face serene. "Don't be. When you need to, you pull strings to get things done all the time, am I right? I just have more and bigger strings than you do, that's all. So let's go."

Sylvia drove them into Westerfield and parked in front of Waldo's house. Blake counted doors and saw they were only four houses from Mary's. A few neighbors gawked at them from their front yards. The house was locked, but there was no crime scene tape on the yard.

Schwartz pulled out a ring of keys, inspected them and inserted one in the lock. It turned and the bolt clicked over.

"Thought so," he muttered, and stepped in, followed by Blake and Sylvia.

"Did the FBI search the house?" Blake asked.

"Don't know. I don't think so, but they didn't say."

"Well, I guess that answers your question," Schwartz said and surveyed the chaos in the house. The first floor looked like Millicent Bass' house, with papers and belongings strewn everywhere.

"I don't think the FBI made this mess. I think they are very professional when it comes to running searches. They wouldn't leave a place looking like this, would they?" He said it positively, but Schwartz heard the doubt in his voice.

"We were in and out. Took his computer, some records, and that's all." He looked puzzled. He had not made the search, Sam and Billy had, and left everything looking perfectly normal...still.

They spent the next hour and a half sifting through files, drawers, cupboards, and cabinets, re-searching the house. Ike rolled back the rugs, checked the bottoms of drawers and even the ice dispenser. Nothing out of the ordinary turned up. Blake removed the grilles on the hot air ducts and reached in as far as he could. The desk turned up only a computer-generated list of names, most of them members of the church. A few Blake did not recognize, and there were one or two more names that did look familiar, but he could not tell why. His name had been handwritten at the bottom, apparently a later addition to the others. It had a question mark penciled in after it. The list probably did not qualify as "church property," but he pocketed it anyway.

Sylvia found a collection of old newspapers from San Francisco and an application for a handgun dated several months before. The approval line was not filled in.

"Ike, can you call somebody and find out if the FBI got here before us? Ask them about the keys, too," Blake added.

Schwartz nodded and pulled out his cell phone.

It took Schwartz several minutes to get through to the Agent in Place, and several more to persuade him to release the information. Schwartz told him he was with a close personal friend of the Governor and looked at Sylvia for confirmation. She gave him a thumbs-up. He muttered "okay" four or five times and "yep" three times and ended with an "I see."

"The feds did not search this property, they assumed we did, and, no, they did not find any keys. Now what?"

"No keys. There were supposed to be two. If Krueger had the files, he was killed for them. The killer took his keys and searched the house but could not find them, so then he must have thought Millie had them and—"

"It's too thin. Blake. The search could just as easily have been done by a hit man. He could have been looking for more evidence that could incriminate the mob. You saw those newspapers. He was scheduled to testify. The only link between the two murders is a mess in their respective houses."

"There is a way to tell."

"How?"

"If we could find those keys, we could check them. Amy said there were two on that ring. One must have unlocked the organ. What did the other one do? If it fits the box, we have a link."

"We don't have the box anymore, remember?"

"And that's another thing. Where is the box?"

"If you ask me," Sylvia said, "it's buried in the town's sanitary landfill."

"But I have a key to the box," Blake cried. "We could match the keys even if we can't find the box. If they match, the murders are linked, but how and why?"

"I don't know. You're right. Unfortunately all we can do is link them circumstantially—not causally. Still, it would be a start. We have to find that key ring."

They left the house, locking the door behind them. Schwartz called his office and ordered a team to the house to reseal it and mark it off with yellow tape.

Chapter Thirty-six

Thursday morning started out cloudy and threatening. By the time Blake ran to the corner convenience store to get coffee and a newspaper, it started to rain. At the cashier's counter his eye caught the word "half-pipe" blazoned on the front of an extreme sports magazine. On an impulse, he bought it.

Back in his office, he put his coffee cup and newspaper on his desk and skimmed the magazine. It took him several tries before he found the reference to a half-pipe, which, he discovered, was a device used by in-line skaters, BMX bikers, and skateboarders. It did in fact look very much like a large piece of pipe cut in half on its long axis. As nearly as he could tell, the skater rolled down one side of the pipe and, propelled by his momentum, flew up on the other side into the air, where he did stunts or tricks with names that made no sense and looked very dangerous. Then, the skater careened down again to the other side to repeat the performance. Very cool, he thought.

He put the magazine aside when Schwartz walked in and tossed a key ring on his desk.

"This it?" Schwartz asked, looking slightly harried.

"Where did you find it?"

"I didn't. It was in an evidence bag the coroner had. Apparently Krueger kept it on a chain around his neck. Unless you were looking, you wouldn't notice. Try it against your key."

Blake searched his desk drawer for the key to the file box. When he had it, he held it up to the key on the ring. No match. He dropped both in the drawer.

"Well, there goes that theory," he said, disappointed. "But I guess we found the organ key at least."

"Don't worry about it. Half the leads I follow in an investigation end up like that," Schwartz said and turned to leave.

"Sheriff, did anybody do a ballistics test on the bullets from Millie and Waldo?"

"We're working on it. By the way, how much do you know about your lawyer?"

"Not much. She lives near Roanoke in an area called Floyd or Flood—something like that. She just started—" Ike held up his hand, palm out. He heard the footsteps. He put a finger to his lips and shook his head. Ike greeted Sylvia, coming in as he left. What was that all about?

Sylvia appeared at his door.

"Good morning, Blake. Are you busy?"

"No, not really."

"I was on my way out," Ike said. He narrowed his eyes and shook his head slightly. Blake guessed he wanted to be sure their conversation about Sylvia stayed mute. He nodded and turned to the woman.

"You were saying?"

"Right. So long, Sheriff. Good, I have a confession to make. No, that isn't right. I have two confessions to make. Have I got that straight? If you go to confession and have more than one thing on your list, do you make confession, or do you make confessions? I've never been sure."

"When was the last time you went to any confession, Sylvia, assuming the church you attended encouraged that sort of thing?"

"Never could find anyone to confess to who I thought was tough enough to hear what I had to say. Anyway, listen. First, I found the letters. You know, the ones that Millie sent to the

Board and to Miss Miller, and I found the ones that clearly exonerated you. I had to clean up the mess and there they were.

"So—here's the confession—I copied the good ones and mailed them to all of the Mission Board members, including the ones whose terms expired but who were on the board when you were hired. I put a cover letter with them that said I did it without your knowledge. I didn't want them to think you were behind it. Might look a little self-serving.

"Second, I called some people I know and told them about the whole plan to deceive, so to speak. These are people, by the way, who shared Millie's 'bad habit,' as you so delicately put it. You can rest assured that the circumstances of your Philadelphia experience are now adequately explained, or will be before sundown. Father, forgive me for I have sinned."

Blake grinned at her. In fact, he wouldn't have sent the letters, and she probably should not have sent them. He thanked her.

He stared at the empty door frame and listened to her as she tackled the task of sorting out forty years' worth of files. He retrieved the key ring and put it on the desk, next to the list he had taken from Waldo's house, and then remembered the envelope with the clipping. He pulled it out from the drawer and added it to the other two items. He stared at them, trying to piece together a story that reconciled all three. He picked up a pad of paper and began a list of questions.

1. Who dropped the clipping in the vicarage and when? Waldo, Waldo's killer, or someone else?

2. Why did he still think the keys were important?

3. Why did Waldo make a list of names and why did he include mine, and who were the people that were not members of Stonewall Jackson?

He reread the list carefully. Dan Quarles headed the church list, which also included Grace Franks, Mary Miller, and three others. Mary Miller? She was not a member of the church when Waldo was killed. How did she end up on the list? The other names meant nothing to him.

4. Who called and left the strange message on the answering machine Monday night?

5. Where were Tommy Taliaferro's files, and what did they have to do with any of this?

6. Why did Ike want to know where Sylvia Parks lived?

He knew instinctively that if he could find answers to the first five questions, he would know who killed Waldo and Millie, and a whole lot more. But try as he might, nothing came to him. He would ask Mary about Waldo when he saw her. Maybe Schwartz would come up with something in the meantime. Sylvia put her head around the door and broke his train of thought.

"I'm leaving now," she said. "You interested in joining me for lunch? I'll take you to Le Chateau."

Le Chateau was a pricey restaurant lost on the mountainside of the Blue Ridge Mountains. It attracted its clientele from the Commonwealth's elite—those who found its location and relative seclusion useful in the world of deal making and maneuvering that characterized the politically connected and moneyed few. It offered polished oak paneling, privacy, and a superb menu. While they ate, Blake ran his first five questions by Sylvia. She thought long and hard and finally threw up her hands, declaring she did not have a mind devious enough to even guess answers. He asked her to think about them anyway.

Chapter Thirty-seven

Bob Franks pulled into his driveway and killed the engine. He was tired and edgy. Grace had spent the last hundred miles of the trip from Virginia Beach singing snippets from *The Sound of Music*. An hour of *the hills are alive with the sound of music* and, *Doe a deer, a female deer...* and he was ready to strangle her.

"Out," he snapped, "before you make me crazy."

"You should complain," she said.

He dumped the luggage on the porch, shuffled into the kitchen, and checked the refrigerator. He wanted to grill but there were no chops, steaks, or even hot dogs.

"We're out of eats," he shouted. "Go to the market and get something for the grill."

"I'm not hungry. I'll just have a salad."

"I don't care what you eat, Grace, I want real food. I've been driving for hours and listening to your caterwauling and I need a break. Go get me a steak—now."

She smiled a secret smile and sailed out the door humming *Edelweiss*.

Back in his office, Blake fought the effects of too much rich dining and the inevitable onset of food coma. He thought about the contrasts in his life, the immediate ones, and the others, the facts he pushed from his mind months ago, but which would not let him go. The luncheon he just ate in a restaurant he could no longer afford, but which six months ago he would have frequented as the guest of one of any number of parishioners. He wondered if he had changed so much. Certainly he felt no great desire to hobnob with the people he met there, but six months ago...?

He liked Sylvia Parks but did not feel the need to curry her favor because of her connections. Six months ago, he would have. She would have been at the top of his "A list." The contrast between Sylvia and Mary, a woman of simple tastes and relatively little sophistication, were vast. Mary he found immensely attractive. But before, he would have brushed her off without a thought. He wondered if he had lost his mind somewhere along the interstates, 95 and 81, as they bore him south from Philadelphia to Picketsville. Six months ago he was a man on the way up, a comer, a sure bet for bishop. He sat on important commissions and committees. He received inquiries about his availability for jobs from all over the country. He'd made the short list for Suffragan Bishop in the Diocese of Maryland. He was a star.

Now he languished in an undistinguished and forgotten corner of Virginia, the vicar of a failed experiment in evangelism. He had no prospects, no influence, and, probably, no future beyond this elegant but dysfunctional church he now led. But for the first time since he arrived, and in his career, the prospect did not fill him with gloom. He'd discovered there were people who seemed to care about him and, equally important, people he cared about in turn. He thought about the doughnut and the hole and his decision to keep his eyes fixed firmly on the former. Life could be worse. He had come a long way, geographically and spiritually, from Philadelphia's Main Line to Virginia's end of the line.

The telephone's insistent ringing woke him up. He sat, dazed and disoriented—the way people are when they've drifted off to sleep in daylight or in an unfamiliar place. On the fifth ring he picked up the receiver. Dan Quarles, voice still hoarse, it seemed, wanted to ask Blake a question. Blake asked how he was feeling. Finally, satisfied that Dan was in reasonably good health, he let him ask his question. Dan wanted to know if the files had been found. Blake said no.

On an impulse—it had become an impulsive day, extreme sports magazines, luncheon with the rich and famous and now this—Blake asked him if he could identify any of the names on Waldo's list. Dan recognized the church people but none of the others. Blake thought he sounded strange and wondered if he really was all right. He asked if there was anything else Dan wanted to talk about. A very flustered Dan said no, and hung up.

He started to leave when the phone rang again.

"Are you still locking your door?" Schwartz said. Blake said he was. "You realize, don't you, that you are the logical next target."

"I guess so, but why? I didn't know you cared, Sheriff."

"I'm not thinking about you, Son, I'm thinking about the folks in your church. Where else can they get a minister who works so cheap?"

"You have a generous spirit and a warm heart. You'd make a great Archdeacon. Anyway, the only reason to shoot me is to get the files, which, as you know, I don't have, and if I did I'd give them up to the right people and certainly wouldn't dream of revealing their contents to anyone. So how does that make me a target?"

"We are not dealing with a simple killing, Reverend. There is something else at play here, something about Krueger. I can't figure out what, but files or no files, you need to lie low."

"I don't understand, but I'll take your word for it."

"Okay, watch your back, and tell your lawyer friend I appreciate her help."

"Okay, but what's with all the questions about Sylvia, anyway?"

"Not important. It's just that Floyd is a community that attracts a certain type of person, and she doesn't fit the mold, so to speak."

"What kind of people are you talking about?"

"People like me." Schwartz rang off.

People like who? County cops who didn't seem to fit the stereotype he'd expected?

He left his office, crossed the parking lot, and let himself into the vicarage. He had the television on and a frozen dinner in his hand ready to be microwaved when he changed his mind. He needed, he decided, a change of scene, a break. He put the dinner back in the freezer, donned his blazer, and left. As he locked the front door, he saw the television's blue flickering through the blinds. He started to unlock the door to turn it off but chose to ignore it. Later he would wonder why, but that night he forgot all about choir practice, about Mary Miller, and the opportunity to try the key. Because he was not at home when his killer came to call, this last impulsive act spared his life for the moment. Small decisions—critical outcomes. The Butterfly Effect.

Chapter Thirty-eight

Friday morning Blake found a note from Mary under his office door. She hoped he was not sick, and did he find the organ key? He smacked himself on the forehead with the heel of his hand for forgetting about choir practice and about the key. He dug it out of his desk drawer and hustled out of his office to the organ. The key fit. He put it in an envelope and scrawled Mary's name and a note of apology, and left it on the bench.

At ten o'clock he heard the organ begin to play a soft prelude and muffled voices, some recognizable—people arriving to set up for Millie's funeral. He resisted the temptation to join them. He had learned from hard experience that his presence in the chancel meant everyone deferred to him, instead of doing their job, no matter how small. Better to stay out of the way.

Schwartz called and told him the results of the ballistics test had not arrived, but he did have a version of the taped message that the county lab had massaged electronically to correct for the speaker's attempt to disguise his or her voice. He wanted Blake to listen to it in the hope he could recognize the caller. Blake said he would, but not until later that afternoon. He had a funeral. Then he remembered his list of names taken from Waldo's house. He told Schwartz how he came by it. He listened patiently to a lecture about the rules of evidence, and asked if Schwartz could try to find out something about the people on the list who were not from the church. He read them to Schwartz, who said he would see what he could do and call back and that he should be prepared to hand over the list.

At ten minutes before the hour, he vested and went into the sanctuary. Mary waved him over. They had not been together since the previous Friday and except for a few phone calls, two of them bad, the rest good, had not had any real contact. However awkward he felt, Mary showed no sign of discomfort.

"Thank you for the key," she said, still smiling.

If the eyes are the window to the soul, he thought, a smile must be the candle in the window.

"You missed all the excitement last night."

"Choir practice with you must always be exciting," he said and basked in her blush. "You mean something else happened?"

"People coming and going. First Dan Quarles came in and walked out. Then he came back and demanded to know where you were. Since nobody knew, he left again. He looked upset, by the way. Then Grace Franks barged in. I thought she wanted to speak to her husband but she just looked around and left. Then she came back and asked the same thing—where were you? She walked out again, and while she was gone the phone rang and it was Dan's wife wanting to know where he was. He missed Rotary or something. Then Grace came back, banging that big purse of hers, and told Bob he'd have to get a ride home, she was leaving for good. Then the Sheriff came and asked where you were. Oh, Blake, life would have been so much simpler, not to mention quieter, if you had just come to choir practice."

It was Blake's turn to smile.

"Nobody seemed to know what music Mrs. Bass liked," she continued, "so I picked some old favorites. Mrs. Garroway seemed to think they would do. They're not all slow, though. Do you think people will be upset if they are too peppy—for a funeral, I mean?"

He assured her that they would not be. She returned to her playing, a small frown on her face.

"I think there may be something wrong with this organ," she said. "It sounds like it is developing a cipher, a squeak, in this register." She ran a scale and he heard the noise, which sounded more like a wheeze than a squeak to him.

"It's an old and overrated organ," he said, and added, "We're still on for tonight?"

She smiled and nodded but kept her eyes on the sheet music in front of her.

He moved away, letting her deal with her peppy hymns and squeaks, and walked the length of the church. Rose and her sister were busy putting photographs on tables and easels they had set up in the narthex. He scanned them. There were dozens of pictures, some recent, showing Millie at any number of church bazaars, her face beaming. There were pictures of younger Millies: on one knee in her cheerleader's uniform, holding a megaphone that seemed as large as she; on a cruise with friends; at ten or twelve years old at Disney World, with a couple Blake assumed must have been her parents. It was an amazing display.

"Where did you get these?" he asked.

"Her attorney let us in the house after we met with the funeral people," she said. "We culled through scrap books and so on. These are the best of the lot. We found all sorts of things."

The hearse arrived at eleven. By then mourners filled nearly two-thirds of the pews. Blake shook his head in wonder. The Wednesday Bible Study had done its homework, it seemed. A limousine pulled up behind the hearse and a middle-aged man got out. Dexter Wayne, it turned out, was the extent of the mourners from Millie's immediate family.

"She had some nieces and a nephew in Ohio. When I contacted them, all they wanted to know was how much they stood to inherit. When I told them nothing, they hung up, every single one of them. I'm the executor of her will, by the way," he added. "I don't know how you people do things, but would it be all right if I said a few words?" Blake assured him it would be fine, welcome, in fact.

He oversaw the placing of the plain white pall on the casket, and with three pallbearers on either side, and men from the funeral home at the head and foot of the casket, the processional into the church began.

I am the resurrection and the life, saith the Lord; he that believeth in me, though he were dead, yet shall he live; and whosoever liveth and believeth in me shall never die.

I know that my Redeemer liveth, and that he shall stand at the latter day upon the earth; and though this body be destroyed, yet shall I see God; whom I shall see for myself and mine eyes shall behold, and not as a stranger.

Blake intoned the ancient anthem as the casket, pulled and pushed by funeral home employees, moved slowly up the center aisle.

For none of us liveth to himself and no man dieth to himself. For if we live, we live unto the Lord; and if we die, we die unto the Lord. Whether we live, therefore, or die, we are the Lord's.

Blessed are the dead who die in the Lord; even so saith the Spirit, for they rest from their labors.

Once in front of the altar, Blake prayed and the congregation recited Psalm 90. He read parts of an epistle and led them in the twenty-third Psalm. Mary played "Nearer My God to Thee." Not one of the peppy ones, Blake thought. He followed with a scripture reading.

He waited and then said, "The number of our days is three score and ten. So the psalmist writes, but someone took from God the right to decide who shall live and who shall die and denied Millie her seventy years. That person ended Millie's life and thereby blew out one of God's candles. The world is a little darker now. I have asked some of Millie's friends to speak this morning, to remember her for us before we say our final goodbyes." He nodded to Rose, who stood and walked to the pulpit.

"I did not know Millicent Bass very well," she began. "And that is a failure on my part. I have attended this church for more years than I care to say. And Millicent was here, too, for twenty of them. How is it that you can share something like worship with someone for two decades and not know anything about her? As I thought about that, I decided that even though any opportunity I might have to talk to Millicent was ended, it was not too late to find out about her, and also decided that I would never put myself in the position to have to say these words again about any of you, or have them said by you, of me. You may rest assured I will be all over you in the next weeks and months.

"Millicent did not have an unhappy childhood. I don't know how else to say it. She never had the experiences many of us have of great joy and excitement, but on the other hand, there were few dark moments either. Her parents were not rich, and what little they did manage to save, they spent on Millie—on cheerleading uniforms, on books and clothes and trips. They died when she was still in high school. She went to work right after graduation. Her marriage failed and she turned in on herself, I think. Yet, as I went through a few of her things, I found hundreds of records, recordings on vinyl, CDs, even old forty-fives and seventy-eights. She kept an ancient record player so that she could play those old chestnuts. Her taste in music ran from forties crooners to the classics. Judging from the books on her shelves, she loved to read and seemed particularly fond of murder mysteries. I suppose there is an irony there."

Blake listened as Rose finished and the others from the Bible Study took their turns speaking. In the twenty minutes or so that followed, he saw faces in the congregation slowly soften. The set expressions, which ranged from bored to openly hostile, disappeared and were replaced with attentiveness and even a few tears. At last Dexter Wayne took the pulpit and introduced himself.

"I am a distant cousin of Millicent's," he said, "and like the speakers before me, did not know her well. I am, however, the executor of her will. I doubt any of you knew it, but my cousin, while not a rich woman, had some independent means. Twenty years ago, an uncle died and left her an income from an annuity. As she had no family, she named this church as her beneficiary. She also willed her property and the few valuables she had to you. The sale of these items, I estimate, should bring something like two hundred and fifty thousand dollars to you, and the annuity will continue for ten years paying the sum of about thirty thousand dollars per annum." The congregation stirred and murmured. They were hearing about a Millicent none of them knew.

"I asked her why she wanted to give so much to you and she said she loved this church. It was her family and you always left your fortune to your family."

He sat down and the room fell silent. Her family.

Blake let them sit in silence for several minutes and then led them in prayer. He placed his hand on the coffin and said the commendation and then followed it out of the church.

Christ is risen from the dead, trampling down death by death, and giving life to those in the tomb.

The Sun of Righteousness is gloriously risen, giving light to those who sat in darkness and in the shadow of death.

The Lord will guide our feet into the way of peace, having taken away the sin of the world.

Christ will open the kingdom of heaven to all who believe in his Name, saying, Come, O blessed of my Father; inherit the kingdom prepared for you.

Into paradise may the angels lead thee; and at thy coming may the martyrs receive thee, and bring thee into the holy city, Jerusalem.

Mary played hymns as the people filed out. Most left to return to jobs or other preoccupations, but a few lingered, waiting to drive to the cemetery for the interment.

An hour later, he returned with the group that witnessed at the graveside. A reception had been set up in the basement. Trestle tables were covered with white cloths, and food prepared by the kitchen volunteers filled plates and saucers. He nibbled at the food, counted it as lunch, and wandered around the room. Rose approached him.

"You were right," she said. "The only thing to do was to find something good in her. You know, I thought about what you told me on Wednesday and I wondered about it. It seemed so contrary to everything I ever believed. But you know what I discovered? That hate, even a tiny bit, is like a glowing coal in your heart, and if you don't extinguish it, sooner or later it will consume you. With Millicent dead, the only way to put out that little fire was to do what you made me do. Thank you."

"It's a lesson for me, too, Rose. I always knew the right words to say, but I never experienced their truth until today. The truth is, very few people have ever taken my advice as seriously as you all did. Now I am a believer in my own words. Isn't that something?"

"You are going to be just fine here with us. You have a lot to teach us, and it seems we have some things to teach you, too."

Dan Quarles slid up to him.

"A question, Father Fisher," he said, looking nervously at Rose and her friends.

"Sure, how about over here." Blake led him into a corner.

"I want to ask you about confession. Do you believe in the seal of the confessional? I know we don't practice auricular confession like the Roman church does, but we do have it, don't we?"

"Most denominations do, Dan. They may not call it that, but in a one-on-one meeting with a minister, a pastor, or a priest, what is said in confidence can and should be sealed. I have only two exceptions to the rule, and I tell people up front about them. I will not seal child abuse of any sort, and I will not seal murder. I know that is a break in the generally held tradition, but I cannot see how withholding that kind of information does God's work. If I know or hear of either of those, I call the cops."

Dan scowled as he spoke. "I see," he said, and stalked off as if pursued by some personal demon.

Ike Schwartz appeared at Blake's elbow. "Got news for you, Reverend," he said.

"That's a nice change. Have something to eat and tell me."

"Already ate. What is this, a wake?"

"Close enough. What's your news?"

"The gun used to kill Krueger is the same one used on Bass," he said. "The FBI is confused. They think the killer believed Millie saw him or something and had to remove her as a material witness, but they know it's a stretch. They are not keen on this being just a local affair—they have jurisdiction issues."

"So we know the killings are linked at least. Now all we have to do is figure out how and why."

"All *I* have to do is figure out how and why. *You* are not part of the equation."

"Well, what about the names I gave you? They ought to give me some part in this. Did you find out anything about them?"

"I did. There's something very funny about those names."

Chapter Thirty-nine

The two men settled in Blake's office. Schwartz managed to fold his long-legged frame into the cracked oak chair in the corner and made himself comfortable. Blake tilted back in his chair, pulled out a top drawer, and put his feet up. He kept the top of his desk too cluttered to accommodate feet. They could hear the rattle of dishes and the murmur of voices in the kitchen below as the clean-up crew removed the leftovers and remnants of the reception. The door slammed from time to time as people left, shouting farewells.

"I'll take that list now," Schwartz said.

Blake retrieved the folded paper from the drawer and handed it to him.

"What will you do with it?"

"Check it for fingerprints."

"Mine and Krueger's?"

"Presumably." Schwartz pocketed the paper.

"No question about the ballistics test? The bullets came from the same gun in both murders, that's certain?"

"As certain as those things ever are. Both victims were shot at close range with a .32 caliber pistol. The lab guy guesses it was an old Colt automatic. Does that sound familiar to you?"

"You think someone used my gun to kill them?"

Schwartz stared at him.

"Oh no, Sheriff, you are not going to put me back on your list. And until you find the gun, you have no reason to, and I have a lawyer."

"Speculation is not the approach I want to take. Frankly, I like you for the murders as much as the next guy, if only there was a next guy. The problem here is you are the only guy at the moment. I hope you don't find that too reassuring. I will keep you off my list for the time being."

"Thanks a lot. So what's so funny about the list of names?"

"There are three lists, as near as I can tell. The first, call it the 'A' list, has seven names on it, all of them from your church. That is if you count Miss Miller. The next list, 'B', has four names. They are all people who live within three blocks of Krueger's house. Miss Miller belongs on that list, as well, which means it is five names long and the 'A' list, six. Go figure. And finally there is another list, 'C', names I cannot place. There are six names on that list. The best I could do is check a phone book, and that didn't tell me much except all the names that matched those on our list live in and around Roanoke, Salem, and Buchanan."

Blake looked at the list again. He discounted Mary. Schwartz was the sheriff—let him suspect Mary. Blake chose to exonerate her. The most familiar names were Dan Quarles and Grace Franks. Well, she had a key and could break into his house to lift a gun; so could Quarles, and he wanted to confess to something. But then all of the church names could, too—everybody has a key. The others were relatively unfamiliar to him. He told Schwartz he thought Quarles and Grace were his choice for suspects.

"These others are off the charts as killers with a motive. The others are folks in what we call the Christmas, Easter, Sometimes Sunday pool. They come to church rarely, high holy days and so on. Almost never see them otherwise. I leave it to you to figure what the acronym for that pool is, by the way. I cannot see any possibility there. Unless…."

"What? Unless what?"

"Unless Waldo, that is, Krueger, knew something about them that I don't."

"Like what?"

"No idea. Secrets probably. People like to keep them. If some-one discovers what they are, and they are damaging.... Well, it was just a passing thought."

"If any more of those thoughts pass by, give me a call. Now, you want to listen to this cleaned-up tape for me?" He pulled out a small tape deck and played the tape.

"Anything?" he asked.

"I can't be sure. The voice is very familiar, but it could be any one of several dozen people I have met in my few months here. I'm sure I have talked to this person on the phone, but I talk to a lot of women—I am right in assuming it is a woman? It's not some mechanical or voice alteration? In my line of work I deal with women a lot, but this time not often enough to sort out the voice. If it were accented or distinctive in some way, I might be able to recognize it, maybe, but not now. You know how it is when someone calls and says 'It's me' and then they rattle on about this or that and you can't figure out who *me* is? You know it's someone you should recognize, but until they say something that identifies them, you are at a complete loss. This is an *it's me* kind of voice. Sorry."

Schwartz stood, inspected the diplomas on the wall for a moment, shook his head, and walked out.

Blake scrutinized the list again. He swiveled around in his chair and tried to think. The sheriff's car pulled away from the church. Everyone had left the kitchen or the church, as nearly as he could tell. Should he be afraid? Schwartz thought he would be the next victim. He wanted him to stay locked in the house or always around other people. Blake decided he would not live in fear. God did not bring him all this way to let him go now. There was a tap at the door and then Dorothy Sutherlin poked her head around the jamb. She sneezed and excused herself.

"We're all finished, Vicar," she announced. "I'll be leaving now." Blake thanked her. Now he was alone.

The leaves on the trees were already turning, partly as the result of an unusually dry summer, and partly because it was

September and time. He never ceased to wonder at the difference a couple hundred miles made—in the weather and in his life. Thoughts about Philadelphia and what he had left behind did not upset him as much as they would have a month ago. He watched as the boys from the neighborhood appeared, almost on cue, to set up their skateboard run. Apparently they'd found a new box, and he watched as they rolled across the asphalt and up the ramp to sail through the air a few feet, sometimes successfully, and land with a crash on the other side. The rumble of their boards blended with the few cicadas singing in the sycamore beside the church. One of the boys tried to bend a piece of plywood into a half circle. Half pipe, Blake thought. Then: why not, the money is available.

He picked up the phone and called Lanny Markowitz to run his idea by him. Lanny taught school. He would understand, and if he did, he would be the one to spearhead the project. Lanny said he wanted to think about it.

The phone rang just as he hung up. Philip Bournet sounded concerned, but then Philip almost always sounded concerned, probably because he genuinely cared about people. He even cared for people he did not like, although they might not believe it after he finished telling them what he thought of them, but he did care.

"Blake, are you busy tomorrow night? I know this is very late in the day to call, but Betsy has presented me with a major calamity." Blake heard the irony in his voice. "Could you fill in for a sick friend? We need a fourth for bridge. We'll feed you, of course."

"Tomorrow, Philip? Tomorrow is Saturday night. That is the eve of Sunday, in case you've forgotten. Do you always play on the night before the Sabbath?"

"We won't keep you late, and if you are telling me that you haven't got your sermon ready yet, shame on you. That is supposed to be done by Thursday. Didn't they teach you anything in seminary? If you really get stuck, I'll give you one of mine. Might be an improvement over what you've been dishing out."

"Philip, I'll have you know I was once nominated for the Pulitzer Prize in Preaching."

Philip laughed and said, "I'll take that as a yes and expect to see you tomorrow evening at six."

Solly Fairmont complained to the mayor, and the mayor called Ike. A meeting took place in Ike's office. Fairmont insisted his zoned air movers were state of the art. Ike said his people were being treated like prisoners, which, by the way, opened another issue: the fact that the planners in Fairmont's office thought the cells should be kept hot and uncomfortable because the occupants needed to be made to realize the dim view society held of them. Ike, as the town's chief law enforcement officer, believed he should make that sort of decision, and, furthermore, it represented antediluvian thinking. Fairmont appeared lost at *antediluvian*. Ike reminded them that the mayor's son recently spent a night in one of them on a drunk and disorderly charge, and did they want to hear from him? Fairmont offered a compromise, and Sam's air conditioner was returned to her, along with Billy's missing chair, which he had removed because it was not properly marked with an inventory number.

Ike found Sam hunched over her keyboard.

"Sam," he said, "your air conditioner will be brought back this afternoon."

"Great. Thanks, Ike."

"No problem. Sam? We need to talk."

"Yes, Sir?"

"About your personal life and about business—the Krueger case."

"What about my personal life?"

"Krueger first. Those pictures you found on his computer. Where are they?"

She pulled a file from her drawer and handed it to him. Ike turned each photograph over. Without labels he couldn't be sure, but he had a good idea now what he was looking at—neighbors and some FBI history. Krueger was their boy and a blackmailer on the side. It had to be. The real estate business was a small side line—a cover. He figured to make a fast buck and embarrass his keepers in the process.

He glanced at what appeared to be a financial statement.

"If this is what I think it is, it looks like he was a substantial investor in some property in anticipation of the Ibex and Crane development."

"Then he lost his shirt," Sam said. "I checked. The Ibex and Crane site was, in fact, a mouse trap. The industrial park is going in south of here, nearer Roanoke. All the land options they need have been acquired by their people. What about my personal life?"

Ike held up his hand and shook his head. If Bullock and his crowd had in fact turned Krueger and then lost him, he was standing in deep kimchee.

"Ike...?"

"Okay, here's the story. I'm sorry, Sam, but Karl Hedrick is not using up leave time to hang around Picketsville because he and you...that is you and he...well, he's not. He's been appointed Agent in Place and he's here to find Krueger's killer. He'll use you and anyone else he can to do that. Krueger started out in their witness protection program and they lost him. They need to cover their—"

"I know. He told me. It's okay. See, just because someone is in one place professionally doesn't mean they can't be in another personally, does it?"

Ike frowned and shook his head. "This is like—what—a version of Heisenberg's Uncertainty Principle for relationships or something, is that it?"

"Whose uncertainty...whatever?"

"Important physicist. Sorry, I read about it...."

"Well, I don't think so. I wasn't too good at physics. It's more like there's work and there's everything else and the two don't always have to mesh, right?"

"No, I guess not. I'm not sure I'm the person to ask about that. So you're telling me you may not be putting in all those extra hours anymore?"

Sam beamed. "I sure hope not."

Chapter Forty

Mary was waiting for Blake when he drove up, and once again she opened the passenger side door before he could help her. She slid easily into the cramped front seat and said, "Where to?"

"I found a theater with a film we can watch. It's a bit of a drive but worth it."

He drove east to the expressway and south toward Roanoke. They found an uncrowded place to eat, no mean feat on a Friday night, and then went to the only G-rated film in the area. It was a charming film with complicated animation and a reasonably funny story line. As he watched a chorus line of cows cross-stepping and bellowing something that sounded suspiciously like Wagner's *Liebestod*, Blake realized two shocking things about himself. In his previous life, BP—before Picketsville—he wouldn't be caught dead in a film like this one, except, perhaps, to take his nieces and nephew to the movies. On top of that, he was actually enjoying it. None of the women he used to date would have endured it for five minutes. Mary sat smiling and laughing and occasionally turned toward him to measure his reaction.

After they left the theater, he offered to buy her dessert, but she declined.

"Just take me home, I have something else planned," she said. "And besides, you already spent too much money."

They walked to the car. The night air was cooler but still very pleasant. He left the top down.

Forty-five minutes later they were sitting on the patio in her back yard. She lived in a charming little town house, narrow front to back, with a living room, kitchen, and dining area in the front, a stairway up to the second floor to the right. The furniture and pictures were scaled to the rooms and the whole effect quite pleasing. Her back yard showed the results of what he guessed represented hours of work. She had him sit and disappeared into the kitchen. He heard the clink of cup and saucers, silverware, and the refrigerator door slamming. Then silence. He waited.

She backed out of the door, both hands laden with a tray. He jumped to his feet and held the door open for her. He offered to help, but she shook her head, maneuvered around, and put the tray down with a thump.

"There," she said, satisfied. "I made you a pie and I have ice cream and decaf coffee. Now isn't that better than a crowded Starbucks?" She stood back and smiled. Blake gaped. She had on the beaded dress from Classique. Sometime during the last week she must have bought it. He swallowed a sound that might otherwise have attracted a gam of whales, and stood transfixed. Mary had always been beautiful in his eyes. In the dress she was drop dead gorgeous. Still smiling, she folded herself into a chair.

"I was right about the dress, when...wow!"

She shifted in her chair self-consciously.

"I hope you like it. I've never done anything quite so impulsive before. I feel positively wicked."

She didn't look wicked—she looked elegant. He couldn't take his eyes off her. After a few minutes, she excused herself, went into the house and returned with a sweater over her shoulders. He was at the same time disappointed and relieved.

"I felt a little chilly," she said. That wasn't his problem.

They talked. He discovered she had a brother who taught eleventh and twelfth grade English in a private school in Maryland somewhere and an Uncle Oscar who retired from a drug company and lived nearby. They were all that remained of her family. His gaze kept sliding to the dress. He told her about his mother and father in Bucks County. They shared stories and a bit of their histories. Finally, he worked up enough courage to ask her about Waldo.

"Mary, last week I asked you if you knew Waldo."

"Walter/Waldo, you mean?"

"Yes, and you acted, I don't know, nervous or something. I'm curious. What was that all about?"

A few citronella candles scented the air and cast dim, flickering light on the patio, but even in the uncertain darkness, he could see her blush and squirm.

"It's nothing, Blake, it's just that he was a little weird."

"Creepy?"

"Worse than creepy. He would pop up in the alley back there," she gestured into the darkness at the rear of her property, "sometimes, especially at night. It's not unusual, you know, for people to move up and down that alley. They walk their dogs, take out the trash, but he seemed to be out there all the time."

"That's it?"

She stared into the night for a minute and he could have sworn her face got redder.

"He's dead now, so it isn't important anymore."

"What's not important anymore? Mary, there is an open murder investigation going on. I did not tell you this before, but the police think that whoever killed him killed Millie Bass as well. Almost anything could be important. What is it?"

"If I tell you, you will think badly of me," she said and lowered her head.

"That is not possible, Mary. I...um...it's not possible."

She sighed. "My bedroom window is that one right up there," she said and pointed to the window above them. "I always keep the shades drawn, Blake. You have to believe me. I never have them open unless I am cleaning or something."

"I am sure you do, but I don't see what this has to do with Waldo."

"A couple of months ago I washed my windows—spring cleaning. Vinegar and water, the whole bit. I had to go out that afternoon and left the blinds up. That night I came home, ate my dinner, and decided to finish my cleaning, so I tackled the basement. Well, I got so hot and dirty I decided to take a shower before I went to bed. Anyway, I forgot the blinds were up and when I went into my bedroom without any—you know—and I thought I saw him in the alley looking in my window at me. All I could think to do was turn off the lights and close the blinds."

"He was a Peeping Tom?"

"I guess so. Anyway, I could never face him after that. Whenever he looked at me he would smile this evil little smile, like he knew me, knew me in the biblical sense, I mean. It was awful."

Blake risked putting his hand on hers. She did not pull it away but entwined their fingers instead.

"I'm sorry," he said. "It must have been humiliating."

"It was awful," she repeated softly. "I even thought about moving. I might have if he hadn't been killed. And then I thought, 'I'm glad he's dead.' That's a terrible thing to think, isn't it? What kind of person did that make me? I was no better than he."

"It's a natural reaction, Mary. You don't feel that way now, do you?"

"No, not any longer, but what I felt about him is not the worst part. What he did made me angry and suspicious and so when the letters about you came, I thought—well, I thought you were like him. I didn't mean to judge you so hard, but because of what he did, I put the two of you together. I'm sorry." He saw a small tear roll down from the corner of her eye.

"It's all right, Mary. It's over now. No more Waldo, no more secrets—all done with."

She squeezed his hand and looked at him, searching, he supposed, for reassurance.

The conversation lagged after that, and ten minutes later he stood to leave.

"Blake," she said, "tell me about Philadelphia."

Chapter Forty-one

Philadelphia.

It should have been obvious to him from the outset. Even now, six months later, Blake still punished himself for not recognizing the signs. The topic had been drummed into him in Clinical Pastoral Education lectures, in workshops put on by the diocese, and countless articles distributed to clergy. Blake's only defense: his incurable romanticism. At least that is what he told himself. His former boss, the Reverend William Smart, had a simpler one: his incurable stupidity. Blake admitted now that Smart's analysis might have been closer to the truth. He had been stupid to miss the signs. But then, if Bill Smart was so sharp, why hadn't he said something at the time?

Gloria Vandergrift played an active role at Saint Katherine's. She seemed a perfectly normal, but slightly high-strung divorcee. She chaired the Worship Committee. She worked tirelessly on Annual Giving, the Christmas Bazaar, and various and sundry committees, not to mention a Rolodex full of worthwhile charities and causes elsewhere—the preoccupations of people with money and time on their hands, but little or no direction in their lives. She haunted the church offices on one pretext or another. In addition, she contributed generously, very generously, to the church, a fact that made staff and clergy far more tolerant of her constant and hovering presence than they might otherwise have been.

At first, Blake took no notice of her, beyond the usual physical assessment every man, clergy or lay, makes of a woman. She wore her blonde hair pulled back severely from her face, a practice which made her forehead seem high and accentuated her cheekbones, The result, instead of diminishing her beauty, actually enhanced it. The overall effect—the hair, slim waist, and rather obviously well-endowed body—was stunning.

Blake had not married, and he knew that he should and probably soon. He believed God had destined him for great things. To achieve them required sacrifice and a few calculated decisions on his part. One of those decisions involved a wife and family. He had hoped to fall in love, marry, and be in the process of raising two or three photogenic children by then, but it had not happened. Women seemed to like him, but none were willing to get too close to him.

"What is it about me," he'd asked his sister Irene, after another rejection from a very nice and, Blake thought, promising candidate for marriage, "that makes women run, after two dates?"

"You are too obvious," she had answered.

"Too obvious? What exactly does that mean?"

"Blake, I love you as only a sister can, so I will tell you what you probably don't want to hear. You do not want a wife 'to love, honor and cherish till death do you part.' You want an attractive and charming addition to your left arm."

Blake frowned and stared at her.

"You want someone who will make you look good, give you status and a measure of *gravitas*, that's all. Your ambition, Blake, has buried your heart."

Her words stung at the time, but now, he supposed, she'd told the truth. He'd looked on the women he dated with an eye to how they might look in various scenarios—at garden parties, church functions, Bishop's receptions and, of course, church search committees.

Gloria had the makings of just the sort of woman Blake thought he needed. She had charm, looks, and money. When she asked Blake if she could see him privately, he jumped at the chance. "Counseling," she'd said. She had some issues she needed to deal with and he, as a man of experience, she believed, could help her. He never saw it coming.

Their sessions were never very long, nor did they involve anything he would describe as substantive. The issues Gloria brought up seemed extraordinarily trivial to him. But he also knew it took time for trust between a counselor and client to develop, so he remained patient, waiting. He listened with as much attention as he could muster to revelations of minor past infractions and erotic thoughts. He kept eye contact with her luminous gray eyes and assumed an expression of deep concern. After two months of intellectual fluff, Blake had enough.

"Gloria, I think there are things you are unwilling to tell me, and I think I cannot help you as a counselor until you do. You need to let it out." At that, she burst into tears and fled the office.

The next day, as he drove to the church, his cell phone twittered.

"Blake, I'm so sorry about yesterday. I want to apologize." Gloria said, her voice calm.

"No apology necessary," he said, he thought, gallantly.

"That's very kind of you. I know what a bother I have been and I have not really been very forthcoming with you."

"I shouldn't have been so hard on you."

"No, no, you were quite right in chastising me."

Blake, busy navigating his way through rush-hour traffic one-handed, did not hear the shift in the tone of her voice. He decided then and there to get a hands-free attachment for his phone.

"Blake, I know you're busy, but do you suppose you could stop by here on your way to the office?"

As it happened, he had no appointments that morning. His schedule was blank until ten. She would not know that, would she? He paused and then replied, "I think I can clear out a few minutes. If you don't hear from me in the next five minutes, I'm on my way to your house."

Fifteen minutes later he parked in front of her brick Georgian house in a leafy suburb west of the city and walked up the path to the door. She opened it just as he reached for the bell button, her head just visible around the door.

"Come in. Oh, thank you for seeing me on such short notice," she gushed, face beaming. He noticed she wore a loose, plum-colored robe or housecoat of some sort, and her hair was down. He had never seen her that way and liked the effect.

"You should wear your hair down more often," he said absently, and looked around. The house had a central hall that ran from the front door to a set of French doors at the back. To his right an arched entry opened onto a living room and to his left an identical arch opened onto a dining room. He supposed there were kitchens and dens and so on deeper in. A staircase rose upward to a landing over the French doors, and then turned and climbed on up to the next floor. Judging by the dormers in the roof he saw on his way to the front door, Blake guessed there was a third floor as well. The décor evoked Williamsburg—paint, pewter, and period antiques. Fresh cut flowers filled the rooms with perfume. Very nice.

"You do a lot of entertaining, Gloria?"

"Not a lot, Blake. I used to, before, when my husband and I were still together. Can I get you some coffee? Tea?"

"Well, I suppose coffee would be fine."

"I have some made—fresh pot—we can have it in the break-fast room. This way."

He followed her to the back of the house, past several nice etchings that could have been original Dürers, turned left, and walked through the kitchen to a sunny room that looked over a garden. A round table and chairs filled most of the available space. He sat and admired the early blooming iris and crocuses while she busied herself with cups and saucers, a sugar bowl and a cream pitcher.

"There," she said, putting them down and sitting opposite him, "now that's better." She poured and handed him his cup, Kona coffee.

"Thank you, Gloria. Now, you said you had something you wanted to tell me?"

"I think you know," she said smiling. She had very white and straight teeth.

"Sorry—I know?"

"It's you, Blake. You're the one."

"Gloria, I am not...you have the advantage of me. I'm the one...what?"

"Don't be coy, Blake, you as much as admitted it yesterday. You said I was not letting it out. '*It*,' Blake. You were right and now I have."

"Have what? Gloria, I know I must sound stupid, but I'm not following you." She stared at him for several seconds, her brow furrowed. Then she brightened.

"Oh, I get it. This is part of the counseling strategy. I have to confess to you, is that it?"

"Confess? Confess what? Gloria, seriously, I don't know where this is going."

She sighed, "Have it your way, then. I am yours, Blake, body and soul. You can take me any way and any time you wish. You have conquered me."

As she spoke she let her robe slip away. She was not wearing anything under it.

Blake leapt to his feet, spilling his coffee on the tablecloth.

"Blake? Something wrong? This is what you have been hinting at for months, isn't it? Oh, I've seen how you look at me. I'm no fool. Of course, we will have to get married. It would not look good for a clergyman to have an affair with a member of your congregation, although if you want to, it is all right with me. Shall we go upstairs now or...?"

Blake bolted to the door, raced the length of the hall, and pelted down the sidewalk to his car, his eyes wide and as round as two ping pong balls. He left a twenty-foot patch of rubber in the street as he drove away. Five minutes later, he was sufficiently calm to consider his situation. First thing, talk to Smart. Tell him right away. Then pull Gloria's file. She must have a history of this kind of thing. They always do. Then...then what? Oh man, what a mess.

◇◇◇

Smart, his face thunderous, sat behind Blake's desk when he arrived. Blake opened his mouth to say something, but Smart cut him off.

"You're fired," he said. "Get this office cleaned out and yourself off the premises by noon today."

"Bill? What's going on?"

"You have the nerve to ask me? She called. Said you tried to…to molest her. Said she's filing a complaint with the Bishop's office. You are finished, Fisher. I hope you have a trade or skill, because your days in the ministry are over."

"Bill, I didn't do anything. She asked me to stop by. She gave me a cup of coffee and then…it was her, Bill, as God is my witness, I never…."

"By noon." Smart pushed out of the chair and left the office. The phone rang. Blake stared at it. Now what? He picked up.

"Bishop Farnsworth wants to see you as soon as possible. He said 'right now' would be best." The Bishop's secretary had an imperious air that brooked no dissent. Blake said he would be right over.

The Right Reverend Barney Farnsworth, Bishop of the Diocese of Pennsylvania, grew up, and served all of his time as a cleric before his consecration as bishop, in the Diocese of Fond du Lac. "Fond of Lace" is how Blake and his colleagues referred to it. Farnsworth loved ceremony and style, high church liturgy and all the trappings—the incense, bells and bobbing and weaving that accompanied it. His theology ran modern and shallow, but he was thought to be fair, if not particularly spiritual.

The Bishop's office could have been a movie set for a period piece. It reeked of Victorian busyness, an English study complete with leather wingback chairs, a fireplace, and handsomely bound volumes lining its walls.

"Blake, my boy, you are in a mess. Sit."

"Bishop, I swear to you I did not do anything, say anything, or even imply anything to have caused this. The woman is mad."

"Yes, I know all about it. Just got off the phone with Bill 'not so' Smart. He's a good man but…." He left the rest dangling in the air.

"You know? How do you know?"

"Not the first time, Blake. The lady is a church gypsy, moves around from church to church. Every couple of years she catches the eye of some young curate and then this sort of thing happens. I hope I am right in assuming you were bright enough to get out of there before…well, you know."

"Yes, Sir, no Sir, I mean, nothing happened."

"Good. I have lost two or three young men to this woman, one or two of whom were not that smart. Got involved…very messy. Wives and children involved, divorce, scandal."

"So, it's fixed? I can go back to Saint Katherine's?"

"I didn't say that, Blake. The truth is—nobody is interested in the truth. Your denial, letters from me, all the king's horses and all the king's men will never erase the belief in the minds of too many of your parishioners, that you must have done something. We clergy, you know, do not have the infallible *cachet* we once enjoyed. No, I am sorry, Blake, but you are finished, at least in this diocese. Terrible shame, you had a bright future here, if I do say so."

"Bishop, with the national policy of putting this sort of thing in my permanent record, I am finished everywhere."

"Not necessarily, my boy, but you are going to have some difficult times. I will write to any bishop you want me to. That should get you past a negative background check. I am afraid it may not help much with a committee searching for a new rector or assistant, though."

Blake's heart sank.

"You must know some people. Surely one of them has or knows of a position. You cannot be picky, of course, but keep your head down in some out- of-the-way parish for a while. This will blow away eventually."

"This is so unfair," Blake shouted. "That woman preys on clergy, destroys them, and I suppose their families. Thank God

I have no family—she goes free while her victims are punished, ruined."

"I'm sorry, but that is the way it is."

"She will still attend Saint Katherine's and I have to leave."

"She won't attend long, I don't think. She will find another church, another foolish young man. We will, of course, send letters to the churches, but it did no good the last time. Smart got the old letter. Filed it away. Probably will again. Let's hope she picks on the Presbyterians next time."

"Bishop, what do I do now?"

"Find out if you have any friends, Blake."

Blake discovered, to his dismay, he had only one. Philip Bournet.

Mary walked him to the door. When he turned to say good-night, she leaned forward on tiptoes and kissed him lightly on the lips.

"You're a good man, Blake Fisher," she whispered and closed the door.

He did not remember how he got home.

Chapter Forty-two

Philip had been nearly correct. Blake had let his sermon preparation slip. Not as badly as he might have, but Saturday morning turned into a workday. He read through the lessons assigned for Sunday. He settled on his text and spent three hours scribbling notes, crossing out lines and then, satisfied he had the makings of a talk, put them all away. In the last two weeks he had come to rely on the movement of the Spirit in his sermons and knew that if he had the basics in notes, the rest would come.

He rewarded himself with a trip to the mall for lunch and a little shopping. He needed some clothes, and his shoes were looking a little shabby. His interest in his appearance had slipped enormously since Philadelphia. In those days he was always very conscious of how he looked, the impression he made. But lately he had stopped caring.

Purchases made, he wandered along the walkway, retracing the steps he and Mary had taken two weeks before. He stopped in front of the jewelry store and looked again at the rings in the case. He remembered Mary's pointing to the large one in the center of the display and saying she nearly received one that size. On an impulse he went in and asked to see it. The clerk found the ring and put it on black velvet. The stone flashed, fiery and hot. He asked the price and blanched.

"Is the gentleman considering an engagement?"

Blake murmured that the gentleman was not considering an engagement any time soon and if the ring were a required part of the contract, not for another ten years or so. The clerk did not seem to see the humor and merely nodded and looked bored. He had lied, of course. For the first time in his life, engagement and marriage were on his mind. He shook his head in annoyance. If he was honest with himself, he barely knew Mary and was in no position to propose to her or anyone else. He still clung, however tenuously, to his ambitions. Mary was a dear person, but not a bishop's wife. Then he wondered if he really cared about that any more. Somehow that light no longer burned so brightly.

He did not see Dan Quarles skulking behind him. Dan arranged it that way. When Blake returned to the corridor from the jewelry store and continued his stroll, Dan followed closely, being careful to turn away when Blake stopped. He wanted to wait for the right moment. He thought if he could approach the matter correctly—use the right words—he might be able to persuade Blake to change his mind, so he could tell him what he needed to, get it all off his chest. If Blake would not listen, he might have to take more drastic steps, and there had been enough of them already. Not that anyone would blame him if he did, especially if they knew, but people were funny and so quick to judge. While his back was turned, and he pondered his next move, Blake disappeared from sight and he lost him.

In the afternoon, Blake met Lanny Markowitz at Picket Senior High School. In addition to teaching math, Lanny served as an assistant football coach. With the season about to start, Saturday practices were in order. Blake watched from the sidelines as thirty or forty young men sweated and groaned in the afternoon sun. Most of them were not fully grown, and their pads overwhelmed their bodies. They dashed up and down, shoulder pads lurching on their shoulders, helmets low on the same shoulders, and thin sinewy legs pumping as hard as they could go. An errant pass came toward him and he scooped it in one-handed, flipped it around in his hand, and sent it back, a perfect spiral.

"How far can you throw that thing, Vicar?" Lanny shouted.

"I don't know. It's been a long time."

Lanny threw him another football, which he caught and tucked. He sent a young lanky boy racing down the field.

"Anytime you're ready," he yelled.

Blake waited until the boy had run about forty yards and pumped once and threw another perfect spiral. It dropped neatly in the boy's outstretched arms fifty yards away.

Lanny whistled and said, "You want a job?"

"I think my high school eligibility has expired, Lanny."

"I was thinking we could use you as a quarterback and receivers coach. I assume you played quarterback at one time or another."

"It was a long time ago, Lanny—another life."

"Hey, Mark," Lanny called, "come here a minute, will you?"

A large, burly man in a sweatshirt and black ball cap turned and strolled toward them.

"Do that again," Lanny said to Blake and tossed him another ball. This time two receivers raced down field, and Blake picked the one with the most speed and led him ten yards and laid the pass into his arms on the dead run.

The man called Mark stood with his hands on his hips and stared.

"You wouldn't be interested helping us out, would you? The truth is, we are only a skilled quarterback away from a county championship. Jimmy Slade over there has the talent, but not the tools. Do you think you could teach him how to throw like that? I'm Mark Buskirk, by the way."

Blake shook his hand. He had not played anything more demanding than a little flag football since college. But he just proved to himself and, he supposed, to everyone else on the field, that he still had the arm. What would it cost him to give up afternoons to help this group out? There were a lot of young men on the field, and he knew from experience that while the traditional church did not appeal to them, something else might.

He guessed God just sent him a message. How else had he managed two perfect passes of over fifty yards?

He'd quarterbacked at Williams, and while that college was no football powerhouse, he'd played well enough to attract some attention from the pros. The Patriots used their next to last pick to draft a "local boy," hoping, he supposed, to uncover another Doug Flutie. He passed on that very slim chance to play in the NFL and went to seminary instead, but he never forgot the thrill he felt when the Pats called.

"Okay," he said. "But on one condition—I do not always control my time. I may miss days and not be able to tell you in advance. If that's all right, I'll do it."

Buskirk tossed him a whistle on a lanyard and pointed across the field. "QBs and receivers are over there. They're all yours." Then turning to face the dozen or so young men, he yelled, "This is your new coach...What's your name, Reverend?"

"Blake Fisher."

"Coach Fisher. You listen to him. If they give you any trouble, make them drop and give you ten."

"I remember the drill."

Blake spent the remaining afternoon working with the boys. Mark was right; Slade had the talent but not the tools. But Blake saw more potential in a tall, thin, black kid named Duane. He, more than Slade, had raw ability, but more important, he showed eagerness to learn. Jimmy Slade had been the starter for two years and figured the job was his and he did not need to listen to this new "Holy Joe" coach. Blake guessed there would be some fireworks before they played their first game.

Chapter Forty-three

The sun slid behind the school building, throwing the field into deep shadows. Mark sent his team around the track twice and into the showers. Blake walked off the field with Lanny.

"I really came out here to talk to you, Lanny. I had no idea that the afternoon would translate into football practice. There are some pretty good kids out there."

"What did you think of Slade?"

"Mark's almost right. He has some talent and some tools. If he'll listen, I can help him with his game, but that isn't going to get the job done. He's missing the third piece."

"And that is?"

"Heart, desire, whatever you call it. He wants to play but not work. He's cocky and not teachable. Are we going to have a problem?"

"That depends. Who's your alternative?"

"Duane. My guess is Jimmy Slade will start the season because, work ethic or no, he's still the best you've got. By the third game, when he's hot-dogged the team into two losses, we could have Duane ready, and he could carry the team the rest of the way. A championship is possible only if you can get it with two losses."

Lanny shook his head and made a face. "Mark will be delighted to hear that. But you're right about Slade. I know it,

Mark knows it, but won't admit it. How hard would it be to get Duane ready by day one?"

"Lanny, I'm not a miracle worker, and I'm not that good with kids if you want to know the truth. But, if Duane wants it, and I can find the time, and if we can get the starting receivers to work overtime, maybe."

"Going to create some heat in the Slade household, I can tell you. His dad and mom are convinced their boy is going to a big university on a full-boat football scholarship. You take the starting job away from him, and all that goes down the drain."

"Your call, Lanny, I am just the volunteer, but I don't see Jimmy Slade playing any higher than community college, and any kind of scholarship seems a reach to me. I know. I've been there. Tough problem for you, though. You heard about the father in California who sued the school system for a million and a half dollars because his kid got demoted to junior varsity basketball? I guess he figured that's what he had coming to him for lost free tuition, meals, books and 'pain and suffering.' Not to mention the loss of revenue from big bucks playing in the NBA."

"I heard. And a mom in Alabama sued her school because her daughter didn't make the cheerleading squad after the parents paid huge sums to a cheerleader coach for a year. We had a girl here who plagiarized her term paper. She didn't graduate and her parents sued the school system. It's crazy."

"It's a litigious society, Lanny. Everybody seems to think they're entitled to things whether they've earned them or not. People go after folks for all sorts of phony and self-indulgent reasons."

Lanny caught Blake out of the corner of his eye, and reddened.

They walked on in silence, and finally Lanny said, "I've been thinking about the parking lot expansion and skateboard park. It's a great idea, but I don't think we should do it."

"No? Why not?"

"Well, in the first place, the liability we would assume, for injuries and that sort of thing, would be huge, and I am not sure we could afford the insurance even if we could get it. You know how that half-pipe thing works?"

"Not really. Sort of."

"Kids start at the rim on one side, skate down and up to the rim on the other. When they get there they fly through the air a little or a lot, depending on how good they are, twist and roll back down and up again. Do you have any idea how long it takes to master that, and how many cracked ribs, chipped teeth, and who knows what else a kid will experience before he does? We are taking a big risk for a small return there."

"Why a small return?"

"Who's on those boards? Young kids—twelve, fourteen, some younger, one or two older. By the time they get to be sixteen or so, most of them are done with skateboards and tricks. They'll go to church, be involved in youth activities, but only if they're coerced. Then they get their driver's license and their interests shift. Now the kids you worked with today—they're the ones who have developing spiritual needs going unmet. So they drift away.

"My father started coming to Stonewall the year it opened. Except for a revised prayer book, nothing much has changed in the church since. The choir marches in, something gets said, and the choir marches out. We sing irrelevant Victorian hymns in keys that normal people cannot manage. We worry more about how the candles get lighted than what is taught and, no offense, the sermons are usually safe and cerebral."

"And why would a kid want to go to a place like that?" Blake finished for him. He thought a minute, then added, "If I were to put together a service for them, follow the book, but ditch the structure, the dreary hymns and the choreography, if you know what I mean, say on Saturday or Sunday evening, would you help me with the kids?"

"I thought nobody would ever ask. Yes. And as for the lot, we can do something with it to make it more fun for the skaters, but they will be there anyway. Putting older kids in the picture makes more sense to me. The younger ones will follow them and build continuity over time. Why not put up basketball hoops and a beach volleyball court. That will bring them to the area. The rest is up to you."

◇◇◇

Betsy Bournet bore in on Blake the minute he walked into her living room. He assured her he thought Mary a charming woman, all a man could hope for, the sun and the moon and the stars, indeed whatever Betsy said, but no, he had not thought past the moment. No, he had not contemplated a symbolic gesture like a ring (a lie), and no, he had nothing else to report. Betsy looked disappointed and then said she would check back in a week.

The evening passed pleasantly. Blake played bridge, not well, but skillfully enough to hold his own. The conversation ranged over the current events in the nation and the city. He did not know much about the affairs in Roanoke. He barely knew the major players in Picketsville. Just when he felt comfortable and relaxed, Jackson Bartlett, Saint Anne's attorney, turned the topic to Stonewall Jackson and the murders.

"Has there been any progress, Blake?" he asked. Blake suspected his bland tone disguised a steely will. He had a reputation as a fierce prosecutor before he went into practice for himself. His connections in the city and Richmond brought him clients and a substantial bank account. Blake filled them all in on what they knew and what he supposed. Blake attempted to downplay Taliaferro's missing files, but did not get away with it. Bartlett's eyes narrowed and he bored in on him. He wanted details, reminding Blake that Saint Anne's stood to take a heavy financial hit if the matter were not resolved. Blake knew it, but could offer no hope for their recovery just yet. He told them about the ballistics and the emerging picture of Millicent Bass and Waldo Templeton being killed by the same person and perhaps for the same reason. After a half hour, Bartlett seemed to be, if not satisfied, at least temporarily mollified. The party broke up and the guests said their good-byes. Philip asked Blake to stay behind.

"I am terribly sorry about Bartlett," he said. "I had no idea he would cross examine you like that. He's a lawyer, you know, and that's what they do, I guess. I hope you don't think I brought you up here to have Jackson sandbag you."

"No, Philip, I don't. I think you brought me up here to have Betsy sandbag me."

"Well, that part is true. Betsy has a vested interest in Mary, and you, too."

"Philip, this is a stab in the dark, but Waldo left a list of names in his house. Some of the people on the list are from Stonewall Jackson, some are his neighbors, and rest we cannot identify. Do you know any of these people?" Blake pulled his copy of the list from his pocket. Philip's eyebrows rose and he cocked his head.

"Actually, I do," he said. "But I don't know what interest your late organist would have had in them. They are Saint Anne's parishioners."

Blake let that sink in for a moment.

"They're yours? Does anything else stick out, anything they may have in common?"

Philip studied the names again.

"Well, I don't think it means anything, but they are all people I referred to Tommy Taliaferro for counseling or therapy."

Chapter Forty-four

It came as another small shock to Blake when he realized he'd started looking forward to Sundays again. He had once before, a long time ago. But this was different. Then, Sundays provided not so much a chance to serve, as to be noticed. Then, he enjoyed, no, he positively basked, in the attention he received as a pastor and priest. When he preached, he expected favorable comments and compliments. To the extent such a day went well, he believed he fulfilled his calling to ministry. On those days when it did not, he assured himself that his parishioners had obviously missed the point. As a member of the clergy, he was not alone in that bit of cerebral hoop jumping.

But now, any thoughts he harbored for recognition were buried by a growing interest in the people around him. His eyes were still fixed on his doughnut, but now he also watched the hole with a renewed interest. He knew that if he continued to preach the way he did and promote the issues he felt strongly about, some of them would leave. He could accept, even welcome that. He just hoped the Mission Board would too. But in truth, he clung to the hope they would stay, would embrace change. He hoped.

His eight o'clock congregation drifted in and worshiped their God as only they knew how. They were wonderful people, Blake thought, but firmly rooted in the late nineteenth century, God bless them.

Mary arrived and turned on the organ and began to play. One by one the choir came in, music folders in hand, and practice began. Blake noticed the frown on Mary's face. She paused and manipulated the stops and voices. Then, apparently satisfied, she started again.

The congregation arrived in groups, and by ten-twenty the church was nearly filled. A surprise. It had never been this full before. The rule of thumb he had been taught years before held that in mainline churches, eighty percent of the available pew space occupied equaled one hundred percent occupancy. Today he guessed they were pressing ninety. Not bad, best he had seen so far. He supposed it must be a back to school, end of summer phenomenon.

The service progressed very smoothly. The improvement in the choir led to more congregational singing, and that, he thought, led to an improved spiritual environment altogether. He could not prove it, but he believed that music affected worship in a very important way and that the extent to which the congregation participated in music measured the impact the service had on each of them. He had never really noticed it before, although several friends and colleagues had mentioned it to him over the years. How the congregation became part of and benefited from worship never seemed important to him before.

And at that precise moment, Blake realized how much he, too, had changed in the months since he arrived. He shook his head and then, with a smile, walked to the crossing and began to speak.

"Our first lesson this morning is, as you no doubt noticed, from the apocryphal book of the Wisdom of Jesus Ben Sirac, usually known as Ecclesiasticus. Let me recite a few lines for you.

He that takes vengeance will suffer vengeance from the Lord, and he will firmly establish his sins. Forgive your neighbor the wrong he has done, and then your sins will be pardoned when you pray.

"We all know of the terrible things that have been visited on this church. I should tell you, by the way, that it appears that whoever killed Waldo, also killed Millicent. How these two murders are linked is anybody's guess. But it does seem clear to some of us that the verses I just read may apply. I cannot be sure, of course, but in my prayer time, before I decided on a theme for today's sermon, these words kept coming back to me. I have not experienced that sort of direction before, at least not with the intensity I felt then. I take it as a direction from God and suggest to you that he wants the killer to hear these words. I cannot say I am comfortable in this, and I have never done anything like this before.

"Moreover, I suppose it presumes whoever the killer is, he or she is within earshot and must be, therefore, one of us. That is not a comfortable thought. Then I asked myself, is this God speaking or just me talking to myself? I am sure many of you have felt this way in your own prayer life. Well listen again.

Does a man harbor anger against another, and yet seek for healing from the Lord? Does he have no mercy toward a man like himself, and yet pray for his own sins? If he himself, being flesh, maintains wrath, who will make expiation for his sins? Remember the end of your life, and cease from enmity, remember destruction and death, and be true to the commandments. Remember the commandments, and do not be angry with your neighbor; remember the covenant of the Most High, and overlook ignorance. Refrain from strife, and you will lessen sins; for a man given to anger will kindle strife, and a sinful man will disturb friends and inject enmity among those who are at peace.

"You see how it is? We have an obligation to stand before God without rancor in our hearts and anger toward our neighbor. Not just in the case of this terrible tragedy, but as a people of God who meet in this building on the Christian Sabbath and proclaim the Lordship of Jesus. We are a covenanted people. We are to be faithful to the commandments God gives us. Our hope is to become a community of faith, bound together in love and worshipping in community. We cannot do that if there is enmity in our hearts toward anyone, particularly anyone within the community.

"We will have communion shortly. We will stand in the real presence of the Lord at this rail. I suggest to each of you that, after we have said the general confession, and are to pass the Peace, you should seek out the person or persons, if any, you hold some anger for, or feel some distance from, or whom you may have slighted or hurt in the past, and offer yourself to them in peace. It seems to me that if there is anyone in the building with whom you cannot honestly share the Peace, you are not prepared for communion and should not come to the rail."

As he spoke, he realized that once again, he spoke words that were nowhere in his notes. Indeed, he had strayed away from them within moments of beginning to speak. God, he thought, what are you doing to me? The rest of his remarks were equally unplanned, and he closed with a prayer. Grace, he noticed, missed most of the message for what he assumed was an exit to the ladies room. At the passing of the Peace, a tearful Mary came to him and hugged him briefly. Lanny and several Board members followed suit. He watched the others from the corner of his eye and caught the awkward but, he thought, sincere attempts by many to shake hands with people they rarely acknowledged before. It was a wonderful moment.

He did notice the number of communicants who came to the rail dropped significantly and took that as a good sign. The recessional hymn produced a noticeable squawk from the organ, and Blake caught Mary frowning as she tried with not much success to work around it.

He finished with the hand shaking at the door and walked the length of the sanctuary to the organ, where Mary sat pulling and pushing organ stops and running scales.

"It's hopeless, Blake," she said. "This dinosaur has got to be looked at. The squeak has degenerated into a complete...well, you heard it, and it could all go blooey the next time."

"I'll call a repairman. Is there someone special?"

"This organ is from another age. The people who can understand the electronics, much less fix them, are few and far between. I think there is a sticker on the back with the company's name. Call them. They'll have to take the back panel off to work on the boards inside."

"You want to be there when they come?"

"I can't, I have to work. I'll write them a note. Oh, and by the way, the back panel is fitted with a lock. You'll need a key to open it. Do you have one?"

"I don't know. I suppose so. It must have been the one Amy saw on the ring with the organ key. I'll try to find it and leave it out for them. I'll try to have it done before Thursday and choir practice....Can I interest you in dinner tonight?"

"Dinner again so soon? What will people say, Blake? I wish I could, but I am going to a baby shower tonight. I'll tell you what, do you know that slab ice cream place next to the shoe store? Meet me there around nine-thirty."

Chapter Forty-five

Schwartz called at three in the afternoon. "You have any more passing thoughts?" he asked.

"No, not really, but I do have something for you. Do you remember those names neither of us could identify? Well, they are all members of Saint Anne's Church. And here's the good part—all of them were referred to Taliaferro for counseling or psychotherapy. Does that suggest anything to you?"

"Krueger had the files. Whoever killed him, wanted them."

"But who?"

"That's the sixty-four dollar question."

Blake sat on the edge of his bed. "How about this instead. Millie Bass finds out he took the files and wants them back. I think—no, I'm sure she did her research in them when my predecessor was alive. So, she kills him and takes the files. Then someone else, who is afraid of what she'll find, or has found, goes to her house to get them. Bass comes in, catches the guy and they struggle. The gun goes off and the intruder panics and runs."

"But not before shooting her two more times, and with her own gun? It's kind of thin, Rev. And that does not explain the other names, or the ones from Roanoke."

"No, it doesn't."

"Either way, you watch your back. If that message you got is for real, he or she thinks you have the files now, and you're next." He hung up.

Blake stared at the faded wallpaper in his bedroom, the phone dangling in his hand. He replaced the handset in its cradle and stepped to the front door. He had to release his new deadbolt to open it. Fresh air. He could smell rain. Gray clouds scudded in from the southwest, and the first drops of what promised to be a soaker dotted the steps. He closed the door and made a pot of coffee. While he assembled cups and saucers, cream and sugar, he mulled over what Schwartz told him. Secrets. Secrets and blackmail made a fine motive for murder. But Millie Bass did not qualify as a killer, he knew that instinctively. No, there had to be some other connection, and the files were part of it. Maybe if he could figure out what the local people had to do with the list, he could get the rest. Blackmail?

Mary said Waldo prowled the alley. Maybe he saw or heard something during those nightly walks that convinced him he could extract some money from them, too. The only thing to do was to start asking questions. Were the people on the list being blackmailed?

The phone rang again. This time it was Dan Quarles, sounding upset, very upset, his voice pitched a half octave higher than normal.

"Are you all right, Dan?"

"I'm fine. I need to talk to you, though. Can I come by tonight? You'll be alone, right?"

"Dan, tonight is not good. I am meeting someone at nine-thirty and don't expect to be back until eleven or eleven-thirty. Can we talk tomorrow?"

Dan hesitated but said he would think about it.

Mary waved to him as he walked across the mall. He shook his raincoat out and put it next to her umbrella.

"So tell me more about the theory that the two murders are connected," she said.

He told her about the files and the lists and the similarity of the killings, including the gun. "But what do you think?" she asked.

"I think we need to make another movie, only we can skip the airplane landing."

"You didn't like my airplane?"

"I loved your airplane, only you almost landed it in your mashed potatoes last time and, more importantly, it doesn't fit any more. The killer is local, therefore, no airplane. Let's suppose, hypothetically, that Waldo—"

"Walter/Waldo," she corrected.

"Walter/Waldo was a blackmailer and someone wanted to stop him."

"Well," she said, a frown creasing her face. "If he was blackmailing someone, they would pay, or if they ran out of money—"

"Wait a minute. Let's suppose that this someone—we'll call him Mister X, or Miss X, better make it just X. X is at a point where he or she cannot pay anymore. The spouse is suspicious, or the money is gone. X refuses to pay. Walter/Waldo threatens to expose him or her. X is desperate. Now what?"

"X goes to the church, waits for his or her chance and blam, Walter/Waldo gets a bullet from the three fifty-seven magnet."

"A thirty-two Colt automatic, actually. That would mean that whoever X is, he or she must be from Stonewall Jackson."

"Why?"

"Because no one else would know when Walter/Waldo would be alone. That eliminates everyone else on the list."

"I prefer that option. It gets me off the hook, but it doesn't necessarily follow. Suppose he had his victims come to the church to pay. The church is usually empty that time of night, and it would be a good time to collect his money."

"That's possible, of course, but it seems unlikely. He was a professional—a mobster. Those people don't usually foul their own nests. They keep their dark side separate from their normal life."

Mary finished her cone, dabbed her lips with her napkin and, screwing up her face, said, "Maybe he doesn't even meet his victims. He contacts them anonymously. He sends them some proof of what he has or calls on the phone. Then they send the money to a lock box or leave it in a particular place.

Walter/Waldo makes sure the coast is clear and takes the money. Nobody knows who he is or anything."

"It works, but how do they find him to kill him?"

"Walter/Waldo was smart, but not a genius. Somebody figured it out or, maybe, followed him back to the church. Then he or she confronted him...no, waited. That's it. X waits in the stairwell, maybe. Walter/Waldo comes in, or he's still there after choir practice. X sneaks up and, blam, shoots him with the whatever."

"That's better. But he was behind the altar. What's he doing there?"

"Well, he may have tried to get away."

"Okay then, X has to roll the body over to get at his keys. I suppose X used them to get into the house and then brought them back. That would take a pretty cool customer. No, that doesn't work either. The sheriff said the house was not tossed until after his deputies searched it. And then where does Millicent's death fit in?"

"Can't help you any more, Sherlock. It's late and Doctor Watson has to go home."

She gave him a peck on the cheek, and a look that nearly melted his ice cream.

◇◇◇

His watch read eleven-fifteen when he pulled up to the vicarage. The outdoor floodlights were out again. Usually if he kicked the pole they would flicker on. Not tonight. He jogged to the front door, his collar up against the rain, which had gotten heavier. Only the dim light from inside the house lighted his way. He wiped his feet at the front door and fumbled for his keys. Something, a movement seen out of the corner of his eye, startled him. He turned the key and shoved the door. As it swung open he heard a voice, a familiar voice, say, "Blake? It's me." And then it felt as if someone took a baseball bat and tried to hit a home run with his shoulder. The pain rocketed up and reached his brain at the same time it registered the pistol's report. He crashed headfirst into the house. He did have the presence of mind to kick the door shut and throw the deadbolt. As he rolled away, more bullets thumped against the door. He thought he heard someone scrabbling with a key set. He managed to call nine-one-one before he passed out.

Chapter Forty-six

It would be months before he remembered with any clarity what happened next. He heard voices calling. One sounded like Schwartz's. Somehow the room filled with people. Schwartz—was it Schwartz?—saying, "Is he going to be all right?" and someone else, "Looks pretty good to me, but we won't know until the docs say so." He recalled a jouncing ride on a gurney, and the slightly smoother trip in a boxy ambulance. He drifted in and out of consciousness. The comforting darkness of the ambulance was torn away by the eye-searing glare in the emergency room. He felt the hands on his back, the sharp jab of the needle in his arm. Somewhere in the confusion he heard the clang and rattle of metal in a bowl and Schwartz saying, "I'll take that." Then pain hit him and he passed out for good.

"It looks like he's with us, Sheriff. You can talk to him for five minutes, that's all." A voice, a very officious voice, a voice that brooked no dissent, in fact—the only voice that prompted the same obedience as God's—the voice of a head nurse.

"Can you talk, Reverend?" Schwartz sounded genuinely concerned.

"I guess I don't need a lawyer any more. I'm as good as I can be. What happened?"

"That's what I want to ask you. Somebody shot you. The bullet came in at an angle and glanced off your shoulder blade and lodged in the muscle in your neck. Another inch, they said, and you would be paralyzed from the neck down. You are a very lucky guy."

"Not lucky, Sheriff—blessed."

"Okay, blessed. We can roam that theological field someday when you're stronger, or I'm weaker. Now, what can you tell me about last night?"

Blake told him what he could remember, which was not very much. The nurse came in, shooed Schwartz out, and showed Blake how to push the little button that released the morphine drip. He pushed it and slid back into unconsciousness.

By the next afternoon, he felt better. His shoulder and arm ached, but he could move his fingers and decided he did not need the "pain button" any more. His lunch still sat mostly uneaten on the tray in front of him—thin yellowish soup and green Jell-O. He wondered if a pizza place would deliver if he called. He guessed they would not. He sat quietly praying, first in thanksgiving for the near miss that spared him paralysis and his life. Then, quite suddenly, for the other near miss—the one in Philadelphia, that could also have cost him his life, only in a different way. He never thought of it that way before. Until that moment, in fact, all he'd felt was anger and bitterness at the treatment he'd received.

"Forgive me," he murmured, "for being such a slow student and a poor servant." He guessed *stupid* would have said it better.

"I'm sure he will," Mary said from the door. She smiled and the room seemed infinitely brighter. And he felt very much better.

"You are the medicine I need," he said. "These nurses and doctors have no idea. All they need to do to empty these beds and restore the sick is to send you into the room and ask you to smile."

Mary blushed. He knew she would. It pleased him enormously. She said she could not stay very long. She had to get back to work. At his disappointed look she promised to come back that evening. She sat beside the bed and held his hand. They talked quietly, not about his wound or the violence that seemed to have engulfed the church and its people, but about the future, about what might be. He asked if she would stay and be their full-time organist. She grinned and said she would, and that made him feel even better.

The doctor walked in and said Blake would be able to go home in a day or two but that he was not to exert himself. He looked sternly at Mary when he said it, and she turned scarlet. Blake laughed so hard it hurt.

At three in the afternoon, Lanny Markowitz ushered in the quarterbacks and receivers from the football team. They filled the room with their size and noisy, embarrassed chatter.

"No more fifty-yarders for a while, huh Coach?"

"Maybe never again, Duane. Tell you the truth, I never threw the ball that far that often in my playing days. God gave me a little help to impress you guys, I guess."

He said he planned to be back by Thursday and he expected them to have practiced the drills he showed them. As they left, Lanny said, "You know, Dan Quarles resigned as Chairman of the Board Saturday night. He called and said he could not continue in good conscience. I asked what that meant and he said you would know. Do you?"

"First I heard of it, Lanny. I do know he seemed upset and wanted to meet with me, but we could never arrange a time that worked. He even tried to meet me last night, but I told him I would be late."

Lanny left, and Blake had a few minutes to reflect. Something, some force or forces were moving in his life, and they were good and bad. A struggle was taking place, and he felt his soul sat at its very center. Good and evil, innocence and guilt combined in a struggle, the outcome of which would forever change lives, his and those around him. He thought of Mary and of Gloria Vandergrift and marveled in the difference between them. Not Gloria's dark side, which, of course, was patently apparent to him now, but the other Gloria, the smart, fashionable and sophisticated woman, the archetype he used to seek out and desire.

"Where will all this end?" he said as if to append something to his earlier prayers.

"Where will what end?" Sylvia Parks came in laden with flowers. "You mean the shootings? Soon, I hope. I put my neck on the line with my son-in-law to get our boy Schwartz off the leash. He had better deliver soon or I will be in somebody's doghouse. Here, I brought you flowers and some news." Sylvia busied herself with a vase she found in the closet.

"What news?"

"You know Danny boy has quit the Board. I was with Philip Bournet yesterday when he quit. Philip was very solicitous—you know how he is—and then accepted the resignation. He turned to me and said something like, 'Well, I guess that means I'll have to find another board member,' and I volunteered to be it, at least for the moment. That works out well, because that means I can make the proposal for the new parish house."

"New parish house? What new parish house?"

"Well, that's what I went to see Philip about in the first place. I figured with the two hundred and fifty thousand we might realize from Millie's estate and the matching funds my husband will raise, we have enough to kick off a pretty good capital campaign."

"But...."

"Don't worry. I already talked to the Bishop. He dragged his feet a little and then said okay, provided no diocesan funds were committed. That's good, isn't it?"

Blake lay back on his bed. His wound started to throb again. Where was that pain button when you needed it?

"Sylvia, you are going too fast for me. Mind you, I appreciate the thought, and all the effort you've put into this, but decisions like these need to be the collective desire of the congregation as a whole. Otherwise they feel no ownership in the project and will not accept it. Please forgive me for saying it, because I know your heart is in the right place, but the last thing the church needs is a 'Lady Bountiful' coming in and building them a parish house they haven't dared to think about for forty years."

Sylvia looked annoyed and a crease formed between her eyebrows.

"Look," he continued, "we will want that building, probably in a year. You have set the plan in motion. Bring your resolution to the board, but leave out the parts about the Bishop and the certain money for now. Let the Board take it to the people and let us begin to build the desire. It should not take long. Then tell them about the Bishop and the money. Make sense?"

"You must think of me as an overindulged woman who is used to having her own way. Democracy is a tough discipline for those of us who think we already know what's best for everybody. Okay, we'll do it your way." And then she added, "…for now."

Chapter Forty-seven

Blake stared at the grey, overcooked roast beef swimming in a sea of suspicious brown gravy, the side dish of lukewarm apple-sauce, and the ubiquitous green Jell-O and sighed. Was he hungry enough to eat that or not? Schwartz stepped into the room, bringing with him the distinctive odor of fast food—fried, calorie dense, and nutritionally unsuitable Junk Food. Schwartz looked at the tray, shook his head sadly and said, "I thought so. I hoped I would get here in time." He picked up the dishes on the tray and dumped their contents in the trash. Then he placed a bag on the tray. Blake peered in—burgers and fries,complete with little pods of catsup, high-sodium dill pickles, and a caffeine-laced Coke.

"You deserve one of those life-saving medals for this, Sheriff. Tell me who to write and I will recommend you."

"Actually, that would be me. Don't bother. Unlike you, I have no snappy paneled walls to hang my honorifics on, but I appreciate the thought. By the way, the bullet they dug out of your neck came from the same gun used on Krueger and Bass. No surprise there. You look much better. Anything else come to you?"

"Did I tell you about the voice in the dark? No? It was—it said, 'It's me.'"

"'It's me'? That's it? It wasn't the voice from the tape?"

"It sounded familiar, like I had heard it before, but I couldn't be sure. It might have been the same one—I don't know....I suppose it had to be. So, now we have three shootings by the same person. All directed at someone in the church, someone on the staff of the church, in fact. What do you make of that?"

"I don't make anything of it. Being on the staff isn't important, I am sure of that, but being in a position to access the files is. They are the answer. Find the files, find the killer. By the way, you notice that the last two followed close on the heels of your sermons? You might want to tone them down a bit. You are driving people to homicide."

"Very funny. You have any more words of wisdom for me?"

"Three things—we have to find those files. I am sure they still exist and are stashed away somewhere. Whoever is doing the shooting knows it, and thinks you have them or you know where they are. The killer will try again, Blake. I'm putting a guard on the door, by the way. In the meantime, rack your brain. Where might those files be?"

"And the second thing?"

"That list of names—fingerprints."

"Krueger's and mine?"

"Just yours." Schwartz started to leave.

"You said three things. What's the third?"

Schwartz turned and looked at him.

"No offense, Reverend, but Billy told me the joke you used in church—the one about Moses and the Law."

"Yes...and?"

"Very funny."

"I'm glad you liked it."

"Right. Let me ask you something. If you heard that Rabbi Schusterman told a Jesus joke in synagogue, even if it was very funny, how would you and your congregation react?" He cocked one eyebrow, turned and left. Blake frowned. He'd never really thought about that.

"Out of my way, Billy," Rose Garroway ordered and pushed past a flustered Billy Sutherlin.

"Sorry, but I have to see some ID," he said.

"ID? Billy, I've known you since you were no bigger than a pup. What do you mean you need to see some ID?"

"It's all right," Blake said, "she's harmless."

"I don't know which I resent more," Rose snorted, "this boy thinking I'm dangerous, or you thinking that I'm not."

"Good evening to you, too, Rose," he said.

"Brought you some contraband," she whispered and produced a thermos of cocoa. "This ought to help you sleep, at least until they come wake you up to ask if you were asleep. Why do they do that, anyway?"

He put the thermos on his table, out of sight behind Sylvia's flowers.

"I also come bearing news. Are you ready? Here's the news from Picketsville," she said in measured tones, mimicking a talking head from the television station. "On the crime scene, Mrs. Grace Franks narrowly avoided arrest today when police, called at her neighbor's request, arrived to remove her burn barrel. Only the assurance of her beleaguered husband persuaded them to let her go after she tried forcibly to prevent them from hauling away the barrel.

"You know she's been at that for years. Apparently the thing almost exploded and the smoke and noise finally got to the people across the street and they called the cops. Big brouhaha down at the Franks'. Also of note—our own Amy Brandt, whom we all assumed was several cards short of a whole deck, has been accepted to graduate school. She's going to study particle physics, whatever that is, and so won't be able to come to Bible study any more. Our loss, physics' gain. Speaking of Bible study, we all voted to meet here or at your house if they let you out by Wednesday, so you don't have to worry about that. And—we are all very sorry about what happened. Do you think God has forgotten us?"

He smiled at the rush of words and the question.

"No, Rose, God never forgets. We frequently forget him, but it's never the other way round. I know that now. Someone in our midst has forgotten, however, and decided to solve her problems without him, and look where it led her. No, God is near and waiting for us to come to him in this."

"Her? You think the person responsible for all of this is a woman?"

"It seems so. Nothing is positive. Just a voice in the dark, but it sounded like a woman to me."

Rose looked distressed and left after a few minutes.

Blake lay back and relaxed. He reached for his thermos when Mary entered. She apparently had no trouble with the guard.

"You are just in time for some hot chocolate," he said. "Rose brought me this." And he hoisted the thermos.

"Not now," she said. "Too much caffeine in chocolate. I just came by to say good night."

"What's that?" a new voice interrupted. Blake took his eyes off Mary to notice the nurse in the doorway.

"Nothing," he said, feeling like a schoolboy caught with a comic book in his desk.

"Looks like something to me," she said and took the thermos, opened it and sniffed the contents. "Ah, a sleeping potion. Don't tell anybody you have this—there isn't enough to go around. Here, take this," she said and handed him a small paper cup with pills in it. He swallowed the pills obediently.

"Visiting hours are almost over, dear," she said to Mary. "Better drink up before you have to leave."

The nurse left and Mary sat down.

"You look better than you did this afternoon. Have you been behaving yourself?"

"I'm fine, Mary. Before I forget, I didn't call the repairman for your organ. I'm sorry."

"Of course you didn't. I'll call tomorrow. It's not that important, you know, not with everything else."

They talked for a while and then his medication kicked in. She was still holding his hand when he drifted off to sleep. His last thoughts were not, however, of her, but of his sermons. Ike wanted to know what he'd said that could have caused all this. Ike Schwartz had been joking. Blake wondered if it was a joke after all. Maybe the joke was on him.

Chapter Forty-eight

Wednesday morning Blake managed to ease down the stairs to the basement. He heard the sounds of the Bible Study members on the other side of the door. He let go of the banister and opened the door left-handed. They were all there. In fact, it looked like a lot more than the usual dozen. Twenty or twenty-five people were gathered around a sheet cake. They cheered as he came through the door.

"Please, don't sing," he said with a grin. "It will make me cry."

The cake had been decorated with what looked vaguely like a woman in black pointing a pistol at Quick Draw McGraw. *Ha Ha, you missed!* was scrawled in blue icing across the top.

"I guess this means we will not be spending any time with Matthew this morning," he said.

"Man does not live by bread alone, Matthew 4:4," Rose recited, "but he certainly can use a piece of cake now and then. Is that enough Matthew for one day?"

"I guess it will have to be."

After they had eaten and regaled one another by misquoting Bible verses that absolved them of any guilt for eating a scandalously rich cake, Sylvia asked, "Why would anyone want to shoot at you? I understand the reasons for Millie and Waldo but—"

"What do you mean, you understand?" Rose interjected. "What about Millie and Waldo? Why shoot them?"

Blake brought them up to date on the facts as he and the police understood them. They were shocked about the missing files.

"It's like a movie," Minnie said, clearly pleased.

"Hush, Minnie," Rose said sternly. "This is not a *Murder She Wrote*. This is serious and real." Minnie tried to look abashed, but failed.

"I miss that show," she said.

"Is there anything new?" Sylvia persisted. "Do you have any idea why you were shot?"

"Can't say, for sure. She must think I have the files or know where they are, or, and this is a guess, thinks I will soon find them and figures if I were dead, the case would turn in another direction, away from the files and what they might tell them about the killer, and toward something about me. Maybe they thought they'd get them after I was shot, but the door was locked."

"So you really don't have any idea where they might be?" Sylvia asked.

"Not a clue. But I will tell you this—if I did, I would destroy them immediately and make sure everyone knew it. Then the killing would stop."

"But you have to find them first. What if the police find them?"

"Then I guess they will be a step closer to the killer. I am positive whoever is behind this is a person with incriminating or compromising material in those files. And I think I have said enough— probably too much. Sheriff Schwartz will skin me alive."

"Well, this has been the most exciting Bible study I've ever attended," said Minnie. "It's too bad there aren't more exciting things in the Good Book to talk about. No offense intended, Vicar, but Jesus isn't exactly Clint Eastwood, is he?"

"Minnie," Rose protested, "what a thing to say."

"I'll tell you what, Minnie, when we finish Matthew we will take up the Book of Judges. Stirring stuff in there—intrigue, murder, war, and betrayal—Sampson and Delilah, Jael and Sisera. I call it 'The Book of Rambo.' You'll love it."

Cake eaten and coffee cups emptied, the group filed out with goodbyes and wishes for Blake's speedy recovery. Dorothy Sutherlin lingered.

"Vicar, when we cleaned up after the…you know…after Waldo, we missed some spots of….Well anyway, yesterday I came back with some cleaner Billy said you all used to clean up blood, and I got to crawling around on the floor and under the altar. Some spots we missed were under down there. Well, now, I bumped my head and sort of looked up and there it was."

"There what was?"

"This here key. It was velcroed up under the edge." She handed him a key. He took it.

"It looks like a spare organ key. Waldo probably forgot his keys once and put a spare up under the altar in case he did it again. Thanks." Dorothy left to catch up with the others.

He made his way slowly up the stairs to his office and collapsed into his chair. The wound started to throb and he felt exhausted. He started to put his head down on the desk when he saw the note. Mary had arranged for the organ repairman to come the next day, and would he please try to find the key to the back panel?

He rocked back in his chair and tried to remember—the key? The one on Waldo's ring locked the organ. What about this new one? Was it possible it did something else? But why would Waldo have hidden that one? He fished the key Dorothy just gave him from his pants pocket. It had gone in easier than it would come out. He had to struggle left-handed to retrieve it. He heaved himself out of the chair and made his way painfully through the sacristy, out into the sanctuary and across the aisle to the organ. He bent over slowly, trying to minimize the pounding in his shoulder. The key fit. He turned it and tugged on the panel. It dropped open quickly, as though it had been opened lately and often. His curiosity led him to pull it aside, and that is when he saw the files. They were stacked in the narrow space between two of the circuit boards. Somehow two or three of them had become dislodged and fallen against the circuitry and, presumably, caused the short that made the organ malfunction.

He forgot the throb in his shoulder and knelt down and retrieved the stack. He carefully replaced and locked the panel. He took the files to his office, shut and locked both doors. His heart pounded in his chest. The locks would not stop anyone who wanted to get in, but they would give him a warning if he had to make a dash out the other door.

He sat and arranged the files into stacks. That was when he discovered that there were other items in the packet besides files: newspaper clippings with dingy pictures that looked vaguely familiar, letters, a large manila envelope, some tape cassettes, computer discs, and folders. He reached into his desk drawer and retrieved the clipping he found in the vicarage. It was of the same vintage and topic and seemed to belong with the others. The thick manila envelope he set to one side. A quick inspection of the folders confirmed them to be Taliaferro's notes, each with the name of the patient on the tab. There were many more files than names on the list he found in Waldo's house. He supposed some of them contained no secrets.

He picked up the phone and called Schwartz. The sheriff was out. He told Essie Falco it was urgent and sat back to wait. Next, he turned his attention to the manila envelope. He pried open the clasp and dumped the contents onto the desk. Pictures, dozens of pictures, some of couples in less than innocent situations, taken through windows, some of people, mostly middle-aged men, getting in or out of cars or standing in front of hotels or houses, all taken with, he guessed, a telephoto lens.

He recognized only one person. Mary stood tall and beautiful, fresh from her bath, looking like Botticelli's "Birth of Venus"—only with darker hair. He fumbled through the stack until he found all her pictures. He took them to the shredder and destroyed them. The police, he decided, did not need to see them. He supposed the other pictures were Mary's neighbors caught in compromising situations. He also found the master draft of a note mixed in with the pictures. Waldo threatened to post the pictures on the Internet, or mail them to spouses or employers.

Schwartz called, and Blake told him what he found and asked him to hurry over. He was feeling a little faint. He checked one more time for any trace of Mary, and, satisfied there was none, replaced the pictures in the envelope and was fumbling with the clasp when he heard the footsteps on the stairs.

Chapter Forty-nine

A tap on his door. Blake froze.

"You in there, Vicar?"

He was alone in the church, could not move his arm, and a potential murder suspect stood outside his door.

"Vicar? I need to speak to you," Dan Quarles said.

Blake glided silently across the room to the other door. He could slip out and hide in the sanctuary. Dan knocked again. As Blake reached for the knob, he heard the sound of car doors slamming and children's voices. He glanced out of his window and saw them—Cub Scouts—a whole den of small boys in blue uniforms. Soon the basement would be alive with them. He was safe.

"Just a minute, Dan," he said and gathered the files and envelopes together and put them in a pile under his desk. He unlocked the door and gestured Dan in.

"Sorry for the delay. I got caught up in some paperwork."

"I'm glad I found you, Vicar. I have to tell you something. I meant to tell you sooner, but we couldn't meet Sunday, and then...well, then you were in no condition to see me. How are you, by the way?"

"I am fine most of the time. To tell you the truth, I could use some rest about now. Could we make this quick?"

"Sorry, yes. Well, it's this way...do you mind if I sit? I resigned as Mission Board chairman. You probably heard that by now. I wanted to explain why."

"Dan, I don't see—"

"Vicar, bear with me. Do you remember me asking about confession?" Blake nodded. "I asked you that question because I have a confession to make. But when you told me of the exceptions to the Seal of the Confessional, I hesitated."

Here it comes, Blake thought. He is going to tell me about Waldo.

"It's not about Waldo," he said. "Although in a way it is. I am not doing this very well. Look, I did you a great disservice. Because of that, I cannot continue as chairman."

"Disservice?"

"Yes. See, years ago I was accused of child abuse. It was when I was in seminary. Nothing happened, I swear to you, but at the time, many people, including my own family, turned against me. It was the worst time of my life. I will not go into the details, but it is enough to say that the child who accused me of terrible things made a convincing case. I had to drop out of seminary....I do not know why she did it, and if it had not been for her brother's testimony, I might be in jail today. But he realized that the joke they played on me had gone too far, and when he understood what the consequences to me might be, he finally told the truth. Even so, many of my friends and neighbors would never look me in the eye again. I moved out of state and started my life over.

"You understand the situation, of course. You were accused and, though cleared, had to leave your home and career. And that's the problem. You see?"

"I'm afraid I don't, Dan. I understand how you feel but don't see what this has to do with today."

"I was your severest critic, Vicar. When we got those letters, we did not want anything to do with you. Bournet insisted and made it clear we would accept you or he would close the church. You see, I should have known, or at least suspected, the accusations might have been trumped up. I, of all the board members, should have shown some mercy, but I did not. When we finally got the letters in the mail, it hit me. I am like the reformed smoker who is the hardest on the person with a cigarette in his hand. I came to say I am sorry and to ask your forgiveness."

Blake slumped in his chair. Fatigue washed over him.

"Of course, I forgive you, Dan. But let me ask you one small question. You know about the missing files. Your name appeared on a list we found in Waldo's house, and I gather you were seeing Taliaferro for counseling or advice. Can you explain why Waldo listed you?"

Dan stared at the floor for a moment and then, quite unexpectedly, pounded his fist on the desk.

"Someone sent me a blackmail note. I assume now it must have been Waldo. I did not know it at the time. The note came anonymously and demanded money in return for silence about the incident."

"But nothing happened; what could you be blackmailed for?"

"You know how it is when an accusation is made. It never goes away. Besides, there were the notes in the file."

"Notes?"

"I haven't told you all of it. Even though I never touched that child, never even went near her, I thought about it. Do you understand? Children have a way of knowing about adults, and that child instinctively knew that I was the perfect victim for her lies, because in my heart, it was not a lie. So I was guilty, in a way. I never could deal with that part. Dr. Taliaferro was helping me with those feelings."

"Dan, thank you for being so open with me. I want you to reconsider your decision to quit. I think I am going to need someone like you in my corner in the future."

"But I understand Sylvia Parks has already been appointed in my place."

"Sylvia can wait. Amy Brandt is going to graduate school soon, and Sylvia can have her place. Please stay."

Dan stood and shook his hand. He said he would pray on it and let Blake know soon. He passed Schwartz on the stairs.

"You look terrible," the sheriff said good-naturedly, "and I gather you have some news for me." He sat and placed a thick folder that he had brought on the floor beside him.

"The files. I found the files."

Blake told him about the organ and finding the files. He pulled them from under the desk and placed them in a stack on the desk. Schwartz sifted through them. He opened the envelope and raised his eyebrows at its contents. He rifled through folders, clippings, and letters. Finally he sat back and stared at Blake.

"This the lot?"

"That's all I found, except one clipping, the one about missing kingpins. I found it in my house before, if you remember. But otherwise that is it." Blake was aware of the shredder in the corner and felt his collar get hot.

Schwartz picked up his own folder and opened it. He placed copies of most of the pictures in a pile on the desk next to the originals. He scooped up the pictures of Mary and handed them across the desk.

"You'll want these, too," he said. "Don't say anything. I would have done the same thing. Now, let's see where we are. We have the list, so we can eliminate all the folders of people not on it. We can assume these pictures," he sorted some into one group, "are from Krueger's neighborhood, and the clippings and these other pictures are related to his other life in San Francisco. You don't recognize any of these guys, do you?"

"One or two look familiar, but that could be coincidence. All those guys look like they should be called 'The Silver Fox,' don't you think?"

"Well, the ones with hair, anyway. The rest look like the cast of *The Sopranos*. No names," he said, "too bad about that. There are some numbers, though. They must correspond to a list somewhere. Did you happen to see a list?"

"No, I got distracted with...." He looked sideways at the shredder.

Schwartz pushed a pile of letters at Blake, copies of the Philadelphia letters. "Except for that bullet you took, these would have kept you on the suspect list. So now we do police work. I will have to interview most of these people."

"How on earth will you ever sort them out?"

"Oh, it shouldn't be too hard. I'll ask them to supply an alibi for all three shootings. It's possible they may not be able to account for their time for one or two of the shootings, but the likelihood that more than one of them will be unable to account for all three is pretty slim. When we find that person, we have—" His cell phone interrupted him in mid-sentence. He scowled and muttered into the phone, and then his face brightened. He disconnected and turned back to Blake.

"You'll never guess what they found in the bottom of Grace Franks' burn barrel—a .32 caliber Colt automatic."

Ike welcomed Grace Franks' arrest, but something still nagged at him. Something someone said, something they weren't supposed to know. He called Ruth from his car.

"Late date?"

"Maybe a beer on the porch, but that's it, Ike. Bad day."

"More money problems?"

"Same money problems."

"Your people tentatively okayed a new tenant for your art storage facility," Ike said. "That should ease the strain a little."

"I'm afraid to ask. Who is it?"

"You don't want to know."

"Not your old CIA pals? Please tell me it's not them."

"Hey, it could be worse. They're discreet, tidy up after themselves, and are willing to pay a bundle to bury something in a place where no one would think to look."

"You really know how to put me on the spot, don't you?"

"For the good of women's higher education, not to mention your career—eat the crow and take the cash."

"Could they have a name?"

"You mean something like, *The Institute for the Advanced Study of Geopolitical Resources*?"

"Yeah. Something like...my God, that *is* the name, isn't it?"

"You have to admit, it has a nice ring to it."

"I've been had!"

Chapter Fifty

Thursday morning started warm and sunny. As the morning moved toward noon, it turned hot and humid as only that part of the country can. Summer made one last stand before being banished south and away for the next six months. Blake smacked the antique window air conditioner and breathed a sigh of relief when the compressor chugged back to life. He settled into his chair and sipped his coffee, his third cup for the day. The doctor told him to cut back, that the caffeine would elevate his blood pressure and cause his wound to throb. The doctor did not lie. He popped four ibuprofen and shuffled through the mail. He had neglected it for days, and gunshot wound or no, he still had a job to do. Sylvia poked her head around the door and said good morning.

"You here? I thought you were done with cleaning up those files," he said, slitting open an envelope, glancing at its contents and dropping it into his wastepaper basket.

"I was, but I figured with your bad shoulder and all, you could use some help for a few more days, although I can't promise you anything. I may have to go out of town."

"Well, I appreciate it. I guess you heard about Grace?"

"Only that the police think she is the person who shot you, Millie, and Waldo. What happened?"

"Schwartz will be here in a minute and can fill you in. Frankly, I probably don't know as much as you."

As if on cue, Ike Schwartz climbed the stairs.

"Well," he said, sitting in the only other chair in the room, "it certainly looks like a wrap. We have Grace Franks in custody and have a pretty tight case against her. It will be up to that son-in-law of yours to put her away," he said to Sylvia, who had pulled a chair in from the other room and seated herself by the door.

"You want to walk us through it, Sheriff?" Blake asked. "I still can't see her as a killer. I suppose she was one of Waldo's blackmail victims."

"You all understand that anything I tell you here can't leave this room. Are we all clear on that?"

Blake and Sylvia nodded.

"I guess you two earned it. When the deputies took Mrs. Franks' burn barrel, their only thought was to haul it away and toss it at the county landfill. One of them noticed a hole in the base, a round hole. The metal around its edge was still bright—that meant it was a new hole. It looked suspicious. Remember, the neighbor who complained and called the office said she thought she heard an explosion. That is what drew her to the window first, not the smoke from the barrel."

"Let me guess. It turned out to be a bullet hole," Sylvia said.

"Right the first time. So they rolled the barrel over to a clear place in the parking lot and dumped it. Lots of old half-burnt papers, ashes, and junk. And at the bottom—this."

Schwartz fumbled around in his pocket and produced a plastic bag with a discolored automatic in it. "This your gun, Reverend?"

Blake inspected the pistol through the plastic and shook his head. "I don't know, Ike. It could be. It certainly looks like my gun, or what's left of it. So you think Grace got in my house and took the gun?"

"I guess she must have. She has been lugging this thing around in that purse of hers for weeks. It has a clip that holds eight bullets, you know. Figure one chambered for a total of nine. Krueger gets two, Bass, three—that's five. You get one, two in the door—that leaves one chambered in the pistol. She thinks eight and out, drops it in the barrel and, bang. Anyway, we checked the ballistics and it is the gun used on you, Waldo, and the Bass woman. Now our lawyer friend here will probably say, 'Anyone could have put that gun in the barrel. What other evidence do you have?'"

"You got that right," Sylvia said. "You better have a tight case or I might take poor Grace on as a client and defend her. It would be a real hoot beating that wet-behind-the-ears son-in-law of mine in court."

"Well, in that case, I probably shouldn't say anything more."

"I'm kidding, Sheriff. Given what I've done so far, I'd have to recuse myself anyway. Proceed, please."

"Well, we hauled her in and questioned her. She swears she didn't know anything about the killings or the gun. She said, 'Why would I take his gun when I have one of my own?' A good question, by the way."

"She didn't want a traceable piece," Sylvia said. "I mean, if she had one of her own, there would be some trace on it, some history, wouldn't there? But if she uses someone else's, it introduces the element of reasonable doubt."

Schwartz eyed her steadily for a moment, his expression blank, dark eyes unblinking.

"There is that, of course," he said slowly. "Well, anyway, she did not have an alibi for any of the times when the killings and shootings took place. I should add she is an excellent shot with a handgun, Blake. You're lucky she missed the first time. Her father collected guns, all kinds, and taught her how to shoot, and about ammunition, safety, and so on."

"It's still circumstantial," Sylvia pressed.

"Then there are the fingerprints," he continued, ignoring her interruption. "We found them in the sacristy, Bass' house, on some of the papers in the office, and—this is the clincher—a partial we are sure will be hers, on the gun."

"How could there be a fingerprint left on it?" Sylvia asked. "It has been in the fire. Look at it. The grips are melted and it's a mess."

"Well, that's an interesting point. It seems some people, in high-stress situations, excrete more electrolytes, salt and organic compounds in their perspiration than others." He looked at the quizzical expressions on their faces.

"I learned all this from the kid in the lab. Anyway, this salty stuff will precipitate out on the metal. When it is heated, like in a fire, it etches the metal like acid. So we have a partial."

"That's pretty definitive," Sylvia said, frowning. "You're sure about that print?"

"As sure as I can be, given the state of the art. There'll only be a few identity points, four maybe, I think, and six is sort of the accepted minimum needed to convince a jury, but when you put it all together...."

"Sounds like you got your killer," she said brightly.

"But why, Ike? What drove her to it? What did Waldo have on her that drove her to murder?" Blake asked.

"It seems she was having an affair with the guy next door. Poor man has an invalid wife. Mrs. Franks has a clod for a husband. They sympathized with one another and then, well, you can imagine. Funny thing about that—Franks, the husband, said he knew all about it and they were working it out. He took her to the beach recently to talk it through. But I guess she'd gone too far by then."

"I still don't see how she's connected to Waldo," Sylvia said. "I thought he worked anonymously, somehow."

"Why did you think that?"

"If he hadn't, as soon as he got shot, you would have heard from at least one of his victims and you would have had a motive. The FBI might never have been called in the first place."

"Very astute. Actually he did. She admitted she received a note from someone threatening her and giving instructions to leave money in a certain place. She did, and she must have followed him back here. She denies it, of course, but I don't see any other way."

"So she follows him back here, waits for the moment and shoots him," Sylvia said. "You left out the business with the water bottle."

"Yeah, why did she use the bottle?" Blake said.

Schwartz paused and seemed to study the two of them. "She must have picked it up from the trash on the way in."

"Then she thought her problems were over until she hears something that Bass said that convinced her that the files, and therefore the potential blackmailer, had moved. There must have been a confrontation, and that explained the next killing."

"But why me?" Blake asked. "Surely she didn't think I had the files. I told the Board that. Bob Franks is on the Board, and though he was not at the meeting, he knew. Dan Quarles told him."

"That part I think I can figure out," Schwartz said. "As I said, she spent the evening denying everything, but she did say that you, Reverend, were the cause of all her problems."

Chapter Fifty-one

"Me? Why me?"

"I warned you. I said you should check your sermons—that all the shootings followed one, and here we are, Reverend. It seems your preaching the last three Sundays caught her—'convicted me,' she said. Every time you made a point about adultery or anger, or forgiveness, she thought you were looking straight at her. Thought you knew about the affair and therefore must have seen her file."

"That's it?" Sylvia asked.

"Pretty much. I have one or two loose ends to tie up, and then I'll turn it over to your boy," Schwartz said and stood.

"Thanks, Ike," Blake said. "I would get up and walk you out, but I am in no condition to. My sermons, huh?"

"Just quoting the lady. You should be more circumspect in the future. I'm not all that keen on corpses popping up all over town every Monday."

"Yeah, yeah. I'll go see Grace in the morning."

"You'll do what?" Ike and Sylvia said in unison.

"Go and see her. Whatever she may have done, she still needs ministering."

"Get someone else," Schwartz said sharply. "You are our star witness. If you are caught talking to the defendant anytime before trial, you compromise the case. Tell him, Madam Lawyer."

"He's right, you can't do it. Ask Bournet or someone else to go. Don't even return her calls." When Sylvia said it, it sounded like an order.

"That's it for now," Ike said. "We'll just tie up a few loose ends and—"

"You don't still have some doubts?" Sylvia asked, face serious.

"It's like a jigsaw puzzle. I still have a few pieces missing. You know how that is. Seems pretty good, but...too bad one of your parishioners had to be the heavy in this, Reverend."

He left. Sylvia watched him disappear down the steps, a frown on her face. Then she rolled her chair around the corner and back into her space. Blake stared at the paneling on the wall. His eye wandered over his diplomas and certificates. They were the proofs of his intellectual and career achievements, years spent in the pursuit of position and power. A very impressive array, he thought, but not worth a cold fried egg when it came to working with people. That skill came from the heart, not from the head. Cerebral machinations could not equal a tear, a pat on the arm, a respectful silence. A few minutes later, Sylvia called out that she was sorry but she had to leave. Blake said goodbye.

Something nagged at Blake. Something someone said, or the way they said it, something did not fit. Schwartz reminded him of jigsaw puzzles. He once attempted one and got one piece out of place. The pieces looked so much alike, it was possible to force two together that really did not belong, leaving pieces that did not fit anywhere. That one misplaced piece stymied him for days. He finally had to pull almost all of it apart and start over before he finally finished. He sensed a piece out of place somewhere but he could not see where.

He slept most of the afternoon. He would never recommend getting shot, but it did get him off the hook from a number of chores he might otherwise have had to do. Besides, he wanted to be ready and refreshed for the evening. He planned to attend choir rehearsal that night. Afterward, he was going to have some time with Mary and, if he had the courage, tell her something he had never told any woman since he was sixteen.

At seven, he polished off his microwave meal, dropped the plastic dish in the trash, and walked to the church. The choir, minus Bob Franks, filled their pews and greeted him as he entered. He sat where he was out of their line of sight but had a clear and unobstructed view of Mary.

The rehearsal went well. As far as he was concerned, he was listening to the Mormon Tabernacle Choir. He found himself humming along and then, in response to several disapproving looks from the back row, stopped. The session ended at eight-thirty. The choir filed out and he was left alone with Mary.

"The organ suitable?" he asked. He knew it was.

"Fine. Actually more than fine. How's your shoulder?"

"Better every day," he said. The silence after he said it began to stretch into awkwardness.

"Well," she said, "I'd better be off." But she made no move to leave.

"Mary?" he said and cleared his throat. The phone rang in the sacristy. "Excuse me," he said, temporarily relieved, and went to answer it. He picked up the receiver.

"Blake? It's me," the voice said.

"Grace?" he stammered.

"No, it's Sylvia."

"I'm sorry, Sylvia, I didn't recognize your voice. After our session with Ike, I have Grace on the brain. What can I do for you?"

"I have to leave town and I wanted to talk about the board position. Dan withdrew his resignation. He said you told him to. I'm a little hurt, Blake. I thought we had an understanding." Her voice was harder than he remembered, harder and edgy.

"It's no problem, really, Sylvia. Amy Brandt will be resigning soon. By the time you return, there will be a place—"

"I still need to see you. There is more to this than just a board membership, as you know. Tonight?"

Blake's face knotted into a frown. "All right, meet me here in the church."

"I'm on my way."

He stood staring at the phone for nearly a full minute. He went back to the organ. Mary had gathered her things. She looked at him expectantly.

"Mary," he said, "I have two things I need to tell you. One of them is extremely important and the other extremely rude. I want you to hear the first and forgive the second."

She stood still, waiting.

"Mary, I love you. I love you very much. But I want you to leave right now. Go home, get out."

"Blake?"

"Please, Mary. Hear the first. Do the second. I'll explain later."

"I love you, too, Blake Fisher," she said, and left.

Chapter Fifty-two

He almost missed hearing the door close. Because of his bandages, he had to sit slightly sideways in his chair, and that made it creak when he swiveled. It did so as he quietly closed his desk drawer and faced the door. Then he was sure. He heard the footsteps on the stairs.

"Anybody here? Blake?"

"In the office, Sylvia. Just finishing some paperwork and calls. You know how it is, no rest for the wicked."

Only his desk lamp illuminated the room, leaving the rest in deep shadows. The door to the sacristy stood slightly ajar. The pool of light cast by the desk lamp lighted Sylvia from the waist down as she crossed the space from door to chair and sat, purse in her lap. Once seated, he could just make out the contours of her face. The dim light exaggerated the streaks in her hair and cast deep shadows on her face. The effect was a little frightening. As always, she was beautifully turned out in a dark gray silk suit and eggshell blouse. He guessed her purse alone cost five hundred dollars. He recognized the accessories from another life, a life now far removed, probably never to be his again. This woman could change all that. He had no option but to wait and see.

"I was very upset when I heard you'd convinced Quarles to stay on the board. Can I ask why? I mean, we have a lot of work to do, and that man is not the person to get it done."

He watched her carefully. This kind of woman could always fool him. He did not see it coming with Gloria Vandergrift. But this time, he would not be taken in. This time he would see it through, even if it killed him. He stayed seated, unmoving.

They both sat in the semi-darkness, faces caught in the yellow glow of the lamp light. Finally he said, "You didn't come over here tonight to talk about the board, did you?"

She did not answer right away. Her eyes bored into him as if she were trying to read his mind.

"You know, don't you?" she said finally. "You figured it out. I knew it as soon as I said it. It was stupid of me. You called me Grace. That's when you knew, am I right?"

"Yes, not entirely sure then, just suspicious. Then I remembered the water bottle."

"What water bottle?"

"The one you used as a silencer when you shot Waldo. I never told anyone about the bottle. Schwartz never told anyone either, but you knew. You said something like, 'You left out the part about the bottle.' Do you remember? I knew something was out of place this morning but couldn't put my finger on it. Then you called and said, 'It's me,' and I recognized the voice. The voice I heard when I was shot. When you're excited, you lose your nice, cultured way of speaking, Sylvia, and revert to a nasal, what—New York, New Jersey? Not Philadelphia. I'd know that one."

"Jersey."

"So…yes, I know, but I don't know why. I guess all that will come out at your trial."

"There isn't going to be any trial, except for Grace Franks. She's the killer, remember? Our slow but predictable sheriff will see to that." She removed a light automatic from her purse and pointed it at him. "Now the question is, what shall I do with you?"

"Do me a favor, Sylvia. Before you decide and shoot me again, tell me why. I think I've earned it, don't you?"

"You want to hear my confession, Father?"

"Something like that. Who knows, I might even give you absolution. Either way, I'd like to know why I have to die."

"Of course you would. Hand me one of your water bottles, please, I'm a little dry, and I may need it in a minute or two."

Blake handed her the bottle and opened one himself.

"How much do you really know about Krueger?"

"Only what we talked about. He held some kind of insider position with the San Francisco mob, and he was about to rat out most of the leadership. I gather the feds had slated him to sing to a grand jury, but he jumped their ship."

"He was all those things and more. He managed the books. He knew where the money came from and where it went to be laundered. Money laundering is a very important part of organized crime. Did you know that?"

"I heard, but it didn't mean much to me."

"Believe me, it is. There are some men who specialize in it—make it a career. A man can make a lot of money in that business. The skim can be as high as ten percent. You figure out what that comes to in a two billion a year business."

"A lot of money, but what has that to do with us?"

"Not with us, Blake, with me. How do you think my husband made all his money? He's their east coast money manager. When the feds picked up Krueger, we all ran for cover. Luckily, Krueger didn't have names. That was a security precaution my husband insisted on. We were just numbered accounts. He put money in and took it back later. The only time my husband might have come in contact with him was when he went to San Francisco for a meeting. Krueger was never allowed to be part of those meetings, so there was no reason to think we had a problem. But Krueger was a resourceful man, and if he didn't get a name, he got a picture. He had a camera with a telephoto lens on it."

"I know about his camera."

"Do you now? Ah, so that's what he had on your little goody-two-shoes girlfriend. What did he catch her doing, Blake? Shall I guess?"

"You were telling me about Krueger and your husband."

"Nothing too naughty, I hope. Well, yes. Robert never met Krueger. How were we to know he would show up here as an organist? You want to figure the odds on that? My husband is not much of a churchgoer, but he came to your installation as a favor to me, and Krueger saw him. Two months later we got a newspaper clipping in the mail."

"CRIME KINGPINS STILL AT LARGE," Blake recited. "You left it in the vicarage. Is that when you took my gun?"

As she spoke, Sylvia's carefully measured speech slowly flaked away and east Jersey emerged.

"I wondered what happened to it. Yeah, that's when I lifted your gun. I didn't have a reason to. It just seemed like a good idea at the time. You never know when you will need a cold piece. It turned out to be a stroke of genius. Then we get a call. Krueger had his picture on the TV—dumb bastard, and I get a commission to snuff him. I'm setting that up, you know, we are sort of settled in here and I don't want to have to blow town, so I think, I'll take my time on this one.

"So anyway, this note comes telling us where and when to leave the money—a lot of money, by the way. Do you believe that? Krueger thought he had his backside covered. The jerk didn't have a clue he'd already been fingered, but you know how it is with guys like that. They always make a mistake somewhere along the line. I wait for the moment and…you know the rest."

"You shot him, not your husband?"

"Robert's a killer in the financial markets, not on the ground. He faints at the sight of blood. I'm the shooter. That's how we met. I pick up a job in San Francisco and he's in it and we hit it right off. Funny, isn't it? I have my specialty, he has his. No, I capped Walter and now I am going to send you off to that heaven of yours."

"Why did you wait so long to kill him? I mean if he'd been fingered—"

"I like it here and I needed time to set up a patsy to take the fall. He wasn't going anywhere."

"It's none of my business, but how did you come to be a…whatever you're called?"

"A killer. That's the word you're searching for, and since you are about to become a score, I guess it is your business. My old man ran a tire store in Camden. He sold new and used tires—retail and wholesale—stuff like that. One day the guy who sells us protection asks him to handle some merchandise that they will supply. It's not like we had a choice, so my father says 'Sure.' And that's how we got dug in."

"Stolen tires and—"

"You could say. Well, one day this mook shows up and threatens us. He's figuring to muscle in on the other guy's territory. So, we call our guy and we think it's all taken care of, you know? But then the creep comes back. He's busted up pretty good by a guy we know named Angelo, who I hear bought it around here somewhere, but I don't know about that for sure because he went solo. Anyway, this piece of crap starts in on my father. I come in and he's got him on the floor and is kicking the shit out of him, so I go to the drawer, get the little .32, and blow him away. That's how it started. Pretty soon, I had me a full-time job. End of story."

"And law school? You are a lawyer, right?"

"Seton Hall, part-time. A reward for being good at what I did for the locals."

"You're still not finished, Sylvia. What about the list? You weren't on the list I found in Krueger's house."

"Oh, my husband had a place on his list, the original list. The one you found was one I left in its place. Adding your name was, like, an afterthought. Good, huh?"

"That explains it."

"Explains what?"

"Why there were no fingerprints on the paper. How was that to be explained, do you suppose?"

"Who'd notice?"

"Schwartz did."

"Woo-hoo!"

"And the search?"

"Easy. After I shot him, I took his keys, copied his house key so I could look later—after the sheriff and his boy scouts got all done. See, they wouldn't know what they were after 'til later anyway, and that way, they'd be screwed big time trying to figure out how the place got tossed after they'd already searched. I looked for his stash. I didn't care about Taliaferro's files. I just wanted whatever he had on us. I didn't find anything but I thought the list would point the police in the right direction. Then, see, if I'm part of 'the team,' I can get there first. After all, the sheriff's office does not have any mental giants working for them, do they? You ever met the Sutherlin woman's kid? The village idiot. That's why I had my son-in-law free up our friend Sheriff Andy—Ike—to run the investigation. I figured in a shed full of dull tools, he's most in need of sharpening. It worked pretty good I thought. Then later, I went with you to Krueger's house—that would explain my fingerprints. I volunteered to help out here, same deal with the fingerprints, and when I visited Millie, she did all the searching, no problem there. You see how it works, Blake. The winners are always a step ahead of the losers."

"What about Millie? Why'd you kill her?"

"Oh, that. I took that silly bitch, Grace Franks, to lunch one day. I'm listening to her moan and groan—what a turkey—I'm getting ready to plant the gun in her purse and then have the cops find it on her. I figured she was one of Krueger's marks, but while we're sitting there, we hear Millie yammering about people and Grace's name pops up. That's when we both decide Millie has the files. Grace almost passes out. I decide to keep the gun for a while. Later, I go to Millie's house to pick up the files. She's a pretty stupid woman, you know. We wasted a lot of nice words on her last Friday.

"She says she didn't have them, you do, and finally, after I make her turn her house upside down, I believe her. I couldn't just leave her after all that, could I? So I popped her, too."

"And me, why shoot me? By then, you knew I didn't have the files."

"Me? I didn't shoot you, Grace did, remember? See, I knew she was ticked at you because she thought you were blabbing her secrets. I had to stay close to her to make sure she had no alibis. She told me she'd called you, so I sort of let it be known to other people what she said. Too bad I didn't get to finish you, though. Would've saved a trip over here tonight."

"Must have made you angry, you being the pro and all."

"Pissed me off. I never miss."

"If you never miss, how come it took two shots for Waldo?"

"It's my style. I always shoot twice, one to stop 'em, one to drop 'em."

"But you missed me."

"Yeah, you're pretty quick. And I didn't know about the damn deadbolt. Actually, it didn't matter much. Remember, it's Grace that missed you. Made her more human, I think."

"But lucky for me. So it was a hit all along. Killing Krueger had nothing to do with Taliaferro's files, local blackmail, or anything else."

"That's about the size of it."

"And now you plan to shoot me?"

"Got to. Sorry about that. Things were just starting to get good around here." She smiled and leveled the pistol at his head.

"Before you do that, one last question—how do you plan to kill me? I mean there will be another investigation. Someone will put all those clippings and pictures sitting in Schwartz's evidence locker together and come looking for your husband. Did you know about the photographs? I bet your husband is in one of them. Sooner or later, they will find you."

"Not this time. They don't have a clue, see, because Krueger is dead. Who's going to say who's who? Besides, I'm not going to shoot you. You're going to shoot yourself."

"Really? Where did I get the gun? Mine ended up in Grace's burn barrel."

"No, no, Blake. This is your gun, pretty nice, too. Needs some work, but you kept it good. No, the one in the barrel is its twin, one of mine. You're going to commit suicide with your own gun which, naughty boy, you reported stolen. Shame on you, Padre, you should not tell fibs to the police."

"And you think they will buy a suicide?"

"Schwartz? Are you kidding? I told you he's dumber than a box of rocks. And he'll believe it because my son-in-law, the Attorney General, will tell him to. And besides, what reason would he have not to?"

"So I am going to blow my brains out. Why?"

"Oh, the tragedies of the past weeks have preyed on your mind. Then, there is your drug habit, which explains the crack cocaine I hid in your luggage in one of those upstairs bedrooms. But mostly, you are feeling guilty for what you did to that bimbo in Philadelphia."

"I didn't do anything to that woman."

"Who cares? In your note, which I will type on your computer, you will confess that you really did assault her. You took advantage of the fact she was known to be a person who misrepresented relationships with men all the time, so you 'had your way with her' as they used to say. Do you think she will deny it? You are, after all, a very moral guy and you would want to clear the record, wouldn't you? Of course, you would. What's her name, by the way? I want to get the spelling right. I don't want to give the sheriff a mental hernia when he does his snooping."

"Gloria Vandergrift. You two have a lot in common."

"Who? Me and the Philly dame? Good for her. I wish her well. Vande…spelled with an 'e' or an 'er' in the middle?"

"An 'er'. What makes you think I will let you walk over here and pull that trigger? I have at least one hundred pounds on you and weak as I am, I can still knock you silly, gun or no gun."

"It's like this," she said and drained the last of the water from her bottle. "I'm going to shoot you from over here with this silencer I'm going to make. Then I am going to put the gun in your hand." She stood and took careful aim.

Chapter Fifty-three

The office suddenly blazed with light.

"That's it. Put the gun down," Ike Schwartz barked. One hand held his service .357 magnum less than a foot from Sylvia's temple; the other still hovered over the light switch.

"What took you so long?" Blake rasped. "I've been asking her questions forever since she admitted killing Krueger."

"Wanted to hear it all. Figured something like this would be my only chance, so I let you hang for a while. You were never in any danger."

"The hell he wasn't. How did you get in here?" Sylvia spat. "I locked the doors."

"I have a key," Ike said. "Everyone has a key. You are cooked, lawyer lady. Nice of you to spell it all out to Blake. He will testify to it in court."

"It's 'he says, she says,' and I can beat it."

"And this young deputy who came in with me heard everything you said as well, didn't you, Billy? Excuse me. This is Billy Sutherlin, sometimes referred to by folks from New Jersey, who don't know any better, as the village idiot. He will back him up."

"You were out there all the time?"

"Most of it."

"That's entrapment. None of this will be admissible."

"Wrong again. You invited yourself over here."

"Bullshit. I say Fisher called me and told me to come. He threatened me if I didn't."

Schwartz heaved a sigh. "Cuff her, and read her rights, Billy. You know, you were right about one thing, though. The bad guys always make a mistake. We know that you asked to come here, therefore, no entrapment. No, no." He waved off her protest. "The phone lines have been tapped ever since Blake got the threatening phone call. Blake insisted it be a court-ordered tap, by the way. If you were closer to your wet-behind-the-ears son-in-law, you would have known that. It was the missing puzzle piece, you see. Then Blake called me and here we are."

"You will never make this stick."

"Oh, I will."

"You said yourself, the etched print on the gun matched Grace's. How are you going to explain that?"

"The fingerprint? You mean the one caused by electrolytes and fire? Well, I'm sorry about that. There never was any print. I made that bit up. Sounded good, didn't it. But acid etched in the fire…? See, as good as Mrs. Franks looked for the murders, I never liked her for them. I worry about something that's practically handed to me on a plate. Puzzle pieces. There was the key on Krueger's ring. He was a meticulous man. He arranged all the keys with the cut sides facing the same way. Someone took one off the ring and then replaced it wrong way out. The question was—who and why. Certainly not Grace Franks. And then there's Floyd. I have associates living in Floyd. They are a suspicious bunch—part of their history—and they tell me things. What ever made you decide to live there, I wonder."

While Ike talked, Sylvia's expression changed from overconfidence to uncertainty.

"You have a weak case, Sheriff, and I've got friends in places that can make it go away."

"Yeah? Maybe so, but worst case, it's my jurisdiction, don't forget, and I have enough to hold you over for arraignment. We can make a case for attempted murder. Blake can positively ID you for his shooting. That gets you behind bars. Other charges may or may not stick. I don't care. Do you want to know why I don't care?"

Sylvia glared at him.

"See, once your pals in San Francisco find out you've been talking to the police and the FBI, you are as good as dead. They will find you and rub you out. And what can poor, dumb Sheriff Andy do about that?" Ike shook his head sadly. "You know what I think? I think you need to get yourself a really good lawyer who can cut you a quick plea bargain and maybe a deal for protected solitary. Then you just might live to see your grandchildren, assuming, of course, they'll want to see you."

Sylvia's face turned ashen. Blake guessed she now realized her chances for survival were slim to none, even in prison.

"I sent a car over to pick up your husband. We have him as an accessory after the fact. My guess is, he's smarter than you, and will give you up and then deal himself into the Witness Protection Program and rat out the rest. Don't you just love it when all the pieces finally fit?"

"What if I deal first?"

"Sorry, murder is non-negotiable, and besides, it's your husband who has the information the FBI wants, not you. No, it's the slammer for you, lady. Take her out," he said to Billy, who grinned and led her away reciting her Miranda rights.

"You know, for a dumb country cop and a Reverend from Philadelphia, we did a pretty good job of work tonight."

"Reverend is not a noun. How many times do I have to tell you?"

"It's a Commonwealth of mind, then."

Blake laughed and then winced at the stabbing pain in his shoulder. "It's been a long day, and nobody will ever accuse you of being dumb again, Ike, least of all me."

Schwartz left humming the theme from *Rocky.*

Blake lifted the phone and dialed. A sleepy Mary Miller picked up on the sixth ring.

"Hi," he said. "I didn't want to wake you but I wanted to apologize for being so rude tonight."

"You don't have to, Blake. You are not the kind of man who would deliberately hurt someone. I know that now. If you told me to leave, it must have been for a very good reason."

"It was. And now the whole business is over. Mary?"

"Yes, Blake."

"The other thing I said to you, I meant it."

"Me too. G'night."

Epilogue

Rose Garroway, in spite of her horrific typing and total lack of computer skills, had installed herself as secretary *pro tem*. She fussed over Blake and tried to make his recuperation as easy as possible. But he knew he needed to hire someone permanently, and soon.

"Big news, Rose," he called around the door.

"What?"

"I'll let you know in a minute. Can you get Philip Bournet on the phone?"

A moment later she shouted, "He's on."

Blake heard the footsteps on the stairs as the Wednesday Bible Study began to assemble in the outer office.

"You might as well use the speaker phone, Rose, since you were going to listen in anyway. It will be easier for the others, too."

"Blake, I never…."

"Philip, I have some amazing news."

"I heard, but I would never have guessed that Sylvia Parks could do such a thing. I thought the husband might be a little shady, you know, but never dreamed he was involved in organized crime—the Mafia and all that."

"That's not the news I had in mind."

"There's more?"

"Yes, but first, you can tell your charming Betsy she can stop worrying about her plans for Mary Miller. We have that under control. The news, Philip, is I just got off the phone with Bishop Farnsworth. You remember the woman who caused me all the trouble in Philadelphia? Well, she got caught in a sting operation—went to the well once too often, I guess. At any rate, I have been exonerated and am now officially in good standing. Funny thing about honor and truth—no one would believe me when I said I was innocent, but when Gloria Vandergrift was splashed across four channels in a very badly reported and quite inaccurate story on the eleven o'clock news, everyone became a believer."

"That's wonderful news, Blake."

"No, sorry, that's just the background, so to speak. Here is the news—Farnsworth offered me the job of Dean of the Cathedral."

"Well, that really does warrant congratulations. It is what you always wanted, Blake. You are only a very short step from a mitre cap and crosier. Shall I call you Bishop now or wait a year or two?"

"Not anytime soon. I turned him down. I'm not going. I want to stay here and be the vicar of Stonewall Jackson Memorial Episcopal Church. There is work to do here and it's real work. That is, if it's all right with you."

"Of course it's all right, but are you sure? You're walking away from a big opportunity. This part of the world isn't known for producing many bishops. Are you sure?"

"I am. But I don't think I can get Stonewall Jackson to independent status in the time left, though."

"I don't care about that, Blake. I told you before, I don't need a mission in Picketsville, but apparently God does and he wants you to be its vicar. Take all the time you need…and Blake?"

"Yes?"

"God bless you."

Blake cradled the telephone and stared at the wall.

"I don't believe I did that," he said aloud, addressing a faded print of Archbishop Cranmer. "A year ago I would have given my right arm for what I just turned down."

"Is that because you did not want it, or because you don't have much of a right arm left to give at the moment?" Rose asked through the door.

"What do you think? Did I make the biggest mistake of my life, or what?"

"Well, me and the rest of the girls are divided on that." He heard them murmuring in the background. "We are divided on the job thing, but unanimous on how happy we are you will stay here with us. Here's one person who is beyond happy," she added and pushed a tearful Mary Miller around the corner. Rose stood beside her and proffered a box of Kleenex.

"Here," she said, "blow. She's a little choked up right now, Blake—can't talk just yet. Oops, add blushing to choked up."

Mary managed one of her thousand-watt smiles and dabbed at her eyes.

"Let's go, girls," Rose ordered, "no Bible study this week either. You two—try to behave."

◇◇◇

"You should get this car washed," Ruth said and kicked at a crumpled coffee cup near her foot.

"Guys on maintenance duty are supposed to do that," Ike said.

"So, what's the holdup?"

"It's a very small operation—Billy to be precise. It may take a while now that he has acquired some stature in the community for collaring Ms. Parks." He grinned. Some things never change.

"What's funny?"

"You haven't said anything about my scent."

"Is that Hugo Boss?"

"I thought men were the only species that couldn't tell one scent from another."

"I'd know Old Spice."

"You're sure?"

"Absolutely."

"This *is* Old Spice."

"Isn't."

"Male pheromones are all pretty much alike."

"Give me a break, Schwartz. And what am I supposed to do with those spooks you put in my basement?"

"They are going to create a museum for you on the top floor. Selected pictures from the National Gallery will be brought in on a rotating basis. They will provide docents and a curator to run it. They will pay you a ridiculously high rent. They will solve more of your problems than you could ever have imagined. Learn to love them."

"You're kidding, right?"

"I never kid, and you're right, it isn't Old Spice."

To receive a free catalog of Poisoned Pen Press titles, please contact us in one of the following ways:

Phone: 1-800-421-3976
Facsimile: 1-480-949-1707
Email: info@poisonedpenpress.com
Website: www.poisonedpenpress.com

Poisoned Pen Press
6962 E. First Ave. Ste. 103
Scottsdale, AZ 85251